ChangelingPress.com

Rycks/Wrath Duet

Marteeka Karland

Rycks/Wrath Duet
Marteeka Karland

All rights reserved.
Copyright ©2022 Marteeka Karland

ISBN: 978-1-60521-832-8

Publisher:
Changeling Press LLC
315 N. Centre St.
Martinsburg, WV 25404
ChangelingPress.com

Printed in the U.S.A.

Editor: Katriena Knights
Cover Artist:

The individual stories in this anthology have been previously released in E-Book format.

No part of this publication may be reproduced or shared by any electronic or mechanical means, including but not limited to reprinting, photocopying, or digital reproduction, without prior written permission from Changeling Press LLC.

This book contains sexually explicit scenes and adult language which some may find offensive and which is not appropriate for a young audience. Changeling Press books are for sale to adults, only, as defined by the laws of the country in which you made your purchase.

Table of Contents

Rycks (Black Reign MC 1) 4
    Chapter One 5
    Chapter Two 15
    Chapter Three 28
    Chapter Four 40
    Chapter Five 51
    Chapter Six 63
    Chapter Seven 78
    Chapter Eight 92
    Chapter Nine 102
Wrath (Black Reign MC 2) 118
    Chapter One 119
    Chapter Two 131
    Chapter Three 143
    Chapter Four 161
    Chapter Five 172
    Chapter Six 183
    Chapter Seven 193
    Chapter Eight 206
    Chapter Nine 230
    Chapter Ten 246
    Epilogue 265
Marteeka Karland 275
Changeling Press E-Books 276

Rycks (Black Reign MC 1)
Marteeka Karland

Lyric: I'm in so much trouble. My orders are to find the highest-ranking member of Salvation's Bane or Black Reign MCs and sleep with him. Worm my way into his bed so I can feed information to Kiss of Death. Little did I know I would find the one man I could never forget -- the man who broke my heart six years ago and left me to fend for myself against a ruthless club who will break me the first chance they get.

Rycks: Lyric ran out on me six years ago. Not that I'd given her any reason to stay. The second I see her again, I want to punish her. She waltzes back into my life with an agenda I can't figure out. When I do, the truth is as scary as it is infuriating. Lyric is my torment. She's sent to me as bait in a bigger plan I can't fathom. Mainly because I'm too distracted by what she reveals. Now I'm questioning my loyalties to both her and my mentor, El Diablo. She pulls at my need to protect at the same time she might just prove herself to be a traitor.

Chapter One
Rycks

If there was a benefit of Black Reign joining with Salvation's Bane, it had to be Topaz. The girl could fucking suck dick like a Hoover vacuum cleaner. I might not indulge often, but at parties, I enjoyed watching all the hedonistic dancing and fucking from a distance. It was even more pleasant while getting sucked off.

Topaz always made herself available to me, though she wasn't my first choice of girls. I rarely refused her, mostly because of that talented mouth. Even though I thoroughly enjoyed her blow jobs, it was a means to an end. Eventually, I'd let her take me over the edge. Sometimes, she pulled out, letting me come on her face. Other times, her tits. Recently, she'd started swallowing me down, and I knew it was time to move on. I was many things, few of them good, but I'd never led a woman on. Good as she was, I didn't want Topaz. Not like that.

"See you're makin' yourself at home." Thorn, the president of Salvation's Bane, chuckled at me. "Enjoying the party?"

"Bane always throws a bitchin' party," I acknowledged. I sat with Topaz kneeling before me. My arms were thrown over the back of the loveseat, resting as I watched her. Sometimes I watched her swallowing me -- which was erotic as hell. Other times I watched the people in the room. Rarely was there a woman who wasn't topless or walking around naked. Some of them were in various stages of sex with one or more men. As parties went, this was decent.

"Any word on our rat problem?"

"Making progress. I gave Ripper the latest when

I got here. He's going through it now." Topaz looked up at me, all wide-eyed as she sucked my cock. It would be easy to just lean my head back and let her take over, but I had shit to tell Thorn. "Got some really good tips. Someone unwilling to risk coming to us directly, so he says, but so far the information has panned out. I think this lead is legit."

"Any idea who your informant is?"

"No, but he says he's close to finding the mole. I believe he's working both sides, or at least has an in to Kiss of Death. He knows too many details."

"Good. We've got more than one being watched already. One I'm pretty sure is working for drugs. The other is still up in the air with means and motive."

"I take it the opportunity's there?"

"Many times over."

I glanced down at Topaz. "Fuck, that feels good," I muttered. She grinned around my cock and worked all the harder on me. Her fingers dug into my thighs as she took as much of me down her throat as she could. I felt her muscles working around my member, trying to milk me of my cum.

"We'll meet later in the night, Rycks. Let Ripper work over the information you have, and he can give us a full report."

"Sounds like a plan," I bit out. I was seriously close to the edge and wanted to hold off. Felt too fucking good to stop now. "Give Lucy my best. I know the pregnancy has been hard on her. If she needs anything I can help with, don't hesitate to ask."

Thorn grunted at me. The offer was genuine, but Thorn would never take me up on it unless it was life or death and no one else could help him. He wouldn't pass it on to Lucy either. At least, not the offer. I didn't take it personally. We might be loose allies currently, but we were still an outside club, and alliances could change.

When Thorn moved on, I let my gaze quarter the room. Sex everywhere I looked. Even one BDSM scene was happening. The crack of a whip on skin followed by a decidedly feminine cry was sexy as fuck. I thought about asking Topaz if she'd let me scene with her, but it would only have been a halfhearted attempt. She just wasn't the girl for me.

So why wasn't I out there looking for my own woman? Or at least a woman I could spend some quality time with? One I could safely fuck every night and not worry about her getting emotionally attached?

That put a damper on my erection. I didn't go soft, but it took the edge off. I wasn't out there looking for a woman because women never stayed in my life. They found someone else. Or they died. While I couldn't lay blame on the former, the latter was my own damned fault. If I couldn't protect my own woman, I didn't deserve one.

Unexpectedly, Topaz let go my member with a loud, wet pop. She slid up my body and crawled on top of me. Already naked, she offered me a tit, which I gladly took into my mouth. My arms stayed on the back of the couch while I pulled strongly. Topaz gasped out, letting her head fall back. I could feel her pussy weeping where it rested over my cock. I nestled between her lips and she rode me, likely putting friction on her clit.

"I could fuck you, you know, Rycks," she purred, leaning down to kiss me. Her tongue found mine and swept into my mouth. She tasted like bourbon and spearmint. Not an unpleasant combination. "Just put that big, thick dick inside my little pussy and ride you all night. Would you like that?"

Would I? Honestly? No. "I'm sure you could." I settled on the noncommittal answer, not wanting to fuck her but not wanting to hurt her feelings.

"You could fuck me 'til I screamed." She rode me faster, rubbing her tits over my face until I caught one, biting the tip none too gently. Topaz cried out, her pussy quivering on top of my dick.

"Oh, that I could." If I could get her to come like this, I could send her on her way without having to actually have sex with her. "Bend you over the pool table and slam into you. Ain't no gentle lover, Topaz. I'd fuckin' take you hard."

"Fuck me raw? Make me come so fucking hard?"

"Oh, yeah. I'd fuck you 'til you came." I grinned at her. "Or not. I use women for my pleasure. Not theirs." Yeah. I knew the words to say. Topaz got off on being used. I knew that. Every woman there had a kink. Many of them were the same as Topaz. Why, I didn't know, but this was what I did. I gave people what they wanted. Secretly or otherwise. "Fuckin' use your little pussy to make myself come."

"Would you come in that little pussy?" Her voice was husky now. Rough in her passion. "Would you fill me with your spunk? Make me take every single drop?"

"Only if I wanted to. If I did, you'd have to lick up every drop you spilled out."

"Oh, fuck!" She yelled and rode me faster, obviously close. She danced over me wickedly enough I found himself getting back into it. Not enough to come, but enough to keep me hard.

"Are you a dirty little club whore, Topaz?"

"No, Rycks," she gasped. "I'm a fuckin' *filthy* club whore." She gave me a wicked grin and continued to rub over me with her wet pussy. Yeah. It would be so easy to just slip inside her. She'd be fine with it, but I just couldn't make myself reach between us and do it. I didn't want to come inside this woman. And definitely not bareback.

I took my gaze from Topaz's face for a split second and something caught my eye. There was a woman. No. It couldn't be. She watched us with wide, dark eyes. Like she'd never seen people fucking before. Being at a party like this, she had to be part of one club or the other, or a close friend of a member. I knew she wasn't as innocent as she seemed, because I'd had her already. Six years ago. The sex had been the most explosive of my life. She'd only been eighteen at the time, but I hadn't scared her with my appetites. I'd been with her two days before she disappeared. Those two days had changed my fucking life.

I shook my head and centered my concentration back on Topaz. Lyric had been the one to leave me. Not the other way around. At least, I hadn't left her yet. Sure, I'd planned on it and she knew it, but I hadn't gotten the chance. I tried to hold on to that, but I knew the fuck better.

As my partner's eyes slid shut, mine strayed back to the dark-eyed girl. *My Lyric*. She was slight of build -- even slimmer than I remembered -- wearing short cutoffs and a tight tank. Long, pale limbs were finely muscled and lean. Her stomach rippled with each ragged breath she took, her nipples standing out behind her tank. Was she even wearing a fucking bra? I didn't think so. Long curly hair spilled down her back and over her shoulders. I could easily imagine those large eyes looking up at me, much like Topaz had, all that dark hair caressing my dick as she stroked me with it. Because she'd done it more than once over our two days together.

Instantly, I was hard as steel, in danger of coming. Thank God, Topaz cried out and her pussy shuddered over my cock as she came. Had she not, she'd have just gone without, because I'd reached the point of no return.

I shoved her off me and to the floor between my knees, gripping her hair in my fist. "Fuckin' suck me," I growled.

Topaz's eyes got wide, but she grinned and did as I commanded. "I love it when you go all Alpha on me."

"You ain't seen Alpha and you never will," I said, my voice hard. "Suck me off. Don't swallow." She must have taken the whole thing as a challenge, because Topaz got a determined look in her eyes. She was definitely going to swallow unless I forced the issue. She was fucking with the wrong guy if she didn't think I'd make her do as I wanted, no matter what it took.

Lyric's ruby-red lips parted on a gasp, her breathing ragged as she watched me force Topaz's head up and down by her hair. I wasn't gentle. Topaz dug her fingers into my thighs again but didn't resist. I gritted my teeth, continuing to hold Lyric's gaze. In my mind, it was her I was forcing to swallow my dick. All that untamed hair spilling around me instead of the straight, blonde hair I currently held in my fist. Lyric had so much it wouldn't all fit in my hand and would caress my legs as she sucked me. As I studied her closer, I could see arousal, but also a healthy dose of hurt. Not that I cared. *She'd* left *me*, dammit!

I glanced down at Topaz to find her watching me. I bared my teeth at her, and she lowered her eyes. When I looked back up, Lyric was hurrying away.

"Fuck," I was so fucking close! I'd gone from a

cool-down to a near meltdown in the space of a minute. No way I could let Lyric get away without knowing why she was here. And who the fuck she was with. "Off," I barked to Topaz, pulling her up by her hair. I tucked my dick back in my pants and stood. I should have said thanks or acknowledged her in some way, but my focus was on the retreating form of my little brown-haired minx. It looked like she was following Thorn, and that just wouldn't fucking do.

Vaguely, I knew Topaz stomped her foot at me, furious that I'd kept her from her prize, but, honestly. She got to come. That was enough of a reward for a club girl. She knew the score. She was there to fuck the men who wanted her. If she wanted it different, she needed to set boundaries. Topaz had been with Salvation's Bane a long while. In the short time I'd been here, I'd personally seen her with just about every single man there was in the club who hadn't claimed an ol' lady. Hell, she'd sucked off half the guys from Black Reign who'd come to party at Bane. I respected women. But I also respected the choices these women made. If she wanted out, I'd help her. I wouldn't fuck her.

I stalked after Lyric, my gaze focused on the tight little ass encased in the short denim. What was she doing here? If she was after Thorn, she knew nothing about the club or its members. Which meant she shouldn't be here. That was a huge red flag for me. Didn't diminish my attraction to her, or my need to punish her for leaving me.

When I caught up to her, I grabbed her upper arm gently. She sucked in a breath as she turned around, stepping back, trying to get away from me.

"Easy, there. I'm not gonna hurt you."

"Rycks." Her voice was like a breath of fresh air.

A gentle caress. I loved the way she said my name. It was one of the many things about her I'd never been able to forget. Just like I'd never forgotten how I'd fucking failed her six years ago.

"What are you doing here? Who you with?"

"I'm not with anyone." She looked confused as she met my gaze. She had to crane her neck. Her answer was enough to keep me focused. Her getting in here alone was a huge problem given the security issues Bane had right now.

"If you're not with anyone, how'd you get in?"

"Oh. That." She shrugged one pale, delicate shoulder. "I know Wrangler." The man she named was a trusted prospect. For some reason, she twisted her hands together, but stopped the second she realized I'd noticed. "But I'm actually here to see Thorn and the highest patched member of Black Reign."

OK, now I was on full alert. Beguiling as she was, Lyric was getting nowhere near the president of Salvation's Bane. "Then you've found the right person. I'm the ranking member of Black Reign here. State your business," I said crisply.

She winced, glancing around nervously. "Not here. This is private, and I need to tell Thorn as well. I only want to do this once so I can get out of here."

"Honey, cute as you are, you're not getting near the president. I don't know why you're here." I grinned at her to take the sting out of my words, but I'm sure it wasn't a pleasant smile. "But I will."

She shivered, rubbing her arms. "It's important."

"I'm sure it is. You can tell me, and I'll pass it on." I held out my hand, intending to lead her to the room I occupied while at Bane, but, if I were honest, just wanting to feel her silky-smooth skin again. She took it.

"Will he listen to you? You're not the same club."

"Keeping tabs on us?" Lyric knew me and that I was with a club, but I didn't wear colors. No one in Black Reign's hierarchy did. It was just something El Diablo decided for us when we took over the club. So how did she know which club I was with? A guess? Or did someone tell her?

"I didn't realize it was a secret. Everyone here is talking about how only you represent the head of Black Reign. They figure that either means the others are using you to take all the risk and keep themselves safe, or..."

I narrowed my eyes at her, not liking how she or the others saw El Diablo, El Segador, or myself. "Or what?"

She gave me a sheepish grin. "Or maybe you're just that good."

I grinned, tightening my grip on her hand. "Let's go talk."

I took her to my room. It wasn't as nice as my home at Black Reign, but it had room enough for everything I needed and a little extra to spare. It also had its own bathroom. Most of the rooms on the first floor didn't. They were mainly used for prospects and patched members, including Beast, the club's enforcer, and any he'd tasked with security. Offices were on the second floor along with the club girls who stayed at the clubhouse full time. The club officers took the top floor. The place was a converted firehouse, and the big, open bays were perfect for the main room. There was another huge building where fire trucks had been housed, and they'd made it their garage. All the bikes were parked there. All it all, it wasn't as nice a place as Reign had, but it wasn't a shit compound either.

I took her inside my room and shut the door

before she could change her mind. I had nothing in mind other than finding out what she had to say, but seeing her look around the place and eyeing the bed, her breathing speeding up, made me decide to keep my options open.

"Uh, this really wasn't what I had in mind," she said, looking everywhere but at me.

"What's that?"

"This," she said, finally daring to take a peek at me. The grin on my face must have flustered her because her face turned red and she dropped her gaze. She took a breath, then, surprisingly, met my gaze full on. "Though, now that I think about it, it might be fun." She said the words softly, almost as if to herself. I had to wonder if she was remembering those blistering two days we shared.

"Tell me what you came here for and we can get to the fun stuff." I gestured to the table, deliberately not taking her to the small couch. Or the bed. I didn't mix business with pleasure. Shouldn't even fuck her after the business was done, but she intrigued me on a whole new level. I wanted to see what she had.

She sat, rubbing her hands over the wood of the tabletop as if to smooth the nonexistent tablecloth. "There's someone inside Salvation's Bane feeding information to Kiss of Death."

That brought me up short. Any arousal I had vanished in the time it took her to utter that one sentence. We knew there was a rat inside Bane. It was why I was still here. But, as far as we knew, no one else knew. So how did she?

Chapter Two
Lyric

Thank God, the man was finally taking me seriously. If he hadn't, I was pretty sure I'd forget the whole reason I was here and just let him take me to bed again. Watching him getting that blow job had hurt. Fucking bad. But I hadn't expected he'd lived like a monk, pining over me while I lived my life.

"Explain," he snapped, his easy-going demeanor changing to one of an intense threat quickly enough to give me whiplash. Suddenly, everything I'd heard about Rycks, everything he'd said six years ago, made sense. This was definitely not a man to toy with. Not if I wanted to stay alive. And he'd been right. I could believe he was more dangerous than Rat Man.

"Kiss of Death wants Salvation's Bane out of Palm Springs. Their president has an agenda he's working, and Bane is in the way."

"I'm aware of that. Explain how you know we have a traitor in our midst."

"Because I heard Rat Man and Butcher talking at the Dark before it burned."

"Was that before or after Butcher met an untimely end?"

I shivered at the blatant reminder that he'd been killed in one of the strip clubs owned by Salvation's Bane -- the MC whose compound I was currently trapped in. "Look. I'm trying to help because I've seen the good Salvation's Bane does in the community. They're good men and women. Kiss of Death would swallow up everyone in the poorer sections of Palm Springs. They're a bunch of thugs." It was only partially true, but I had no choice but to keep things from Rycks.

"Who's our rat?" His gaze was hard, focused wholly and entirely on me.

"I don't know. But I know he has a close tie to the club. A relative or best friend. And it's someone you trust, because Rat Man indicated he was getting movements on Thorn and Havoc. I think he plans on taking out one or both of them."

There was a long silence. Rycks looked at me with a hard gaze. This was the man I'd heard so much about. The man who was merciless to his enemies. If he considered me one, I didn't stand a chance.

"Your full name, Lyric. Something I should have gotten from you six years ago."

I nodded. "Lyric Jefferson." I'd expected this. He'd get some information, but not everything.

He nodded but said nothing else. Just stared at me. I'd never been this uncomfortable in my life! He was the most unusual biker I'd ever met. Most men in MCs were covered in ink and had full beards, maybe shaggy hair to go with it. This guy had some stubble, but even that was neatly groomed. His haircut looked expensive. In fact, he looked like he could be at home in either a motorcycle jacket or a business suit. Leanly muscled, he had enough bulk to fill out his T-shirt to perfection, the vein running up his biceps leaving an impression on the sleeve after his skin disappeared under the cloth. The only thing that made it even possible to consider that he was anything other than part of the rich, social elite of Palm Springs was the jagged scar running down one arm and the one bisecting his eyebrow and running the length of his cheek down to his neck. They were raised, but white. Like it had happened long ago, and he hadn't bothered to have any cosmetic surgery on them. He hadn't had them before. What had he done in the intervening years?

"Lyric Jefferson, from Ismay, Montana. Long way from home, aren't you?"

I gasped. "How... how did you know that?" Sure, I expected him to get some information, but that was fucking fast.

He tapped his ear. "Call it outside intelligence."

"The room is bugged."

"No one in this building gets in without a thorough screening. We've been working out your identity since you walked in." Oh, God. They couldn't go digging too deep. Some records were confidential. Others weren't. And I was certain that things hadn't been hidden as well as they should have. It was an insurance failsafe for Rat Man to keep me in line. So I'd discourage anyone from looking at my past. If I didn't do my job and Rycks or anyone at Bane or Black Reign dug too deep, Rat Man's people would know they'd been looking. Then my life would be altered forever. And I'd lose my mind and, likely, my will to live.

"Why did you not know my name then?" Had he done this on purpose? Got me interested in his ulterior motives, which were designed to interrogate me covertly? Did it really matter?

"You seem to be good at hiding. The only photo ID we found was a driver's permit from when you were fourteen."

"Fourteen and a half," I muttered. I wasn't expecting to have to relive this. I guess I never thought anyone would consider me a threat.

"Right," he said after a pause. "Fourteen and a half. You never completed your driving requirements for a Montana license. You didn't open a checking or savings account, so there is no money trail. Your family seems to have disappeared off the face of the earth."

"Easy to do in Ismay."

"In a cluster county that small, I imagine it would be. Census in 2010 was only nineteen. About half of the residents were families. The other half lived alone. I find it difficult to believe one of those families leaves or goes missing and no one notices. Yet your family did."

"It's a personal story," I said, trying to hold it together. "Look. I came here to help. If you don't want my help, I'll leave."

"I'm sorry, Lyric. But I can't let you leave until I know your full story and why you're here."

I glared at him. "You gonna tell me how you got those scars? Everything about you screams rich. Except those scars. And they weren't there six years ago. Looks like you've lived a rough life."

That must have been the exact wrong thing to say. Rycks stood up so abruptly he knocked his chair over. Naturally, I stood, too, backing toward the door.

"I suggest you keep your nose where it belongs. Way the fuck out of my business, Lyric."

"You started it," I snapped. "I was just being nice. Looking out for our community more than your stupid clubs. Why are you so pissed at me anyway? You said you weren't taking me with you. I had no desire to stay there and lose more of myself when you didn't give two shits!"

I was still trying to get to the door, but he saw the move and stalked toward me. With a cry, I turned and lunged the few steps that separated me from freedom, but the bastard caught me, pulling me up against him hard with one steel-like arm around my waist.

"You don't get to leave until I'm satisfied I know all you know, girl."

"My name," I bit out, trying not to let my fear show, "is Lyric. Not girl."

He swung me around and carried me to a chair in the corner of the room. It was soft and comfortable, but as far away from the door as I could possibly get. There was a stool that obviously went with the chair. Rycks sat on it in front of me. He shoved my legs apart so he could move his body to sit between them. It was an intimate position, one that was likely designed to make me feel vulnerable. It worked.

"Now. I want your story, Lyric." His voice was soft. He looked like he was more in control than he was after his initial outburst. I'd definitely struck a nerve. One thing I'd learned in my life was that, when being interrogated, the end result wasn't always about the information, though that was a huge part of it. Interrogation was all about being in control. You gain enough of it, you get the information you want. Rycks was using intimidation to get control of me. Well, I'd been intimidated enough in my life to be able to stand my ground. Rycks might be a dangerous man, but there was nothing he could do to me that hadn't been done in the past. Except for killing me. In a way, I dreaded that the least.

"I'll gladly tell you what I came here to tell you. But you don't get my story. You haven't earned it."

I thought that might set him off again. Strangely, it seemed to calm him. "I concede your point. And don't think we're not coming back around to us later. We will." He gave me a small smile. It wasn't as charming as his smiles had been before. More like he was tired. Strangely enough, that slight vulnerability made me want to soothe him. Had I not just given myself a lecture in power dynamics, I might have tried. "Will you tell me what you know?"

I took a breath. "Kiss of Death is in deep with the city's administration. Mayor. DA. But mostly, people who've been in their positions for a while. It's all good to be in with the mayor, but if he gets voted out of office, you're back to square one. Somehow, Kiss of Death has managed to find a group of people who stay in their jobs even when there is an administration change. Those people are able to influence the elections just enough to keep a certain people in their elected positions. Like the district attorney. Though it's possible the DA can be voted out, they manage to keep people in office without too much trouble. I don't know the particulars, but I'm sure it has more to do with who posts the results or something. Something no one would notice. But whoever is at the top of this is keeping people they can manipulate in power. Kiss of Death is part of it. Again, I don't know what they do exactly, but I know the reason they want Salvation's Bane out of the way is because they know you guys can't be bought off or bullied into staying quiet. They also know you'd never do their bidding like Kiss of Death."

"This is a lot more information than just what's going on inside Kiss of Death. You're on the inside. Working for the city."

I swallowed, looking away. "Was. Well, technically am, but only because quitting would be a red flag for them. If I leave my job, they'll suspect I'm up to something. Whether I am or not."

He narrowed his eyes. "If they knew you were here, wouldn't you be in the same situation?"

"Yeah," I said, not wanting to divulge the rest. Oh, well. I'd known this would likely happen. Though I'd hoped to keep my secrets, I knew Rycks and Thorn were too intelligent to just let my involvement in this slide. "I'm supposed to be a plant. To bring information back. Even I don't know who your rat is, but my job was to seduce my way into the club. It's how I got inside in the first place. Wrangler thinks I'm with him tonight. He brought me here to impress me. After I slipped off, though, I doubt he'll bring me back. I was supposed to get into the bed of one of the patched members. Not as a club girl, but as a regular sexual partner. That way I could glean information and bring it back to Kiss of Death."

Again, that hard mask fell over Rycks's face. "You fuck him?"

"Not yet," I confessed. "Trying not to. I'm sure several people saw me leave with you. You weren't exactly subtle about dragging me out. He won't want your leftovers."

"Sure, he would," Rycks said without hesitation. "I'm a novelty to the women here. Unless you guys are exclusive partners -- and from what I've gathered about Wrangler, that's not his style -- he won't care. I outrank him in a big way." He crossed his arms over his chest. "The question is, do you want to stick with him or set yourself up with me?"

OK. That was unexpected. "What do you mean?"

"If you leave here, you'd have to go back to Kiss of Death. Right?"

"Yes. I go to work, then I'm back at their compound. They always want information about what's going on in city administration, then they lock me up until it's time to go back to work."

"They hurt you?" He slid the question in so unexpectedly, it startled me.

"Why would you ask that?"

"Not your business. Now, answer the question."

"If I do what they tell me to, no."

"What will they do if you go back to the club tonight?"

"They'll want to know who I slept with and what information I got." I shrugged.

"How will they know you're telling the truth?"

Of course, he'd ask that. Rycks was cunning as they came. This was something I absolutely could not divulge to him. I was certain no one had been in Rycks's room to plant a bug, but I had no idea how many other rooms they'd reached.

"You know, Black Reign is getting a reputation."

He gave a small chuckle. "Yes. Though how is something we wonder about."

I noticed he didn't say they didn't know. Was this a test? "Kiss of Death spreads a lot of stuff, but I have no idea where they get their information."

"No worries on that account, Lyric. What we don't already know, we soon will." "You're not distracting me. How will they know you're not lying to them if you go back to the compound and tell them you've got a lover on the inside?"

"For someone so tight-lipped about his own details, you're sure as hell interested in my private business." I wanted to get angry, but I was just scared. If he knew the place was bugged, I was in more trouble than I realized. And Bella would be good as dead.

"I'll figure it out. I assume there are bugs or something?"

"No idea," I said, hoping like shit I was angry enough he couldn't see my lie.

"Assuming you leave here, you tell them you slept with me. What happens then?"

"They pump me for information. I'm supposed to get you to talk to me."

He focused sharply on me. "They know we have

a past?"

"You know they do or I wouldn't be here," I snapped. Taking a breath, I tried to calm down. "Look. Kiss of Death is after Salvation's Bane. They haven't said anything much about Black Reign, but if they take out one club, it will embolden them. They'll come after El Diablo next."

"And that will be their death warrant," Rycks said softly. "You know you won't stand a chance if you go back tonight. Right?"

"I'll be fine. If I go back, I might be able to convince them you didn't want sex with me after I ran last time."

He actually laughed at me this time. "Are you fucking kidding me? Who in their right fucking mind would think I'd turn you down?" Before I could argue he continued. "You're naive, innocent-looking, and in obvious trouble. Normally, that would be enough to get you my protection, but you showed yourself to me at the perfect time. You waited until another woman was swallowing me down before you chose to reveal yourself."

I blinked, taken aback. Did he see me like that? Now I was questioning what he'd meant by appeal. "You're not making any sense. Everyone knows you're protective over the two girls you consider your wards. Do you have sex with them, too?"

Rycks looked like I'd slapped him. He actually jerked upright. "You honestly think I'm fucking those girls?"

"Well, from what I hear, they're not girls anymore. They're grown women." I couldn't back down. *Control.*

Seeming to shake it off, his face hardened. "I know. But they're still vulnerable, and I would never take advantage of a woman who needed my protection."

"But I'm different," I pressed. This was how I took back control. The chink in his armor was his need to protect those weaker than him. Particularly woman.

"You're very different," he said in a hushed tone. "You're the reason I'm the way I am, Lyric. I fucked up six years ago. I let you down." He shook his head. "I'm not about to let you down again."

This sounded bad. For the first time since I saw Rycks, I got the feeling I might be in real trouble. Because I was truly afraid he might regret not taking me with him. If that were the case, could I convince him to let me go now? Everyone knew he was protective to a fault. He'd risk his life for anyone he thought of as his. No matter what capacity. If he wouldn't let me leave, Bella was good as dead.

"Stay here. With me. I'll make it known you're with me, and that you're not to leave here unless I give permission. If you're right and we've got a rat, it will get back to Kiss of Death. Before you say anything, know that this will mean you're mine. I'm not letting you go until this is over. After that, if I've fucked you out of my system, we'll see."

"Wait a minute. If you think I'm sleeping with you again, you're out of your goddamned mind."

"You telling me you don't want to see if we've still got chemistry? Maybe we'll both realize we want nothing to do with the other."

He didn't sound like he believed that. "Uh-huh."

"You don't have much of a choice, Lyric."

"Fuck you," I muttered. If I went back and didn't give them something, that would be it. They wouldn't give me a second chance to seduce one of the other guys and pump them for information. They'd simply put me in the rotation of girls they fucked. And that first night would be horrible. Hell, who was I kidding? It would be more than a night. Way fucking more. Worse than all that, they'd kill Bella in front of me. Likely with her begging for me to help her. But was staying with Rycks tonight going to get me anywhere? I had no doubt he could make me enjoy anything he did to me. The question was, would he? Also, would he give me something to take back to Kiss of Death? Something of value. I just didn't know. I decided to test him.

"Look. I can't stay here past tonight. But if I go back with something that looks important, you could control the information I'm giving them." Was it my imagination or did he look disappointed?

"I don't like it. I'd have to discuss it with Thorn, and he'd have to decide what you tell them, but it's not something I want to risk."

"It's the only option I have."

"Why?"

"I'm sorry?"

"Why do you have to go back, Lyric. You're here with me now. You're safe."

"All you need to know is that I have to go back. I *want* to go back." If the look on his face was any indication, I'd just thoroughly pissed Rycks off.

"You're staying. End of discussion. You want to go back, you tell me why."

"It's personal. That's all I'm saying so don't ask again."

Rycks sighed and reached for me to pull me onto his lap, straddling his hips. He stood up and turned to sit in the same chair he'd plucked me out of. Those strong hands held me still. Like I'd dare move.

"Are you telling me you want to go back to that

lot? They'll use you until there's nothing left. I'm surprised they haven't already. You'll die in that place if you go back. You have to know that."

"No. I don't know that. Dangling information from someone high in rank at Black Reign would keep them off me. Plus, they need me working at my job in the city. It's the only way they're able to get their information."

I tried to ignore how good it felt to be in his arms again. Rycks was my first lover. He'd made me feel special despite his refusal to keep me. Even that had been because he'd thought any danger I faced wasn't anything like what I'd face with him. I had no idea if he'd been right, but I knew where I was now was as deadly dangerous.

"You're a damned fool," he snapped. Then he did something unexpected. He slid his hand into the hair at the back of my head and pulled me to him. "Girl, I'm surprised they let you leave at all. Surprised they haven't already made you a whore in the most violent way possible. It would be Rat Man who'd start with you. You know that, right?"

I shivered. Rat Man. Even saying his name gave me the creeps. The man knew no depravity he didn't indulge in. If there was a repugnant sex act out there, chances are he'd done it.

"Yes. I can see you do know. I can also see you're afraid." He sighed, loosening his grip on my hair, but not letting me pull away from him. "I suppose that's something." With a sigh, he pulled me to him until my head rested on his shoulder. "You're going to be a problem, I can see. Not sure the word brat even covers you."

"Why would you call me a brat?" Maybe I was, but it was only because, for some reason, I felt safe to let that side of myself out when I was with him. Sure, he tried to come across gruff and dangerous -- and I was sure he was under the right circumstances -- but I knew in my heart he wasn't like anyone at Kiss of Death. He was a protector first. A killer only when someone he was responsible for was threatened.

"Because you're testing me when you should be following orders."

"Never been much good at following orders."

"I can see that. Also," he said, taking a deep breath, "you've got to tell me why your family went missing from Ismay. And why you're the only one of them ever to turn back up."

Chapter Three
Rycks

If Lyric truly thought I was letting her go back to Kiss of Death, she was either not as smart as I'd first thought, or braver than I gave her credit for. To my question about her family, she let go a bark of laughter before pressing her fingers to her mouth to keep in her amusement. She tried to pull away from me, but I wouldn't let her. It felt too good to hold her. Thing was, cuddling had never been something I was fond of. I liked my own space. Women were pleasant in bed, but I didn't linger after sex. With this girl, I could see myself wrapped around her lithe body throughout the night.

No. She wasn't going back to that fucking club. Even if I had to tie her to my bed and lock her in my room. And that wasn't something I could do here, at the Salvation's Bane compound. I needed to get her back to Black Reign. It would put her in the most secure environment and lead the danger our way. Bane was perfectly capable of handling Kiss of Death, but Reign could do more than handle that fucking club. We'd annihilate them.

"You don't give up, do you?"

"Not in my vocabulary. I have to know your past before you left here. You want to go back? This is part of what you have to do." I stroked her back up and down because I couldn't help myself. I think she might have enjoyed it too because she arched into my touch ever so slightly.

"Fine. I was taken, OK?"

I tried not to pause in my movements, wanting to keep her as relaxed as possible. If I gained her trust, I'd have control of the situation. Of the flow of information from her. "What do you mean, taken?"

"I mean, shortly after I got that driving permit when I was fourteen and a half, someone came to my house, killed my parents, and took me with them."

"Kiss of Death?"

"His name was Gremlin. I'd met him at a football game a few nights before. He was older than me by quite a bit but kept following me around, trying to get me to leave with him to go to a bar."

"But you wouldn't go."

"No. I finally went to my dad and he got the attention of a cop at the game. There was always one with the local ambulance service at every game in case they were needed. Gremlin took off, but I knew that wasn't the end of it. You could see it in his eyes. He wasn't one to let something like that go. Had I just ignored him, he might have. But by calling the attention of the cops to him, that wasn't something he was going to forgive."

"What happened then?"

She shrugged. "Less than a week later, he and a few of his buddies broke into our house, killed my parents, and kidnapped me. They tied me up, shot me up with a drug that made me sleep, then shoved me in the trunk of their car. Next thing I know, I'm in Nashville, Tennessee."

"This fucking club is in a bad need of putting down," I muttered. It was more for myself, but she readily agreed.

"I thought they had been. Gremlin and his father, their president, were both killed several months later. I thought I might be able to escape. Several of the women and kids being held did. But either they kept me dosed higher than everyone else, or I was just more susceptible to it. I could never get my wits about me long enough to form a plan."

She snuggled closer to me. Maybe for comfort, I don't know. But her little hand curled into my shirt, and I was fucking lost. Lyric was no stray I'd picked up. No kid in need of my protection. She wasn't even penance for my failures long ago. No. This girl… No. She wasn't a girl. She was a young woman. And she was fucking mine.

I cleared my throat. "How did you end up here?"

"Came with the club. Rat Man came in and took over. Couple of the older members objected. He shot them. He had a couple men with him who were loyal, and they helped convince the rest of the club Rat Man was the guy for the job. He promised them they'd all be rich, and the club did seem to be bringing in more money than ever before. So they let him take over."

"How did you keep from being raped all that time?"

She shivered, her hands tightening even more in my shirt. "At first, I didn't think I could. Gremlin wanted me bad, but his father wouldn't let him. Slash was his name. He wanted to find the right buyer for me. He said the only way to get top dollar for me was for me to remain a virgin. Gremlin snuck into the room they held me in several times. Almost managed to get what he wanted a couple of times. Then Slash moved me into his room."

"I take it by the tone of your voice that wasn't much better?"

"Well, I knew I wasn't safe. And I always felt threatened, like, if I did one thing wrong, he would let Gremlin have his way with me. Also, I had to watch him fuck woman after woman. Some of them weren't much older than me. Some were younger." She stopped a moment, a hitch in her voice. "Those times, I was grateful he kept me drugged. I tried to keep my head down, my mouth shut, and just do as I was told."

"Where in there did you meet me?" She flinched back, trying to pull away but I wouldn't let her. "You're fine where you are, Lyric. Tell me."

"I was supposed to get you to sleep with me."

"Which I did. Six years ago."

"Yeah. They'd been looking for you. Rat Man said you were the key to controlling some guy name El Diablo. Said you were his muscle, and if he could control you, he could bring El Diablo to heel."

"He had bad information if he thought that. Go on."

"They found you in El Paso."

"Where we met."

"Yes," she buried her face in my chest and gave a heavy sigh. I thought I'd have to prompt her, but she continued on her own. "They had me 'meet' you at that bar. Told me to just be friendly and let nature take its course."

"It did," I said, remembering all kinds of things about those two fucking days. "So, why did you leave when you did?"

"It was time. I was only supposed to stay one night, but you kept me in that motel room for thirty-six hours."

"Loved everything about you. Never had a woman satisfy me like you did." I took a breath. I had to ask the next question, but everything in me tried to hold it back. "That why you got beat up?"

She gasped and looked up at me. "You knew about that?"

"Baby, I looked for you the night you left. At first, I tried to tell myself it didn't matter. I'd told you you couldn't stay with me. Figured you'd just gotten mad and left. Then I'd met up with a guy who was selling Fentanyl for us. He's a paramedic in El Paso. While I was doing business with him, he and his partner got paged out to a young woman, late teens, found walking on the side of the road. Facial and head trauma." The memory still brought on a visceral reaction. I broke out in a sweat and had to fight to keep my breathing even. "Anyway, I told the guy I'd give him a fix of Fentanyl for free if he'd get the name of the girl, a picture, and tell me the hospital he took her to. He readily agreed, and I went back to my room to wait.

"An hour later, when he finally sent me the information I wanted, I sat there and stared at your lovely face, swollen and beaten until you were unrecognizable. The only thing that helped me identify you was the two little freckles on your top lip." I brushed my thumb over those two little dark spots on her mouth. "I remembered tracing them with my tongue and how you surrendered to me when I did."

"If you found me, why didn't you come for me?" I hated the hurt in her voice. It fucking gutted me.

"I did. But you'd already gone. I bribed one of the hospital security staff into showing me camera footage of you leaving. I took the footage back to El Diablo, and he put his best people on it. We identified a guy called Pretty Boy and Butcher."

"Yes. Pretty Boy is the one who messed up my face. He left me with one of the prospects -- I can't remember his name, but he's dead -- and the guy dropped me off a few miles away from the club and told me to get lost before Rat Man killed me. He was trying to be nice, but I was so out of it all I could do was put one foot in front of the other. The cops eventually saw me and stopped. Everyone was trying to help, but no one could. Rat Man had Pretty Boy beat me because I was late. He was OK with me staying the extra twenty-four hours, but I hadn't checked in and gotten permission. Even though I was doing what I was supposed to do, he still had to make an example of me."

"I could have helped you," I muttered. "That picture of you he sent me haunted me, Lyric. You tried to tell me."

"I didn't tell you what I was facing. I just felt you out. When you weren't interested, I moved on."

She was killing me. All this was like a raw, gaping wound that she'd just rubbed salt into. How much worse could this get? Needing to put all that out of my mind for a while, I changed the subject. "So the club moved to Palm Springs."

"Yes. That was after Gremlin and Slash were gone. Rat Man moved us here. I think it was because he knew you'd settled here. It's why he sent me back. To see if you'd bite again. If not you, he wanted me to get as high as I could in the ranks of either Salvation's Bane or Black Reign."

"Well, you've made it as high as you're likely to go in either club."

She pulled back. "Rycks, I honestly don't care how high up the ladder I go with this. I didn't want to come here in the first place. I just knew that if I didn't, Rat Man would make my life worse than it already is. I'm not trying to sleep my way to the top of a club to get all the president's secrets. I'm just... I don't know..." She foundered for an explanation. She didn't have to put it into words. I knew exactly what she meant.

"Trying to survive?"

With a sigh, she dropped her head, looking as ashamed as anyone I'd ever seen. "Yeah. I guess."

"Look at me, Lyric." I waited until she reluctantly lifted her head. "I don't blame you for this. No one here or at Reign would. This isn't your fault. You're caught in a bad situation between some really violent people, myself included." I waited to see if she'd say anything. She didn't. "I'm also aware that you're exactly the type of woman Kiss of Death would send to me. You could just as easily be my downfall as I could be yours. So what's going to happen is this. We're going to trust each other. Do you think you can do that?"

She looked at me suspiciously. "What do you mean?"

"I mean, I'm going to trust you're not using some elaborate mind fuck to set me up. In return, you're going to trust me to keep you safe from anything to do with Kiss of Death, or anyone else out there who might want to hurt you. Even my own club."

"Black Reign would want to hurt me?"

I didn't pull any punches. I was serious about us trusting each other. More, I was trusting she wouldn't figure out I was the vulnerable one. If she was giving me a song and dance, and she was intent on playing her part with Kiss of Death, I was fucked. Because the longer I spent in her presence, the more I realized I wanted her. Not for a night. For a very long time indeed.

"If they thought you were playing me to hurt the club, they wouldn't hesitate to slit your throat right in front of me. I'm telling you now, they'd have to kill me for that to happen. So I'm all in. I need you to be, too. Do that, and I'll see to it you're free of Kiss of Death."

"It's not that simple, Rycks. I have to go back to them tomorrow. After that, you can come get me or whatever. But I have to go back."

"Why?"

"Just as I'll trust you to get me out, you're going to have to trust me when I say I just can't. Once you come charging to my rescue, you'll know. For now, though, this is all I can give you safely."

I stared at her, willing her to say more even as I knew she wouldn't. Control. We grappled for it. Why did she need it so much? Somehow, I knew it was important. Just a gut feeling I had, but what the fuck was it?

"Fine. But tonight you're mine, Lyric. We're going to get used to each other again. I'm going to see your scars, and you're going to see mine. Then we're going to kiss and lick every single one. When we're done, we'll talk about this again."

"I'm not opposed to that," she said with a small smile. "But I'm still going back, and you're still coming after me. If you're successful, I'll explain everything to you."

"I guess that's as good as I'm getting." It was the best I was going to get. It'd have to do.

"What now?"

I grinned. "Now, I get to stake my claim on you in front of everyone. You think this mole in Salvation's Bane is here tonight?"

She thought about that. Biting a fingernail, she looked away. "I'm not sure. If I had to guess, I'd say yes. It's someone close, so if the whole club is at this party, the mole will be, too. I know there were several of us. Only one knew who everyone was. The rest of us were kept in the dark. Kind of like, if we don't know who the others are we couldn't give anyone up if we got interrogated. Kiss of Death wants to find a way into Black Reign as well. Never hurts to have too many options."

"Makes sense." I stood, urging her to wrap her legs around my waist. When she did, her denim-clad pussy came hard against my cock. I'd managed to calm myself down. Mostly. With that one touch, my cock grew by the second.

"Holy shit," she whispered, her eyes wide and looking into mine. "I'm... I'm sorry." She tried to wiggle free, but I wrapped one arm around her waist and smacked her ass with the other. She gave a startled yelp but jerked up straighter. "What was that for?" The little demand in her voice only made things worse.

"Keep squirming, baby. You'll end up in that bed quicker than I'd planned."

"What are you doing?" Her voice was a little husky, which told me she was more turned on, too.

I filled my hands with the globes of her ass. Those cutoffs were so short, I could feel the crease of her thigh. I squeezed. Hard. "Gettin' you ready to show off," I murmured. The flannel she wore was knotted under her breasts. I'd admired the lean muscles of her abdomen earlier, now I wanted to see if she really was braless. "Lose the shirt."

Her eyes widened. "But --"

"Lose the fuckin' shirt or I'll lose if for you. Won't be much left if I do."

She nodded slightly, her eyes wide, glazing over as she undid the little buttons down the front and untied the tails. Her pale skin blushed becomingly. She was, indeed, braless. Her little breasts were still barely more than nipples on her chest jutting out for me to suck. If they seemed a little larger, it wasn't much. I did notice a couple of veins that stood out more than I remembered, but it had been six years, and I'd only had her two days. I might have just missed those small details in my hunger for her.

"Yeah. Put you in one of my shirts with your nipples hard and everyone will know what we've been doing up here."

An adorably confused look creased her face. "But, we've not done anything."

"Yet."

Her eyes widened. "Oh..."

"Don't worry, baby. I'm not gonna fuck you. Yet."

Something in her expression changed. "You think I can't take you on? I did it once, I can do it again."

"I know you can take me on. But we've both changed. We're gonna take this slowly." I grinned sheepishly when she raised an eyebrow at me. How could she know me so well after only forty-eight hours six years ago? This girl was fucking meant for me. "At least as much as I can."

Oh, yeah. That was the exact best thing I could have said at that moment. Lyric got a mulish look on her face and she finished shrugging out of her shirt. Then she reached between us to deftly dip her hand under the waistband of my jeans. When she found my aching cock, she squeezed and stroked.

"Oh, I think you want me as much as I want you," she said, her voice a breathy moan. "If everyone's going to think we've been fucking, I think maybe we should." She cocked her head to the side. "Besides, I'm a horrible liar."

"Fuck," I bit out between my teeth. "You're gonna be the death of me, Lyric."

"I've been given a hardcore sex education in living color since you took my innocence six years ago, Rycks. I haven't done a whole lot since then, but I've seen everything you can possibly imagine."

"Don't equate what you saw with what we're about to do. I can imagine some of those scenes weren't very pleasant." That thought should have brought me back under control, but her soft palm continuing to stroke and caress my dick was more powerful than the images swarming in my head.

"They weren't. But some -- like the little show you put on with your girlfriend downstairs -- were different. Not all the men in Kiss of Death are pigs. Just most of them."

"First, she's a club girl from Bane. Not my girlfriend."

She shrugged. "So she's fine with you being up here with me?" Was there a note of vulnerability in her voce?

"She's a club girl. She's been with almost every man in this building. By choice. Hell, she probably moved on to another patched member without batting an eyelash when I left her."

"Sounds like you don't much care."

"I don't fucking care at all. She's doing what she does by choice. Most women hanging around the club are either looking for a high-ranking member to make her his ol' lady, or just get off on being used. Some stick around for years. Others get their fill and move on. You know this."

She shook her head. "Works differently in Death. Some are like that, but most are hoping to be picked up by a patched member to either protect her or set her free."

I grunted. "Figured as much. Now. Enough about that shit." I thrust against her palm. "I want to finish unwrapping my present.

As I'd hoped, she giggled. "Present, huh?"

"Yeah. Not every day I get the woman who got

away back in my bed." As much as I was looking forward to this, I still felt guilty. "I'm so fuckin' sorry I didn't really listen to what you were saying that night, Lyric."

"You couldn't have known, and I wasn't telling." Her smile was the sweetest thing I'd ever seen. I was so fucked. "And I wouldn't have changed a single thing about those two days. If I'd actually gotten to pick to who took my virginity that night, hands down it would have been you." As I laid her down on the bed, she placed her palm on the side of my face. "You're not a good guy. I know that. But I believe in my heart you would never have left me in El Paso if I'd told you what was going on."

"Don't bet on that, baby. I wasn't the same person back then. I think you know that."

She shook her head. "You'd have fussed and rejected the idea at first. But you'd have helped me. You wouldn't have been happy about it, and you wouldn't have left me, but you'd have gotten me away from them and protected me until I was safe."

"You're in a precarious position, Lyric," I said in all seriousness. "You're a spy from a rival club." Then my gaze trailed to her unbuttoned shorts and I lost focus.

"I know. But I swear I won't let you down. You let me go back to them, then come get me, and I'll be the model semi-prisoner." She grinned.

My gaze jumped to her. "What was that? You won't be a prisoner."

"I could leave?"

The thought filled me with dread. I didn't say anything, but she laughed out loud this time. "Yeah. That's what I thought."

Chapter Four
Rycks

"You're the biggest brat I've ever met," I said as I stood to remove my jeans. "Think I'll have to find another use for that mouth of yours."

She stretched, her nipples calling to me like a siren to a hapless sailor. No way I was resisting that. "Promises, promises," she sang.

Then I whipped my shirt off and lay on top of her. She wrapped those strong legs around my waist, immediately finding the ridge of my shaft like a pro. When her eyes widened slightly, I knew her clit was right where she needed it.

"You're going to fuck me now." Her breathy voice didn't ask a question. She fully expected I'd just plunge into her.

"Oh, no, little brat. We're not there yet. You're not ready, and I'm not ready for it to be over."

"One-shot chump, are you?"

"Fucking brat." I chuckled before taking her lips.

In my lifetime, I'd kissed literally hundreds of women. Some had been for business. Some for pleasure. Some had been for less-than-honorable motives but all of them had provided varying degrees of pleasure. The second my lips touched Lyric's, my world flipped upside down, just like it had six years ago.

Lyric was a puzzle. I believed everything she'd told me. I didn't get where I was and still be alive without being able to see through lies. She was the woman in trouble calling me to her like a moth to a flame, but it was even more than that. Some things she did -- like rubbing her sex against me to find the spot that pleased her most -- spoke of experience. But her kiss was hesitant, unpracticed, leading me to believe she may not have had many lovers after me. There was no artifice, and she mimicked my actions instead of kissing me back with movements all her own. It was almost as if this was her first kiss. Like she hadn't done it often. With that realization came two thoughts.

First, I was more fucked that I realized. If I did this, if I took her again, I'd be the slimiest slimeball on the face of the fucking earth. She was a good girl caught in an impossible situation, and I was taking advantage of her for reasons she couldn't begin to fathom. She was a link in a chain that would lead me to the threat inside Salvation's Bane that was looking for an in for Black Reign. I could protect my club and our allies if I kept her on my side. Also, knowing she came from an enemy club, I couldn't just let her go back. I'd told her I would knowing I'd never let her leave.

Second -- and this was the worse of the two in my opinion -- I loved that innocence in her. In all women. It was why I protected women like Serilda and Winter. It was why I'd protected and goaded Mae so much before she'd been kidnapped. After that, I'd just coddled her. Before, there had been nothing sexual about my need to protect those women. It had been a means to assuage my guilt. Now, with Lyric, it was entirely about sex. How could I shock her? What would she do when I did? Would she like it? How far could I push her before she pushed back? How much would I like it when she did? That bratty side to her was the icing on the fucking cake. It hadn't been there before, but now it was a fucking turn-on like nothing else could be. If I pushed too hard or too far, she'd let me know it with fireworks flying. And I'd keep pushing because I couldn't help myself.

Even knowing what a bastard I was, when Lyric

opened her mouth, I swept my tongue inside and coaxed her to do the same. She moaned in my arms, following my lead as if she'd done so all her life. Her little nails dug into my shoulders, the bite like spurs urging me on. Thank God I still had my boxer briefs on because I could have easily slid into her. Instead, I rubbed my cock against her, creating friction where I could. As before, she wiggled until she had her clit positioned exactly where she wanted it. Then she tightened her legs around me and thrust her pelvis at me.

"You're really getting into this, huh?" I chuckled.

She froze, her eyes opening in a flash. "'M'I not supposed to?"

"Oh, yeah. You're supposed to. You had anyone since we were together?"

She stiffened a little but nodded. "Couple times." Just the tone of her voice told me they hadn't been good experiences.

"By God, Lyric. You're going to enjoy this if it fuckin' kills me."

"Well, then," she said, shifting a little, her body relaxing once again. "Can't make it too easy for you. I think you should have to work for it."

I barked out a laugh. When had I enjoyed the simple sexual banter between a man and a woman like I was now? Had I ever even tried it? Yeah. I had. Once. Six years ago. "You're priceless, you know that?"

"That a good thing?"

"The best."

I kissed her once more before sitting up and grabbing the waistband of her shorts and sliding them down her shapely thighs. "Not sure I've ever seen a body like yours," I muttered. I ran my hand up her legs, over her hips and ribcage to frame her tits with my hands. Next to me, she was so small, her body young and clean where I was scarred and old. Yet another thing that made me a bastard. I was forty-two. She was twenty-four.

Unable to wait another second before I tasted her sweet skin, I kissed the valley between her breasts. As she lay on her back, those delicious mounds practically disappeared into her chest, but her nipples protruded nicely in her lust.

I licked over her soft flesh until I took one puckered nipple between my lips. I flicked and sucked the little nub, stretching and pulling it out, making it stick out farther until, finally, I took it between my teeth. Gently, I bit down, looking up into her flushed face. She gasped, her lips parting on a cry. Lyric arched her back, thrusting her chest at me. I opened my mouth to take in more of her tit, flicking the nipple with my tongue until she screamed sharply.

"Fuck!"

"Mmm."

Her body erupted in sweat. Her breathing came in little gasps. I looked up at her lovely face and felt something like wonder. I knew it was there. Knew she could see how this affected me. For the first time in my life, I didn't care about control, about getting what I wanted from someone. I wanted her to feel good, to enjoy this like no other woman before her ever had. Her body continued to undulate beneath mine, and I had the fleeting thought that this was what I'd been waiting for my entire life. This one woman and her sassy mouth. How had I not recognized it before?

Needing to keep her on the edge, to drive her insane with lust only for me, I moved to her other tit. Again, she gasped and wiggled beneath me. Her eyes closed, and she laid her head back on the mattress. Her hands tunneled in my hair, pulling me to her so sweetly. Her cries filled the air, and I found myself growling around her nipple, eager for more.

Against her protests, I let go of her breast. She looked down at me with a glazed look in her eyes as if she had no idea where she was.

"Rycks?"

"It's fine, little brat. Just breathe for me."

"Did I… did I do something wrong?"

"What? No, baby," I soothed, realizing she thought I was stopping. "We're not done yet. But there's someplace else I want to kiss." She whimpered, but pulled her knees up to her chest, spreading her legs wide. "That's it. God, you're wet!"

And she was. Her pussy was glazed with her dew. A tuft of dark, curly hair sat on her mound, but she was trimmed around it. I stroked her slowly, watching her body quiver with each touch. Her little clit was swollen and pulsed with her rapid heartbeat.

"I'm going to lick and suck this pretty little cunt, Lyric. I'm going to suck your lips and lick all around them. Then I'm going to get you right on the very edge before I fuck you."

"Will it hurt?"

"Did it hurt? After me?"

She nodded. "But I wasn't… I wasn't wet."

"Honey, that's not going to be a problem. But I'm going to make you wetter so that, tight as you are, I'll just slide right in." When she nodded, I continued, "Gonna take you right to the edge and hold you there. I'm not going to fuck you until you're screaming for it. Then I'll fuck you 'til you come."

"Please. Yes!"

I would've laughed at her eagerness if I could have. My cock was diamond hard, and I knew the pleasure that awaited us. It was then I made one more decision for us that I knew was a dick move. No fucking way was I using a fucking condom. As I remember it, I'd made the same decision last time, and she'd welcomed it eagerly. Lyric was all mine. If she got pregnant with my kid, all the better. I was keeping her. And I'd use everything in my power to make that happen.

One thing at a time, though. First, I needed her so out of her mind she didn't know up from down.

Her pussy was delicious. Her cries even more so. It wasn't long before I completely lost myself in her. Lyric's legs were draped over my shoulders, her heels occasionally thumping against my back, but I barely felt it. Pulling open her lips, I sucked on the most decadent little clit imaginable. It throbbed beneath my tongue. I delved my tongue inside her. Fuck! I needed inside her like I needed to breathe. When she shrieked her frustration, I felt an answering growl from my chest.

"Rycks! I can't take it anymore! Please! Now!"

"Fuck," I muttered, crawling up her body. "I'm not using a condom, Lyric. I need you to tell me you're good."

"I'm good! I'm good! Just please don't wait any longer! God!"

Yeah. I was going to hell. That knowledge didn't make me hesitate even a single second. Once I was over her, pinning her down, I tucked my cockhead at her entrance and eased inside. I thought I was going to lose my whole Goddamn mind. The pleasure bordered on pain as she strangled the head of my dick. Lyric still squirmed and wiggled around me, but she didn't appear in pain. She seemed to be trying to work her body down my shaft whether I wanted her to or not.

"Still!" I snapped at her. "Be fuckin' still a second!"

She opened her eyes and bared her little teeth at me, hissing like a little angry cat. "Don't tell me to be still, Rycks! Get the fuck inside me now before I fucking kill you!"

If I hadn't already been on the verge of coming, that would have gotten me there. I let my head fall back and counted backward from twenty, her pussy still gripping my dick like a vise.

"If I fuckin' come before I'm ready, I'm gonna spank your ass, Lyric."

She reached up, aiming for my face. I thought she was going to rest her palm on the side of it, but instead she slapped me. Hard.

"MOVE!"

"Fuck!"

Next thing I knew my full weight was on top of her, and I was fucking her like a rabid beast. It was like an out-of-body experience. I could hear myself snarling and growling, panting and groaning. I could even taste her skin where I bit her neck. She did the same, crying out with every surge forward of my body. But it wasn't in pain or even disgust. Oh, no. My little brat was urging me on, digging her heels into my lower back and using the leverage to buck on my dick, meeting me with every stroke. The sharp *slap* of skin on skin punctuated our cries and shouts.

It would be only a matter of seconds before I came. I knew it like I knew my own name. And I wasn't ready. Not yet.

With a hoarse shout, I shoved myself off her, pulling her with me by the arm. When she didn't move fast enough, I grabbed her hair close to her scalp and pulled her up. She gave a sharp cry but didn't fight me.

Instead, she simply did what I wanted and moved quicker.

Once she was on the way, I led her quickly to the bathroom in front of the vanity. The mirror reflected us, which was what I wanted. Not wasting a second, I shoved her leg up so it rested on the counter, then found her pussy with my dick and sank back inside her.

She cried out but kept her eyes open. Not looking at me, but at herself. Which was also what I wanted.

"You see that woman in the mirror?" I gripped her silky hair again and tugged her head higher so she could see the marks of my possession on her neck. Fuck, I'd left some big hickies. A first for me. I brushed damp tendrils of hair away from her face where they'd stuck. She was flushed and panting, her lips parted and her eyes shining. I had one arm around her waist and one above her tits. "She belongs to me." I bared my teeth at her before dipping to her neck again, making another hickey.

I started moving inside her again. She fought to stay upright, circling my head with her arm. The harder I fucked her, the harder she gripped my hair. I couldn't fucking get enough of her! In the back of my mind, I knew I needed to take it easy with her, to go slow and be careful with her because it was obvious by how tight she was she hadn't been with many men after me. But her demands and the way my cock felt inside her simply wouldn't let me.

Finally, knowing I had to make one last, violent run at her, I pulled her leg down to place her foot on the floor. "Spread your legs," I snapped. "Fuckin' wide as you can."

She did. Eagerly. Then looked at me over her shoulder. "Get back inside me, you bastard."

"For such a skittish girl when you first got here, you're a demanding little thing."

"Please, Rycks!" She looked desperate as I felt. "I don't know what's happening to me!"

"Me neither," I muttered. But I did as she demanded. I guided my cock to her entrance, then pulled her hips back to me. Then I proceeded to fuck her as hard and fast as I could.

Lyric screamed, her cry long and loud. Her cunt gripped me so hard I thought she might squeeze me in two. Instead, her little pussy milked me so hard I finally gave up the fight.

I met her gaze in the mirror. "I'm comin', Lyric. Tell me now if you don't want my load inside you."

Her hands flew to my wrists, her eyes going wide. "Don't you dare pull out!" Then made a desperate grab for my ass, pulling me to her as she held my gaze in the mirror. I bared my teeth just before my orgasm hit. When it did, I yelled through my gritted teeth, the tendons in my neck standing out grotesquely. I looked like the monster I'd always thought myself to be. Fitting in a surreal, unnatural kind of way. My body tensed as jet after jet unleashed itself inside her. I held myself deep, not wanting even one drop to spill.

In a rush of breath, my strength nearly gave out. I leaned one hand on the vanity while holding Lyric with the other. Both of us were panting hard. She laid her head weakly back against my shoulder.

"Damn," I gasped. "Not sure I've ever worked that hard."

"Me neither."

For long moments we stood like that. Reality was slowly intruding on our little interlude. There were things that had to be addressed. I just couldn't make myself to voice them first.

"My legs feel like Jell-O," she said softly.

"I know, baby. Mine too. Let's get you cleaned up, then we'll lay down."

She glanced at me in the mirror. "You sure? I mean, we can go back downstairs if you want. I know that was part of the plan."

I scowled at her, pulling out and snagging a washcloth. I still had an arm possessively around her waist as I turned on the hot water and let it heat before wetting the cloth to wash her. "We've discarded the plan. You're staying with me."

"Look," she said, turning and taking the cloth from me. She dipped it between her legs, then tossed it into the hamper next to the tub. "I have to go back. You come get me, throw me over your shoulder caveman style or whatever, but I have to go back."

"You're not," I said in a clipped tone. "You're staying here. Everyone will know I've claimed you. They'll expect us to be together, and you'll be under the protection of Salvation's Bane while we're here and Black Reign from now to eternity. You're as protected as I can make you, and you'll be with me. End of discussion."

I could tell she wanted to say more, but then she shut down. "No."

I cupped her face in my hands, needing her to understand but unwilling to admit just exactly how under my skin she'd gotten. "Let's lie down for a minute before we both fall on our faces. We'll talk about it then."

She nodded, but I could tell I was going to have a fight with this. I needed to get her to tell me why she had to go back. I took her hand and led her to the bed. She climbed in and I followed, pulling her securely against me, my arms wrapped around her. Lyric laid her head on my chest and sighed.

"Thank you, Rycks."

"For what, brat?"

"For giving me something so wonderful to remember when this all ends." Her words were slurred, and her eyes fluttered shut.

I kissed the top of her head, needing to tell her it wasn't going to end, but hesitant to do it just yet. I had to hold on to some semblance of my man card. Otherwise, the guys in Bane would start ragging me, and I wasn't ready for that yet. I needed to process all I'd done tonight. Consider what the ramifications were. Not just if Lyric got pregnant. But what it meant for my club and what was going to happen in the next few days. Kiss of Death wasn't going to let Lyric go without a fight. Not if they thought they had a way into Black Reign. And I intended for them to know I was the one who'd taken Lyric to bed. I also intended them to know I wasn't fucking giving her up.

Ever.

Chapter Five
Lyric

I woke to a female voice in the room, followed by a soft groan beneath me. The woman talking on what had to be the other side of the room was no more than a buzz of noise in my sleep-fogged brain, while the masculine reply was all too clear. And close.

"Do I look like I need company? What the fuck?"

"You've always switched girls in the morning since you've been here. Figured tonight wouldn't be any different." The woman sounded sulky. Like she was disappointed in the extreme.

"Had one woman in here since I came here, though I did run her off. Didn't get a replacement."

"My room's empty without you."

"Was only there once, Topaz. For all of thirty minutes. Now, get the fuck out of mine."

"I don't mind joining you here. If you've worn your little toy out, I'm more than capable of picking up the slack."

"This is why I hate going to other clubs to parties," he muttered. I figured this was the best opportunity to let him know I was awake.

"Everything OK, Rycks?" I stretched my naked body over his, my thigh brushing his cock as I did. It twitched eagerly, and Rycks wrapped his arms tighter around me.

"Fine. Go back to sleep. Topaz was just leaving."

"If you didn't want a club girl in here, you should've locked the door," Topaz grumbled.

"I did. I heard you picking it before you opened it. Just so you know, that's not something I tolerate. I'll be letting Vicious and Thorn know I don't like the invasion of my privacy."

Without another word -- and after closing the door much more firmly than was necessary -- Topaz was gone. I wasn't really sure what to say or do, so I lay still for long moments, waiting to see if Rycks would say anything. When he didn't, I had to fill the void.

"I can leave if you want to go to her. I know men in MCs generally don't stay with the same girl long. Especially when they just met.

"Hush. Go back to sleep until at least dawn. It's fuckin' early."

I nearly giggled. "My. Are we grouchy in the morning?"

"You have no idea. Now hush. Or I'll find something better to do with that smart mouth of yours."

Now, that was an invitation if I'd ever heard one. If anything could turn the morning around for him it was a blow job. I stretched once more, then ducked under the covers.

"The fuck? Lyric, what the fuck are you doing?"

I took his semi-hard cock in my fist. "What does it feel like I'm doing?"

"Girl..."

Still under the covers, I took his cock into my mouth and pulled with force. He was instantly hard and pulsing in my mouth. Two strokes, and I tasted precum leaking from the tip.

"Fuck... fuck... *fuck*!" Rycks thrust his hips at me, urging me to take him even deeper. He threw the covers back and tunneled his fingers into my hair, fisting the thick mass. He held me as he fucked my mouth in measured strokes, never going too far, but pushing my comfort. I fucking loved it! I liked knowing that he was taking control, that he obviously needed it. He didn't push me away from him, but took what I offered.

Seconds later, he pulled me off him. I yelped at the sharp sting to my scalp where he held my hair securely in one large fist. He urged me to my back before covering me with his much larger body.

"Little brat. You think you can get everything you want when you want it, don't you?"

"I didn't say that," I denied. "Just thought you might like a little pick-me-up."

"Ain't opposed to morning sex. But you've got to be sore." He stroked a stray curl from my forehead. His cock was nestled between my pussy lips as he rocked his hips back and forth. I knew I was wet, easing his way so that he moved in a silky glide. "I wasn't gentle with you last night."

"Never said I wanted or needed gentle." The counter was automatic, but it was the honest truth. "I wouldn't have traded one second of what you gave me for an entire night of gentle."

"Damn," he whispered. The moonlight filtered through the blinds in his room, illuminating his face. He looked like he had no idea what to do with me but desperately needed to figure it out. "You're going to be the death of me."

"Don't plan on killing you." I grinned up at him. "At least, not if you give me what I want."

"Back to being a brat, are we?"

I pulled him down to kiss him, darting my tongue inside his mouth. "If it gets you to fuck me, I'll be the biggest brat in the history of the world."

With a defeated groan, Rycks angled his hips just a little lower and slid inside me with one smooth, silky stroke. God, it felt good! I was rapidly becoming addicted to sex with this man. It was every bit as good as I'd remembered and then some. Granted, my experience from age fourteen -- other than those two glorious days with Rycks -- hadn't been exactly geared toward finding my own sexual gratification, but no woman in the Kiss of Death compound had ever indicated she enjoyed sex. Now, I couldn't imagine having sex and not experiencing this intense pleasure or the associated rush of knowing what was ahead. Over the course of the night, Rycks had taken me more than once. Always, it had been filled with near-blinding pleasure. This time was going to be no less intense.

The sex was slow and giving. He kissed me over and over, making me drown in his taste and touch. His cock filled me, and I couldn't deny the twinge of discomfort, but he moved his hand between our bodies and flicked my clit several times. The result was a meltdown of my senses. Before I realized what was happening, I was cresting a wave of pleasure and falling from the height in a freefall. I cried out once. An instant later, I felt his cock pulsing inside me and Rycks grunted, shuddering over me. Emptying himself inside me. I was secretly thrilled at that. It felt naughty. Dangerous somehow. I didn't say a thing, just squeezed with my inner muscles, trying to hold both him and his seed inside me. One more reminder of the last time. It should have given me pause, but I was going to trust him to fix this. To let me go back to Kiss of Death. I'd get Bella, then Rycks would rescue both of us.

And we'd all live happily ever after. Right?

All too soon he rolled, taking me with him. I expected he'd tuck me beside him, my head on his chest and my thigh over his. Instead, he rolled us over completely so that I straddled his hips, lying completely on top of him.

"You're gonna be the death of me," he panted.

"You said that before." I had to stifle my giggles.

"Yeah, well, I mean it this time."

We lay there very still for a long time. His breathing rising and falling lulled me into a drowsy state. It was kind of like being in a boat on a gentle sea. I was about to drift off when his phone buzzed on the nightstand beside the bed.

"Motherfuck," he muttered, snagging the phone. "This better fucking be good." He was silent for long moments, his body tensing while a male on the other end spoke. "You sure?" Another pause. "Fine. Give me ten minutes." He laid the phone back on the nightstand. I expected him to tell me he had to go, but he said nothing. Just lay there, his arms tightening around me. Something was wrong, though. He was no longer relaxed. In fact, he seemed to be contemplating what to do next. Rycks didn't strike me as the indecisive type. By all accounts he was quick with his decisions and cunningly smart. Hadn't I been told to be wary of him?

When he spoke next, his voice was hard. Cold. "Get dressed. We need to go to church."

Wasn't "church" their meeting room? Where the club met to do club business? "You want me there?"

"I do." He didn't shove me off him, but he lifted me slightly so he could roll under me off the bed. He slung on jeans and a shirt in crisp motions.

"What's happened?" Had Kiss of Death come for me already? Was he regretting telling me he'd help me?

Had they done something to Bella and were sending a message?

Instantly, my heart pounded, and I felt like I

couldn't get my breath. If anything had happened to her, I had no idea what I'd do. Or how I'd go on. She was all I had in the world.

"Get dressed," he repeated softly. "I'll be back in a couple of minutes." Rycks left the room, closing the door behind him. Well, he was the one Kiss of Death was most afraid of since he came from Black Reign to help them ferret out the mole Kiss of Death had inserted. I hadn't really seen why, but I was beginning to understand. The tone of his voice alone put me on high alert. I didn't know him well, but I guessed this was the side of himself he showed to others. What I'd experienced the past night and this morning wasn't something he gave on a whim. Or maybe I was wishful thinking.

With a sigh, I did as he told me. No sooner had I slipped on my shoes than Rycks opened the door. His face was expressionless, and he didn't look at me directly. Instead, he looked over my head. Holding out his arm as if reaching for me, he stood in the doorway. When I would have taken his hand, he dropped it, turning to walk down the hall.

"Follow me," he said, belatedly.

"Rycks, what's going on?" I was nervous now. OK. More than nervous. I was in the middle of an enemy club and the one person I trusted was acting very strange. I hadn't lied to them. They knew I was from Kiss of Death and that I'd been supposed to seduce my way into the bed of a patched member. I'd told Rycks everything last night, except for the few bugs I'd been ordered to plant. But I'd put them in public places. Places they couldn't do any good. Truth was, I'd simply forgotten about them with everything else he'd asked of me. Other than that, he knew every single humiliating detail of my life there. I thought about telling him now, but if that was why we were here, that ship had sailed. To my chagrin, he said nothing. Just marched down the hall to a door in the back of the building.

He opened the door then stood back to let me enter first. There was a single flight of stairs, well lit. At the bottom, there was another door. Instead of reaching for it, I waited for Rycks. Like the perfect gentleman, he opened it for me and, again, waited for me to precede him. He still didn't look at me.

My heart was pounding. Something wasn't right. When I entered the other room, there was a long, semicircular table. In the center, in front of the table, was a chair on a black mat. Men sat at the table while more stood in the background. Wouldn't you know it, Rycks led me to the center chair and indicated I should sit.

I looked up at him. He didn't meet my gaze.

"You'll answer their questions truthfully and completely," he said softly. Then, finally, he met my gaze. When his eyes locked with mine, I knew I was looking at death itself.

Sucking in a little gasp, I swallowed. Then I nodded. "I've got nothing to hide."

"You'll address yourself to us, Lyric." Havoc, the vice president of Salvation's Bane, instructed. "Rycks isn't a member of our MC. He's here out of courtesy to him and his club since he's helping us with this ongoing matter." Havoc's tone wasn't unkind, but it wasn't gentle either. The man meant business. Whatever had happened to lead to this meeting was serious. And more than just me confessing something to Rycks in an effort to help their club. "Do you understand?" When I nodded, he continued. "You told Rycks last night that you'd been sent by Kiss of Death to glean information from us."

It took me a second to realize he expected an answer, that it wasn't rhetorical. Then I responded simply, "Yes."

"Did you pass on anything you saw? Anything you heard?"

"No. I was with Rycks from the time I met up with him until now." I thought about the bugs. Was now when I needed to tell them? What was the protocol? Before I could answer, I was interrupted.

"We're aware of that," Havoc said. "What I want to know is, did you make it so that Kiss of Death could gather information on our club from the inside. Did you plant any listening or video devices?"

So they had found them.

"Yes. Not tonight, but when I was here before with Wrangler. In the common room. Last night, I was searched before I came in."

"So you had nothing we could readily see or detect if we didn't know what to look for."

What was he getting at?

"Sir, I was with Rycks the entire night. Yes, I did as I was instructed and planted three bugs. I have no idea if they were visual or audio, but they had to be pressed into a wall or flimsy piece of wood. I didn't go anywhere other than the common room, and the bathrooms I was allowed into all have tiled walls."

"But you were there an hour and a half *before* you left with Rycks."

I paused, thinking. "I suppose so, yes. But I was in the common room the entire time."

Havoc nodded once, then used a remote to turn on a big TV across the room. My attention automatically focused there. On the screen, I saw myself at the bar with the time stamp. After a couple of seconds, the camera zoomed in. It focused on my left hand where I had apparently removed something from the pocket of my shorts and placed it under the lip of the bar. Then another scene with me doing the same at a table. And a couch. All of them out-of-the-way places that were easily accessible, but wouldn't be noticed if they hadn't been looking for them.

"I didn't do that." I said softly. "If you pan back, you'll see it's not me. I didn't have anything that stuck to anything. It had to be pushed into the wall. Like a thumb tack."

He did. And it was me.

"After checking the places in question, we found listening devices. There were also a couple of video devices. Then, you left the room. You stopped to talk to a club girl and get directions to the bathroom. She pointed you in a direction down the hall, which you followed. Only you didn't go to the bathroom. You went to Thorn's office."

The next video on the screen was of her, rifling through the drawers in the president's desk. Again, it looked as if she planted bugs all around the room.

"I'm going to need you to show us where all those bugs are, Lyric," Havoc said. "We found some of them, but they're extremely tiny. There were at least three places where it looked like you planted something, but we couldn't locate the device."

"But I didn't --"

"Stop lying!" Rycks growled. "I gave you a chance to come clean with me, Lyric. You told me about Kiss of Death expecting you to infiltrate Bane and set yourself up with a patched member to feed them information. You neglected to tell me you'd already bugged the whole compound. How many times have you been here with Wrangler?"

"Only once. It was when I planted the bugs I was given. I didn't lie to you, other than not telling you about them. I intended to, but our conversation was pretty intense and emotionally draining. Other than this, I've been completely honest with you. It was an honest omission."

"Bullshit," he spat. I felt like he'd slapped me. I even flinched a little before I could stop myself. If I'd lost Rycks's protection, I was fucked. Whatever happened down here, I had no hope of preventing. At that moment, I wasn't sure I cared. Because, no matter what Salvation's Bane did to me, it was going to be so much worse for Bella. And she'd never understand what was happening. Rycks had just ripped out my heart for more than one reason. I loved Bella with everything inside me, but I hadn't realized how much I was beginning to care for Rycks. I hadn't realized how tightly he had a hold of my heart until he ripped it from my chest. If they killed me, at least the pain would go away. But what would happen to Bella?

"Back off, Rycks," Thorn said. "Rein it in or go upstairs."

"Like hell! She played me!"

"It looks like it, but Data said to give him some time with the footage. See what he could find with his computer shit." Havoc didn't sound hopeful the man he mentioned would find anything, but he made it clear they would wait for the final verdict before passing sentence.

"So what now?" The one they called Vicious asked the question softly. From what I knew about Salvation's Bane, Vicious was the equivalent of a chaplain or therapist. Or something.

"Now we question her." The woman who spoke was dressed from head to toe in hot pink. Her hair was the same vibrant shade, as were her long, pointed nails. She spoke with a thick Russian accent. "Start with how to find bugs we missed."

"I told you, I didn't plant the ones you saw there. I planted three. All in the common room. I'll be happy to show you where they are. But I didn't plant them anywhere else. Only the main room. The reason I was sent here tonight was to gain the trust of a patched member. Highest ranking I could so I could get the most information."

The woman nodded to Rycks. "Looks like you fulfilled at least part of mission. Rycks is third in command of Black Reign. Can't help you with stuff going on at Salvation's Bane, though." She shrugged. "I hate to see wasted effort."

"I explained all that to him," I said, beginning to feel desperate. There was obviously a reason they let this woman take over. I'd seen her before and thought they called her Venus. Though all the pink should have made thinking she was dangerous silly, I knew better. One only had to look into her eyes (also a hot pink from what had to be specially made contacts) to know she was just as dangerous as any of the men.

"One last time, precious. Bugs. How do we find them?"

"I don't know --"

Venus backhanded me. Hard. So hard, I actually saw stars. I didn't cry out though. In that moment, I resolved myself to take this silently. I glanced at Rycks. His gaze darted away, above my head. His jaw was set in anger. His fists clenched.

"So be it," I said. The absolute only chance Bella had to survive this was if no one found out about her and who she was. The only place I knew for sure wasn't bugged were any bathrooms with tiled walls, and their church. But telling them about Bella now meant them checking out my story. If they did that and raised the wrong flags, Bella would be dead within the hour. If Bane killed me, there was a possibility Bella would be handed off to an orphanage or something. Slim, but Rat Man had dangled it in front of me low enough that I'd bitten. I was holding out hope. Maybe if I hadn't been so despondent and disappointed with my decision to trust Rycks, I'd have told them. But I had no guarantee they'd go looking delicately. And they were getting ready to inflict more pain on me than I'd ever felt in my life. No. Telling them about Bella wasn't happening. I took a deep breath and sat back in the chair. I looked at Venus, meeting her gaze. "Might as well get it over with."

Chapter Six
Rycks

When Venus backhanded Lyric the first time, I hadn't felt the satisfaction I thought I would. In fact, I'd had an almost visceral *negative* response. Before I could stop myself, I'd taken a step toward. Vicious, the bastard, laid a restraining hand on my shoulder. I was both thankful and irritated. If Vicious had noticed my discomfort, had anyone else?

Then Venus hit Lyric again. Lyric said nothing, just rocked back in her seat before looking back up at the other woman. She didn't give Venus a defiant look or in any way challenge her. Lyric just met her gaze steadily. Resigned. She didn't look defeated, exactly, but she looked like she knew the situation was only going to get worse from here, and there was nothing she could do about it.

"Trying to be brave, my little precious?" Venus grinned at her, as if she were getting ready to deliver the punchline of a great joke. She lifted her hand where those long, pointed, razor-sharp nails of hers hung like a guillotine in front of Lyric. "I have something that might make you think twice about holding back."

Venus was going to cut Lyric. Maybe her face. Maybe her arm, or something else. All I knew was that I absolutely could not watch it happen.

"Stop," I said softly.

Venus glanced my direction and shrugged dismissively. She raised her hand for the blow.

"I said *stop*!" Shrugging off Vicious, I moved to Lyric's chair, stepping in between her and Venus. "She's my responsibility. I'll take care of things from here. I'll get this out of her."

"This is Salvation's Bane territory, Rycks," Thorn

said. The man had a hard mien about him. Harder than I'd ever seen him. To say he was furious over this was an understatement, and I couldn't blame him. If someone came into Black Reign and bugged the place, we'd likely not take the time to get the location of all the bugs. We'd kill the fucker and drop the carcass on the offending organization's doorstep. "She did this in our fucking home. Her punishment is our right."

"She's Black Reign. Punishing her is my responsibility."

"And you'll be responsible for letting us take over," Thorn growled at me. "Our house. Our rules."

"Would you do the same if she were my woman? Because she might as well be. There's every possibility she's carrying my child even now."

Thorn didn't back down an inch. "Then it's your fucking bad luck to have been stupid enough to fuck the bitch in the raw."

"Everyone just take a step back," Vicious said, coming to stand in the center of the room, between Lyric and me and the table where Thorn had risen and stood with his palms flat on the surface. Vicious was a voice of reason no one wanted to listen to.

The door on the other side of the room shut, and I watched Justice hurry in. "Stop, Thorn," he said, his voice firm.

"Justice, you're my brother and a very important part of this club, but you've tested my patience enough the last month." He stood straight, his shoulders back, every inch the MC president. "This is my club, and I'll take care of the problem how I see fit."

Justice raised his hands in a non-threatening gesture. Rycks had grudgingly come to respect the man. Even if he had taken Rycks's ward as his woman. He was doing right by her, and the girl loved the cantankerous ex-con. Well, not an ex-con exactly, though he had spent the last seven years in prison. Mae had managed to not only get him released, but got his conviction overturned and his record expunged, making him no longer a felon. "I'm not trying to tell you what to do, Thorn. Not even saying you're wrong. I'm just saying, from first-hand experience, maybe we should wait until Data and whoever else he brought in to help is done analyzing the video footage."

For long, long moments Thorn and Justice stared at each other. I only wished I knew what was passing between them. I should be grateful Thorn was good to take on the punishment of Lyric. Women were always my weak spot, especially women in need of help. Was she in need of help? I'd thought she was. In fact, I was beginning to suspect there was something else she was holding back. Because, why, for the love of all that was holy, did the woman want to go back to Kiss of Death only to have us rescue her? It didn't make sense.

Finally, Thorn spoke. "You make a valid point. As someone wrongfully convicted, you'd know better than any of us how big a mistake that could be." He looked at Lyric, his face still a hard mask. "You better hope and pray to whatever deity you hold dear our tech team proves those videos were altered. If you've betrayed us, I'll do this myself. Before I'm done with you, you'll beg me to let you die."

"We done now?" I'd had enough. I'd been angry before. More because she'd also cut me to the fucking bone than because she'd withheld information from me. Never had I been so thoroughly played in my fucking life.

"No." Thorn sat. "You've been given free rein in our house, Rycks, but it stops now."

I raised my chin, knowing this was the logical

step, especially since I'd taken responsibility for Lyric. And because I'd announced to the whole room what a fucking idiot I was. Coming inside her, for Christ's sake! What the fuck had I been thinking? "Lay it out," I said, not flinching. I could leave at any time, I knew this. I just wouldn't be able to take Lyric with me until this was finished.

"You will have a Salvation's Bane member with you at all times, unless you're in your assigned room. I'm moving you to the second floor where there is a layer of security between you and the exit."

"You're not worried I'll be one step closer to you?" Why I said that, I had no idea. Likely the lingering effects of the adrenaline I hadn't expected would hit me so hard when I thought they were going to torture Lyric.

"If I were, you'd be dead, Rycks," Thorn said simply. "No. I want to make sure she doesn't 'accidentally' slip past you and escape the compound. Also, when you're not with her, I want a Bane member on her." He focused on Lyric then. "You don't get even the privacy to take a fucking shit. Someone will be with you all the fucking time, and if you protest, they'll bring you to me and I'll be the one watching you. Trust me when you say you won't enjoy that." Lyric nodded once, but otherwise stared straight ahead, not focusing on anyone in the room. The side of her face where Venus had hit her was red and starting to swell slightly.

"Wanna shove a leash up my ass as well?" I was intentionally antagonizing Thorn. I wanted his anger directed at me. Not Lyric. No matter how angry I was at her, I couldn't let her be the target of his anger. My internal make-up wouldn't let me.

"I might," Thorn said. "Now, I think both of you

should get the fuck outta here before I change my mind."

"I'll be their escort," Justice said immediately. "I'll also take responsibility for them."

Thorn cocked his head, looking for all the world like he wanted to throttle Justice. "You do that and they do something stupid, you'll take their punishment."

"I'm aware," Justice said.

I was having none of this. "That's horseshit. I don't need anyone taking responsibility for me. I fuck up, I'll take my own beating. I appreciate you volunteering to escort us, Justice. I'd be grateful if you'd be the one to look after Lyric if I can't."

"Why are you treating her with fuckin' kid gloves?" Thorn demanded. "She betrayed you more than Bane if she got you to fuck her without a rubber. What the fuck were you thinking?"

"None of your fucking business. And I'm not treating her with kid gloves, I just don't relish the idea of beating a woman senseless. Pardon the fuck outta me if I'm a little old-fashioned!"

"If she were a man she'd already be dead."

"And you might have killed an innocent person," Justice reminded. "I think we all need to take a step back and really think about what we're doing."

"Justice is right." It didn't surprise me Vicious took up the fight. It was what he did. "No judgments until we're sure the video hasn't been tampered with. That could be several hours or a few days."

Thorn sighed, sitting back in his chair. He scrubbed a hand over his face wearily. "Fuck it all," he muttered. "Get her out of my sight before I do something I regret. Only because it would upset my wife, and she doesn't need the drama."

I snagged Lyric's upper arm and moved her toward the door. I wasn't giving Thorn a chance to change his mind. Besides, if she knew anything about the bugs placed in the Salvation's Bane compound, I'd get it out of her. I'd also know if she was telling me the truth. There was a nagging feeling in the back of my mind that she might be telling the truth and that I'd lost my head. I hadn't done that since I was a teenager. The results this time had the potential to be as devastating to me as the last. On the heels of that was the reminder I was sure she was holding something back.

Lyric didn't say a word as we marched up the stairs. Justice led me to our new accommodations on the second floor. It was actually a larger room than the one I had, but it was right smack in the middle of the club girls' rooms. They'd be coming and going at all hours of the night. And be annoying as fuck if I didn't discourage everything from the beginning.

Just as I was getting ready to usher Lyric inside, a club girl lunged for her, pulling her free of my grip and taking her to the ground.

"You fucking bitch! I don't know why Thorn let you live, but I'll finish the job myself!"

The fight that ensued was one for the ages. Lyric might have sat there passively when Venus struck her, but she wasn't backing down from a club girl. No sooner had she landed on top of Lyric, straddling her waist, than Lyric shoved her up, getting her feet underneath the girl and heaving. The club girl went flying a few feet down the hall, giving Lyric time to get up. She didn't make a sound, but threw her body at the club girl, grabbing her hair in her fists and banging her head on the floor twice in rapid succession.

With a sigh, I snagged Lyric by the waist and

dragged her up. Immediately, she went still. Justice wasn't quite as quick with the other woman, and she ran the three steps separating them, ramming her shoulder into Lyric's middle. Lyric grunted, but wrapped her arm around the other woman's neck so her head was under Lyric's arm, and hiked her knee into the woman's middle. Lyric kept leverage on the woman's neck, letting the club girl know Lyric could break her neck if she chose.

"All right, that's enough!" Justice pulled the club girl free and swung her around bodily, putting himself between the two women. "All of you get in your rooms or leave the fuckin' floor! Now!"

There was a flurry of activity as about half the women darted into rooms and the other half for the stars. "Fuckin' nosy-ass bitches," Justice muttered. "You OK?" He actually looked at Lyric with gentleness.

"Fine," Lyric said softly.

Justice looked at me and shook his head. "Fuckin' women. When they say 'fine,' it means they're anything but."

"Well aware of that," I said, taking Lyric's arm once again. "Let's get inside before anything else happens." Lyric nodded and went passively where I led.

"You good?" Justice asked.

"No," I answered truthfully. He and I had been through enough that I owed him that much. Like him or not, Justice was actually a good man. He had his own code and followed it religiously, but he wasn't above doing the dirty work when needed. "I imagine that whole thing reminded you of your time in prison."

"Not sure how she fit in with Kiss of Death, but she knows the score with club girls. Just like with inmates in prison. You can't show weakness, or they'll eat you alive."

"She's got spunk," I said. "I like her sass, but…"

"You know you jumped to conclusions," Justice said quietly. "Just admit you're feeling guilty and fuckin' talk it out with her. Before you can fix this between the two of you, you've got to figure out if she's guilty or not. If she is, you've not lost her so much as you never had her to begin with."

"And if she's not?"

Justice shook his head. "I'm not sure what you should hope for."

"Me neither."

Once inside, I locked the door and stood with my back to it for a long time. Lyric sat at the small table, her hands folded in her lap, looking out the window a few feet away. The morning sunlight hit her face, making her look starkly beautiful. Then I moved toward her, and she turned to face me and I saw the reddening bruise on her face where Venus had struck her.

"Christ," I muttered, immediately diverting to the small kitchenette and the fridge. I snagged the clean dish towel and loaded it with ice from the freezer. Kneeling in front of her, I laid the towel against her cheek. She immediately took it to hold it herself, looking away from me. "Look at me, Lyric."

"No." Her soft voice wrapped around my heart and fucking squeezed. She sounded like she felt as betrayed as I did. One thing I'd learned to do in the years since El Diablo had taken me in was to read people. I could tell you an accurate life story about someone I'd known for only half an hour just by watching their body language and paying attention to what they said and the way they said it. My instincts were screaming at me this girl was as innocent as the first snow of winter, yet my mind kept going back to that fucking video of her planting bugs all over the Salvation's Bane clubhouse.

I sighed. "We're going to talk about this, Lyric. You're going to tell me where all the bugs are, and we're going to work this out before Thorn takes matters into his own hands."

"So, you've already decided I'm guilty."

"The evidence is pretty damning."

"I suppose it is," she said softly. This wasn't the woman I'd met last night who had decided to take a chance and tell me as much as she knew of what was going on with Kiss of Death. This girl had lost hope. She'd resigned herself to whatever came next and would take it as best she could. It felt like a knife had just plunged into my belly and twisted.

"You gotta give me something, Lyric. Anything."

"I already gave you everything. I've got nothing left to give anyone." Her statement seemed both literal and metaphorical.

"What rooms were you able to access? Did anyone help you?"

"I already told you. I was alone because we don't know who's in the group. Only one person does so he or she can keep an eye on us and report back. I couldn't get the bathrooms because most of them have tiled walls. I planted three in the walls of the common room. I'll be happy to show you where."

"Who gave you the tech?"

"Pretty Boy at Kiss of Death."

"Where else did you plant them?"

This time she was silent. An annoyed, frustrated look came over her face, but she said nothing. I decided to change tactics.

"You can't have done all this by yourself. You're not our rat. You've not been here enough over a long enough period of time. Who else is working this?" When she continued staring out the window, I swore, slamming the flat of my hand down on the table. "Dammit, Lyric! You may think you're safe here, but you're not! These men are every bit as dangerous and ruthless as the most vicious member of Kiss of Death! They won't like torturing a woman, but they'll do it and never regret a second!"

"I'm aware of that," she said, breaking her silence.

"Then help me help you!"

Finally, she looked at me. "I have no love for anything or anyone at Kiss of Death, Rycks. I gave you every scrap I had. All I wanted..." She swallowed, clearing her throat before continuing. "All I wanted was a way out. When I said I was just trying to survive, I meant it."

"I get that. You planted the bugs to make it look like you were doing what you were supposed to. You did the same thing last night. Just tell me that, and I'll have something to go to Thorn with. I can't promise all will be forgiven, but it might buy your life!"

"Don't you think I'd tell you that if I thought it would help?" For the first time since I'd gotten that fucking phone call this morning, Lyric was showing some fight to her. She raised her voice as she finally started pushing back. "I'd tell you anything I thought you'd believe! I'd tell you how Rat Man told me he'd give his men free rein with me if I came back empty-handed. I'll tell you how I've watched what they did to women who failed them for years and how I watched them die a slow, horrible death and wanted to avoid it myself. I'd even try my best to play on the things we shared last night, how you were special, and I don't regret anything about that or our first night together six years ago or how I never regretted giving you my innocence. I'd throw all that in there and sob like a baby if it would help! Neither you or Thorn would buy any of it. True or not. It wouldn't negate anything you believe I did. You've caught a spy in your home. What does it matter why I did it? A spy is a spy!"

"Are you saying you're guilty?"

"I'm saying that if enough people believe I am, it doesn't matter what the truth is!" She shut her eyes, an errant tear making a trail from the corner of her eye down her cheek, and I wanted to howl in anguish. The last thing I ever wanted to do was make her cry. Again, my gut was screaming at me so hard, I thought I might vomit. There was no way Lyric was guilty. At least, if she was there was a fucking good reason. But I just couldn't let go the damning evidence I'd seen. Nothing made sense. It felt like my whole world was spinning out of control, and I had no way to stop it.

"OK. Look at me." I crouched in front of her. "One last thing. But you have to look me in the eyes. I want your full attention." She nodded, and I asked the one question I absolutely did not have an answer for. "Why are you insisting on going back to the Kiss of Death compound?"

For a moment, her eyes widened just that little bit. There it was. I didn't know what it was, but it was something she was desperately trying to hide.

"I -- I just..." She swallowed. "Rycks, I just have to." This time, she shook her head slightly. Just a little bit. She seemed to be begging me not to go further, but I had to.

"Lyric." I tried to be gentle, but I'm sure it came out stern.

Then, right before my eyes she seemed to just... deflate. Tears sprang up as if some kind of fountain had been turned on and she just started *sobbing*. I pulled her with me to the floor and just held her while she cried. This was a woman who'd given me everything she had, including her innocence. Never once had she cried. She hadn't when Venus had hit her or when the club girl had attacked. In fact, when Venus had started, Lyric had looked like she intended to take everything Venus had to give without a fight. So what the hell was this? More importantly, how did I fucking *stop it*?

"Talk to me, baby," I whispered in her ear. "You know it's safe in here with me."

She shook her head. "I think it is, but I don't know for sure. I may have already set things in motion by agreeing to let you come rescue me at Kiss of Death, though I'm hoping they'll think I was just trying to appease you. Now, if your room is bugged..." She let out a broken sob. "Oh, God!"

"My room's safe. I'm absolutely sure of it because I have this." He brought out a small device from his pocket. It was about the size of a standard die. Only instead of pips to mark numbers, there was only one small LED light. "El Diablo gave me this before I left Lake Worth to come here. It's a jammer. My cell phone works because I have an app that lets my phone read through the signal. Anyone else in here would have any electronics jammed while this thing is on. No one knows about it because El Diablo told me to keep it secret. I have no idea why. I imagine it's to torment Thorn. For some reason, the man sees everyone in authority as a rival. Not necessarily in a bad way, but a rival nonetheless."

She looked at the little cube, then back up at me.

For the first time there was genuine hope on her lovely face. "Are you certain it works? Against everything?"

"Honey, I can't even get a radio signal in here unless it's turned off."

She took a deep breath, nodding several times as if trying to convince herself this was what she wanted to do. She looked up at me, then cupped her hand to my ear and whispered. "I have to go back because I can't leave Bella."

I looked down at her in confusion. Just as softly I asked, "Who's Bella?"

She shut her eyes, fresh tears spilling down both cheeks. For a moment, I wasn't sure she'd answer me. Then she looked up at me, meeting my gaze with intent. "My daughter."

For a long time I sat there, not daring to move. "Your... daughter. Lyric, is she..." She nodded, not daring to say it out loud, but it was painfully obvious. Her gaze clung to mine. "Sweet God, Lyric," I whispered. "You can't be lying about this." When her face crumpled, I quickly added. "I'm just saying I'm not sure I could take it. Not about this."

"I swear to you on all I hold sacred and dear," she whispered in a tremulous voice. "She's five. And she's my entire world, Rycks. Everything. She's alone and scared. If I don't make it back, they will kill her. Eventually."

"Motherfuck," I swore, standing, urging her back in the chair. I stalked across the room. I needed to talk to El Diablo more than I needed to breathe. I needed to see if his eyes and ears knew any more than I did. Then I remembered I had my own set of eyes and ears.

Moving to the door, I opened it. Sure enough, Justice stood outside the door, his arms crossed as he stood guard. Funny thing was, he stood with his back against my door. Like he was guarding us from the rest of his club.

"Come inside, Justice."

The other man did so without hesitation. Again, he snagged a straight-backed chair and planted himself, back against the door.

"You expecting trouble?"

"Always. Can't let anyone take matters into his own hands. Someone kills you, Mae would probably never speak to me again."

I couldn't help it. I grinned at the other man. "She's got you all wrapped up, doesn't she?"

"Without a doubt. Tell me."

"Treat every room in this place as if it's bugged. I'm betting only church is safe."

"What about here?" Justice raised an eyebrow.

"Don't worry about that, brother. Leave it at that."

Justice shrugged. "What do you need?"

"As discreetly as you possibly can, without talking to anyone who could possibly have ties to Kiss of Death, I need to know if there is a child there and what her status is."

Justice immediately stiffened. He glanced at Lyric's stricken face and nodded once. "I can tell you that right now. There is, and word is she's not to be harmed unless Lyric sends someone to rescue the girl, or we start digging."

I blinked. "When the fuck did you get that?"

Justice just shrugged. "When I realized there was a possibility the video footage had been altered. I wondered why they'd go to that much trouble. Didn't seem like gettin' us to kill your woman here was worth all that trouble. So I asked a couple questions. This came up, along with a bunch of shit that didn't matter."

"Any idea why?"

"Oh, yeah. I have a very good idea. But if there is even a possibility you're bugged, we need to go to church. Besides, I think Thorn needs to hear this as well."

I held out my hand to Lyric. "Come on, honey. I'm gonna fix this. I swear it."

"Please, Rycks. You have to be careful. She has a hiding place, but it won't take long for them to find her if they decide her time's up."

"I will. Let's go."

Chapter Seven
Rycks

Thorn listened to me in silence as I explained what I'd learned from Lyric. I could tell he wanted to interrupt but, thankfully, just listened intently.

"You confirmed this?" Thorn looked at Justice. The other man nodded.

"Confirmed the kid. Can't confirm who she belongs to. Not without digging, and I'm not sure I'm willing to risk it."

Thorn seemed to mull this over. I wanted to punch his fucking face in. Finally, he said, "The fact that there's a kid in danger is really all we need to know for now. We can sort it all out once we have her safely with us."

"Took you long enough to decide," I grumbled. "If Bane is the kind of club that has to think over whether or not to rescue a child, I'm not sure Reign needs any of you."

"Watch your fuckin' tone," Thorn snapped. "You're lucky I don't just off the both of you and say to hell with it." He glared daggers at me. I'm sure the look was returned. "There's no question we're going after the girl. I'm just trying to decide whether or not she's lying." He pointed at Lyric. "Could be her kid, sure. But who says it's yours? Hell, maybe it's a girl she took in to protect."

"Does it matter?" I might yet beat him to a pulp before this was over. I understood his caution, but, in my position, I didn't appreciate it. "If she's protecting the girl, if things were as bad as I believe them to be for her, maybe she feels like the kid's mother. We'll never know until we get the kid, now will we?"

"I've had just about enough of you, Rycks,"

Thorn said, standing and pacing across the room. "This isn't your fault, and I don't hold you responsible for the situation, but I will not stand the disrespect in my own fuckin' club."

I should have apologized. Or at least backed down. But I couldn't. I felt like my heart was racing out of my chest. Thorn still had doubts about this kid, and I could even see his point. But I knew in my heart that every word Lyric told me was the truth. She had a daughter. That daughter was my daughter. She was currently in a world of danger. That's really all I needed to know.

"You don't want to do this, Thorn, I'm more than happy to call in Black Reign. We'll put these guy down like the fuckin' rabid dogs they are."

Thorn slammed his fist down on the table. "Shut the fuck up or get the fuck out, Rycks! And if Black Reign comes into this fuckin' city to execute a raid on *anything*, Salvation's Bane will not let it go quietly."

"All right, that's enough," Vicious said softly. "We all need to take another step back. Thorn, Rycks is worried about a girl who could possibly be his child. You can't fault him for wanting all hands on deck." He turned to me. "And you are way out of line."

Justice sidled up to me. "I have a close tie to the bastard, but even if I didn't, I have to agree with him. We need to move quickly."

"Fuck," Thorn spat. "I never said we weren't, but this ain't a fuckin' democracy!" He scrubbed a hand over his face. Other than Justice and me, only officers in the club were present for this meeting. Thorn wasn't taking any chances and I was grateful for it. The man was taking the threat of an infiltration into his club seriously. I wasn't telling him that because he was still a prick. "We do things my way. If I thought for one second you'd actually do what El Diablo said, I'd call the man and have him give you a direct order to take your woman and return to Lake Worth until we got this done."

"He wouldn't issue the order so I wouldn't have to disobey." No sense in letting him think he had that option. "I'm not sitting on the sideline and leaving someone else to rescue my daughter."

"Which is why I'm letting you go with us."

I shook my head. "I'm here to tell you what's going on. So you know what I found out from Lyric. You may or may not believe her, but my gut tells me she's not lying. Knowing that, this is my *daughter* we're talking about! I'm not asking for permission to do this raid, and I'm not sitting back while someone else leads it. I'm going in and crushing every single motherfucker who stands in my way. When I get a hold of Rat Man, I have something special planned for him."

"I feel a nightmare happening," Thorn muttered. "Fine. But only because this is your daughter. And, believe it or not, I do realize that, even if she's not yours, you can't take that chance. Nor should you. You can lead a team in, but Blood is still the cleaner. You make his job difficult, and he'll be the one to deal with you."

"Understood."

"I want to know every detail, Rycks. If you're using my men, I get to be in the loop."

I snorted. "Thought you'd insist on going."

Thorn shook his head. "Normally I would, but you don't trust me, and I wouldn't be able to stop from reining you in."

I shrugged. "You could try."

"So, let's hear it. What's your plan?"

Looking around the room, I knew there was only

one person here I wanted with me. Fucker. "I'll need Justice, if he's willing to come with me." I looked to the other man who simply nodded, his arms crossed over his chest and standing shoulder to shoulder with me. As much as I wanted to hate the bastard, he was a solid ally. My ward had chosen well. "Other than him, I only want a couple of my own men. Assuming El Diablo will spare them."

"Who?" Thorn was a demanding son of a bitch, but he had every right to know. We were still in his territory after all.

"Shotgun and Fury."

"We could use Shotgun here," Thorn said. "He could be your eyes and ears if you wanted to use drones or access remote cameras. I know intel isn't his real strength, but he's still good."

"No. I want him on the ground."

Thorn nodded. "I'll give El Diablo my blessing. Now, lay out your plan."

I did. Which was basically, get in unseen. Get the girl out. Go back in and kill every motherfucker we could find. If there were other innocents, they could get out when everyone else was dead.

"I like it," Thorn said after a long silence. "Simple and effective. Can you do it?"

"I'll get an idea of the layout from Lyric." I hated putting her name out there again to give Thorn something to scoff at, but she was going to be a huge part of this.

"It's your life. If you're willing to trust it to her, who am I to judge?" Thorn was a stubborn, annoying son of a bitch, but maybe he was OK. "When do you want to leave?"

"As soon as it's dark. I'll call El Diablo."

It wasn't long before I had my requested men,

armed to the fucking teeth. This was a rescue and an execution. I found it ironic that I thought Fury was well suited to this. As a doctor, he was supposed to save lives. Not take them. Yet, I'd never met a man more singularly suited to killing than Fury. He'd save the life of my daughter, but he'd also execute her tormentors without mercy. But only if he got there before me.

The plan wasn't that difficult. Get in when they were too drunk to notice, get Bella out. Go back in and kill anyone we felt needed to die. We picked the fucking perfect night to do it, too, though not by accident. Justice was a fucking genius not only at getting information, but distributing it. How he managed it, I wasn't sure I wanted to know, but he convinced someone at Kiss of Death that a raid on one of the local shipping yards was a fantastic idea. He said he dangled an out-of-town rival MC's drug shipment in front of them, then messed with the shipping manifests to make the rival think their shipment would be on a different transport. Leaking the mix up to Kiss of Death meant there were free drugs to be had with little to no security other than whomever they had to bribe. Everyone had someone at the Port Authority on their payroll. Kiss of Death was no different.

We waited for several hours to see if they'd take the bait. Then, sure enough, they took off in force. From what Ripper could get from the city cams and intercepted cell phone messages and calls, the only people left at the clubhouse during the raid were about five prospects and Rat Man himself. Which was great because it meant a quick in and out. We could probably do the rescue and capture at the same time. Thankfully, El Diablo agreed with my brand of justice. He also had money to burn. Which was how I had a

Gulfstream on the tarmac awaiting my instructions for later tonight.

There were several Bane members as well as Reign brothers with eyes on the situation both at the Port Authority and at the Kiss of Death clubhouse. If we got into trouble the four of us couldn't handle, we'd have backup. We wouldn't need it. The prospects were lazy, not keeping guard but rather drinking or fucking the couple of club girls hanging around. Getting past them was easy enough, and Lyric's directions and recall of the layout of the clubhouse was spot-on.

It didn't take long to find the tiny room she shared with Bella. But by the sound of things, Rat Man was only partially distracted with his club's unexpected activity. Given the reputation he was brandishing, I expected him to be absorbed in the activity he'd set in motion with his men. Even if they expected no resistance at all, they were still stealing a big drug cache from a rival club. *And* they were doing it at a heavily guarded port. Which told me he wasn't as good as everyone thought he was. The problem was his focus was on Bella and the fact that Lyric hadn't come back to the club yet. He was preparing to come for my daughter, and I wasn't having that.

Justice took up a point in a hallway nook while I went inside Lyric's room. Not surprisingly, Bella was nowhere to be found. Lyric had said she'd told the child to go to her hiding place and not to come out for any reason. She explained she'd planned for this and Bella had a stash of snacks, water, and even pull-ups so she could go to the bathroom without having to leave her hiding place. The one thing I hadn't really thought about was how to find the girl without scaring her to death.

"Bella," I called softly. "Your mom sent me to

bring you to her." No answer. "Bella, honey, we don't have much time. My name's Rycks. I'm a friend of your mom's."

No sooner had my name left my lips than I heard a scurrying inside the walls. A soft *thump* sounded followed by a soft "ouch!" A small girl poked her dark head from behind a dresser. As I looked closer from my position by the door, I could see there was a loose panel just barely big enough for the small child to squeeze through. When she came out, she clutched a stuffed dog that looked like it had seen better days. She stared at me with wide eyes.

"You're Rycks?"

"Yeah, honey. Ain't got time to explain, but I know your mother --"

Before I could finish, the child had flung herself into my arms and wrapped her skinny arms around my neck. "Daddy!" Her cry was soft, barely above a whisper. "Mommy said you'd come." She had?

"She was right. I'll always come for you. You got that?" She nodded, but said nothing, still clinging to me, her face buried in my neck. "Can you look at me a second, Bella?" When she pulled back slightly and looked up at me, my heart melted and my arms tightened around her slightly. I couldn't help it! God-fucking-dammit, if she didn't look the spitting image of my little sister. My chest squeezed painfully, and my eyes prickled like someone had thrown sand in them. I cleared my throat to dislodge the lump forming. "I'm going to need you to be brave for me. Can you do that?" She nodded. I undid the Velcro of my Kevlar vest on both sides. I'd worn one a couple sizes too large for me just for this purpose. I didn't have a kiddie-sized vest for her, so this was going to have to work. "I'm going to have to put this vest over us both,"

I told her. "Don't think your head will go through the neck with mine, so you may be a little mashed for a bit. Can you stand it?"

"I think so," she replied. Again, she didn't raise her voice much above a whisper.

"Are you scared?"

She shook her head. "Mommy said that when you came for me not to be scared. That you'd take care of me."

Kid was fucking shredding my heart. "She's right. You just do what I tell you, and I'll get us out of here." She nodded as I put the vest over her. "Put one arm through the hole and wrap it around my neck." She did as instructed. "Now, hang on as tight as you can to me and to your dog there. If you drop him, we can't go back for him. Understand?" Again, she nodded. Bella was tucked against my body, the vest over her so that she was covered all but her one arm and her legs, which she'd wrapped tightly around me without my telling her. Kid had good instincts.

I fastened the Velcro at the sides. There was a bit of a gap, but not much. I'd prepared as well as I could, and I hadn't missed the mark much on her size. I checked my gun, then knocked one time on the door -- Justice's signal that I was coming out.

"We don't have much time," Justice said, his throat mic picking up for me and Fury and Shotgun. Communications were, of course, monitored by Ripper. He would know every step we made and exactly what was happening. He could also warn us of incoming danger if necessary. "Rat Man has decided he's through waiting. He's on his way here now."

Bella whimpered, but otherwise stayed silent as we moved through the compound out a door on the north side, as far as possible from Rat Man's most likely path to Lyric's room. We passed one Kiss of Death prospect lying half in, half out of an open door on the way. There was no blood or another sign he'd been stabbed or shot, but his neck lay at an odd angle. Likely Fury's work. He was a hands-on kind of guy.

Surprisingly, we made it safely outside without any incident. Shotgun helped me get the vest off and took Bella, talking soothingly to her as he put her in the booster seat we'd fitted into the back seat of the truck. Probably not strictly necessary, but I didn't want to take any risks I didn't have to.

"Get her back to Lyric," I said. "Justice and I will finish up here. How many of the prospects did you get?"

Fury came up behind us. "All of them. Only people left in there are two club girls and Rat Man himself. Club girls were gettin' the fuck outta Dodge. You guys can't handle Rat Man on your own, you're pussies." He didn't break his stride as he moved around the front of the truck. Shotgun was already at the wheel and Fury opened the passenger-side door, climbing in and shutting the door. "Rip it up, guys. Time's wasting, and you have several hours ahead of you."

"Just make sure Bella's not hurt and tell Lyric I'll be back in a day or two."

Shotgun nodded. "We got you, brother. Rip it up."

"Guard them both for me. Stay in touch."

"Want us to take them to Lake Worth?"

"At the earliest possible convenience." Just knowing they were in our own compound under El Diablo's protection would make me rest easier. Also, I didn't trust Thorn. Not with this. He said he'd wait until he got all the information back from Data, but I honestly didn't care what that video footage showed. As far as I was concerned, anything Lyric had done she'd done to protect our daughter. All was forgiven. Thorn wouldn't see it that way, and I wanted my girls out of there ASAP.

"Consider it done." Shotgun gave me a two-finger salute then drove off with my daughter in the backseat of his truck. Just the mere fact I had to deal with fucking Rat Man before I got to be properly introduced to my daughter made a cold fury burn inside my gut. This man was going to suffer like no one I'd ever punished before. I just wished I could do it here so I could get back to Lyric and Bella tonight. Unfortunately, El Diablo intended to send a message to the Brotherhood with this one. Rat Man's bad luck he'd taken up with the fuckers. It was the last mistake the man would make.

"Don't look ahead, Rycks," Justice said, laying a hand on my shoulder. "That will make you sloppy. If we're doing this, we're doing it right. Otherwise, call someone else in."

"Blood on the way?" I didn't want to think too closely about that because I very much indeed wanted to let someone else take care of it. Only my loyalty and total belief in El Diablo pulled at me to continue with this. Even with that, if I hadn't trusted my brothers from Black Reign as much as I trusted El Diablo, I couldn't force myself to continue. Bella and Lyric were just too important to me to risk if there was even the slightest bit of doubt. There was none. My girls would be fine until I could take charge of them.

"Already here." The man in question stepped from the trees. "You need me to take care of your Rat Problem, too?"

I groaned. "More than I can tell you, but I can't.

El Diablo wants him to be far away when he dies. If the body is found at all, it won't be in Florida."

Blood raised an eyebrow. "Seems a bit overly cautious. I'm very good at my job. No one will find him."

"It's not the authorities he's worried about. He wants to throw the Brotherhood off the trail and to send a message. If he can make them think Rat Man went rogue and left on his own, they might leave us all alone."

"Hate to break it to you, buddy, but that jet waiting for you isn't exactly inconspicuous."

"Don't worry about that. If anyone looks too closely at it, it most definitely won't lead to El Diablo or anyone he's associated with past or present."

Blood shrugged. "He's nothing if not thorough. If he thinks this is necessary, I guess it is." He stuck out his hand. "Good luck, brother. Get in. Get out."

As I took his hand, I couldn't help but think maybe I'd made a friend or two in Salvation's Bane. I mean, they were still uncivilized and inferior in every way, but they came in handy and were good at having a man's back when he needed it. Yeah. This was a good alliance. But Thorn was still a prick.

We went back in search of the Rat in question, which wasn't hard. The first time I lay eyes on Rat Man, I thought he probably was a rat. The fat, furry kind. With a long tail. And fucking little beady eyes. I wanted to squish him like Percy did Mr. Jingles. Only this rat wouldn't have a John Coffey to save his sorry ass. If Justice hadn't been with me, I'd have lost my shit, but I held on with grim control.

"You in a heap a trouble, boy." I tried to draw out a deep Southern accent, keeping in line with my *Green Mile* movie theme. It was the only way to rein in my temper. This man had tormented my woman, kept my child hostage, and had come to this very room, probably to kill her. I was not in a merciful mood.

He spun around, knife in hand. "Who the fuck 'er you?" Justice snagged Rat Man's weapon hand and twisted until I heard bones snap. Rat Man howled, dropping to his knees. Once Justice had the knife from the man's now useless hand, Rat Man cradled it in his other hand. "What'd you do that for? I didn't do nothin'!"

Justice looked at me. "Are you shittin' me?"

I shrugged. "It looks like the guy, but he's not a criminal mastermind."

"Fuckin' pussy if you ask me." Justice's disgust was clear. I could relate.

"Why did you come to this room?" I asked the question calmly enough when I really wanted to take that knife and plunge it into the man's groin and twist. Slowly.

"To kill that brat kid. Where is she anyway?"

"A pussy and a fuckin' dumbass," Justice muttered.

"Obviously, she's gone. Why were you coming to kill her?"

The guy got to his feet slowly and shrugged, still cradling his broken wrist, a pained expression on his face. "'Cause the bosses told me to."

"And who, exactly, are your bosses?"

"Don't know exactly. I do what they tell me, and they pay me."

"Either this Brotherhood business isn't as connected as El Diablo thinks or this guy is a patsy, doing work they know will get him killed."

As the words left Justice's mouth, Rat Man lunged for me, I felt pressure at my side where he tried to stab me with something, but, after dropping off Bella, the vest was large enough on me the sides of the Kevlar met instead of leaving a gap at the sides. He didn't hit it right, and the blade didn't penetrate the seam. But he wasn't finished. Even with his injured hand, Rat Man moved with a speed I had underestimated. And he was a scrapper.

Somehow, he slid under my legs and tried to make a run for it. Just as he broke into a sprint Justice pulled out a gun, aimed, and pulled the trigger. Instead of the report of a gunshot, there was only a metallic click. I glanced at Justice with a raised eyebrow.

"You came into this place, outnumbered as we were, with a tranq gun?"

He opened the other side of his vest where his Gloc was holstered. "Just makin' sure we didn't kill this guy here. You said El Diablo made that absolutely clear. We were not to kill him here."

"He did."

Justice raised an eyebrow of his own. "I'd have thought you wanted to kill the bastard yourself. Now your bitchin' 'cause I didn't?"

"No. I'm bitching because that tranq gun could have been a real gun. With real bullets. And I'm not bitching!"

There was a thump in the distance around the corner where Rat Man had disappeared. Justice and I continued our conversation as we followed Rat Man.

"You always bitch," Justice said.

I scowled at him. "I never bitch. I inform you Neanderthals of Salvation's Bane when you're being idiotic."

"Idiotic? I shot the fuckin' bastard, didn't I? And without killing him."

We rounded the corner and there was the bastard in question. Out cold on the floor. "Yeah. I suppose you did."

I bent and lifted Rat Man by his shoulders. Justice got his feet.

"Heavy motherfucker," Justice grunted.

"Are all you Bane men such pussies?"

Justice glared at me. "One more smart-ass comment and you can get this bastard to the plane your own damned self."

"Guess that answered that question." I smirked. Justice dropped Rat Man's feet and flipped me off. "Fine. If it will soothe your delicate sensibilities, I'll apologize."

"You're an asshole, Rycks." He bent and picked up Rat Man's legs again. "One more comment and I'm fuckin' leaving." We made a few steps before my snicker broke free. "What?" Justice said, a look on his face that said he dared me to say something else.

"Nothing. Nothing at all."

"Remind me when this is over I owe you an ass beatin'."

"Yeah. I'll just call Mae and tell her to remind you since I won't be there much."

Justice grumbled. "Fucker."

Chapter Eight
Lyric

I'd worried myself into a sick mess. Literally. I'd just spent the last half hour kneeling in front of the toilet barfing up everything I'd eaten until only yellow, slimy foulness was left to puke up. If I was wrong, or if Rycks was, and there were bugs in his room, then Rycks would be bringing Bella's body home to me. I wasn't sure I could take that. Just thinking about it brought on a fresh wave of nausea. And tears.

Needing some fresh air, I stumbled to the sink and rinsed my mouth out. Then I made my way to the door of the room I shared with Rycks. When I opened it, Venus was standing on the opposite side of the hall, arms crossed and one foot braced on the wall behind her. She had been looking to one side, but brought her attention to the door once I opened it. She said nothing. Just gave me an assessing look.

"I-I needed some air. Am I allowed to go outside?"

"Da. With escort," she said, pushing off the wall and gesturing for me to join her. "I'll take you."

I hesitated but went. "You're not going to hurt me, are you?"

She shrugged, answering in her thick, Russian accent. "Not unless Thorn says to. I happen to like you."

That was surprising. "You do?"

"You didn't flinch when faced with an unwinnable situation. I could see it in your eyes. If Thorn had told me to continue, you'd have taken your beating better than most men I know. I knew you would never give up that last scrap of information, though I knew you held something back." She glanced at me as we walked. "Now, I know why. Willingly giving up your life for your child makes you OK in my book."

I guess that was something. We continued on down the hall. Venus took me out to the backyard area. It was surrounded by a privacy fence around the rest of the property. No one could see in, but she showed me to a lounge chair well underneath the covered porch they'd built onto the back of the building.

"Stay in this general area," she said. "It's one spot on property no sniper can get bead on."

"You think I have to worry about that?" That was all I needed, but fuck it. What's one more thing?

"Not likely, but possible," Venus said. "Better safe than sorry."

I got that.

I'm not sure how long I sat there, but I could hear the ocean softly in the background. The cries of the gulls off in the distance. Gradually, I began to relax. Or, at least, I felt better in control. I was still wound tight with fear for Bella. Venus sat at the table between me and the clubhouse door. I had to wonder at that. If the encounter I'd had with the club girl before was any indication, Venus was there to make sure something like that didn't happen again.

Deep in thought, I missed the building commotion until Venus stood and turned to face the clubhouse. "Stay there unless I tell you to --"

The door burst open and a high-pitched voice cried, "Mommy!"

I jumped to my feet. Or, rather, tried. I stumbled and rolled to the concrete, all the while craning my neck to see if the girl crying out was, indeed, my Bella. Before I could get to my feet, she threw herself at me, landing hard with her thin arms around my neck. We both burst into tears. Vaguely, I was aware of several male voices murmuring. Looking up, I saw several men in the doorway and on the patio talking to Thorn in low tones. Club girls looked on out the windows, a few squeezing their way through the men to watch the reunion.

Bella clung to me tightly, sobbing uncontrollably. I'm not sure I was in much better shape, clutching her just as close, tears and snot pouring. I was aware of the building crowd, but didn't really give a damn. Bella was here. Safe. With me.

"Wh-where's Rycks?" I managed to get out the question.

"Has some unfinished business," Thorn said softy. "He'll be back either tomorrow or the next day."

I glanced up at the man who had so recently held my life in his hands. I wasn't sure I trusted him, but at least he'd brought my daughter to me. For that, at least, I was grateful. "Thank you, Thorn."

He shook his head. "Don't thank me yet. Jury's still out on your fate."

I closed my eyes and inhaled my daughter's sweet scent. "It doesn't matter. Bella's safe. Do what you have to do. Rycks can take over if he has to." I was trying not to say "if I die" in front of Bella. The kid had been through enough without realizing her mother wasn't in any better a situation than we'd just come from. Bella was safe. I was not.

"Don't worry," Venus said to me softly. "Thorn is thorough. And if it does come to that, I'll make it quick and painless." I knew, to Venus, her words were meant to make me feel better, but I wasn't as brave as Venus gave me credit for. I wanted the fairy tale. I wanted to live happily ever after with Rycks and Bella. I just didn't want to die. I wanted to see Bella grow into a caring, intelligent woman. I wanted a life with Rycks. "Besides. No matter what, I'll make sure nothing happens until Rycks gets back." She laid a hand on my shoulder and stood slightly in front of me. I looked up at her, and her gaze was on Thorn. The man nodded at her as if the two were having a silent conversation and had come to a decision. Did that mean Thorn already knew what he was going to do?

Now wasn't the time. I had Bella with me. We were together. For now, that was enough.

I was aware of people leaving and the murmur of voices gradually receding. Looking up, I saw the men were mostly gone, except for the one called Fury. Likely he was there to make sure Bella was physically OK. As our crying tapered off and Bella relaxed slightly, he moved toward us.

"Bella?" She looked up at him. "I told you I'd bring you to your mother. Do you remember?" She nodded. "Now, I need to look at you. You remember me telling you I'm a doctor?"

"Yes. But I want my mommy."

"Not a problem. I just want to get this part over so you can be with your mother and not have to worry about anything."

"Where's Rycks? He's my daddy. He's supposed to be here."

Fury looked at me before answering her. "He's taking care of Rat Man."

Bella wrinkled her nose. "I hope Daddy kills him. He's an asshole."

Venus barked out a laugh before covering it with a cough. "I like this kid."

Fury nodded. "That he is, little bit."

Thirty minutes later, Fury pronounced Bella healthy and unharmed, if a bit underweight. Probably the result of stress. He'd looked briefly at her skin all over, and asked her questions like, "Did anyone touch you anywhere that made you uncomfortable?"

Bella had looked at me and asked if he meant like "down there." When I nodded, she answered without hesitation that no one had. I hadn't thought she'd been abused that way, but it was definitely a relief to know she hadn't. Fury had taken time with her, reassured her she could tell him or me, even if she was afraid to right now. There was nothing to be afraid of, nothing was her fault, and there was no time limit on when she could tell us if she remembered someone hurting her.

Now, Bella and I sat on that same lounge chair, Bella curled up in my lap with her head on my shoulder as we watched the sun set on the horizon. I wasn't sure we wouldn't just stay here all night. If so, I could wake her gently to watch the sun rising from the ocean view in front of us. A fresh start on a new day. Hopefully, in a new life.

I was just about to doze off when Venus stirred from her spot beside us. The woman had apparently appointed herself our guardian in Rycks's absence. Then I heard female voices.

"Just because Thorn's gone soft since taking Mariana as his ol' lady doesn't mean this bitch doesn't need to die. She's a traitor. Probably the spy the men have all been looking for."

"If we do this and we're wrong, Topaz, Thorn will banish us. Or worse. Rycks has some kind of claim on her."

"Shut up, Mercedes."

"Easy for you to say. I'm not even supposed to be here. I do something Thorn doesn't like, he'll do more than banish me."

"Only if you're lucky," a third voice said. Several

women giggled.

"Fuck this shit." That was Topaz.

Venus looked at me and stood. "Can't help you with this. Can only keep it one on one."

"Club girls I can handle. Any of them patched members?"

"Only me." Venus stepped off to the side into the shadows.

"I've dealt with those fuckers at Kiss of Death. Club girls are nothing. Will you protect Bella?"

"With my life, little sister." That was the most solemn vow I could have gotten from any MC member anywhere. With her calling me "sister," she considered me an equal. Which meant she absolutely would keep Bella safe.

I stood to meet the threat. Topaz smirked, which meant she believed she had the backing of the other girls in a pinch, no matter their reservations. She might have been going to say something, I really had no idea and could give a shit. I just had no desire to listen to the little bitch.

Taking the three steps separating us faster with each step, I launched my attack just as she spoke.

"Listen, bitch -- UMPH!"

I drove the heel of my hand up into her chin, snapping her head back. Topaz staggered back before falling on her ass. She didn't immediately scramble up, but glanced around at her buddies. A couple of the girls backed away toward the door, wanting no part of an actual fight. The other three looked nervously at each other.

Topaz got to her feet and screamed her attack. She threw herself in my direction, intending to take me to the ground. Apparently, blow jobs were the extent of her talent. She might be a good lover, but she was no fighter. I sidestepped her attack and she ended up on the ground once again. This time she was quicker to get up. When she rushed me a second time, I leaned into her. We hit with jarring force, hands on each other's shoulders, but I managed to stay on my feet.

"Thorn's gonna kill you, bitch! You and your fucking little whelp!"

"He might kill me. But he won't touch Bella."

"If you think Rycks is gonna protect you, think again. Guys said he's gone. Back to Lake Worth and his own, snooty little club. You're just like the rest of us. Beneath him."

There might have been a sliver of doubt. I knew how over-the-top protective Rycks was. Even if he left me to face Thorn's wrath alone, he'd never leave Bella. Unless he didn't want the complication in his life.

No. Rycks would never shirk his responsibility.

"You might be right. Rycks might be back in Lake Worth. But if he is, then he'll make sure that any punishment Thorn sees fit to hand down doesn't involve orphaning Bella. He'll make sure she's taken care of, no matter if he arranges for me to care for her, or he does himself."

"Maybe. But if he does come back, that only means he's good with Thorn passing judgment on you. For betraying the club, that's death, you bitch!"

"Not until he gets the final report from his computer people. That's what he said."

"You didn't actually believe that, did you? He's just making it look good to appease Vicious. As the club shrink, he always demands shit like that. Doesn't mean Thorn does it. You're guilty as fuck, and you're gonna die. I just hope he lets me pull the trigger on your skanky ass!"

"You honestly believe that about Thorn? He'd

kill someone for no reason?"

She shrugged. "He has before."

"Careful where you go, Topaz," Venus said from behind me. She'd stepped away from Bella but not so far she couldn't get to the child if she needed to. She was also between the mob of club girls and Bella. "Accusations like that require proof. Can you produce it if I take you before the club?"

"You can't do anything. You're just a club girl in disguise. You're no better than any of us." Topaz said those words with feeling, but the look in her eyes said she wasn't so sure. She kept shifting her gaze, looking back to her friends. The second she'd uttered the last sentence, the other girls backed away farther. The two in the back left the patio and went back inside, leaving me there to deal with only Topaz, assuming the other woman might attack again.

Venus saved me the trouble. Faster than I'd have thought possible, Venus lunged for Topaz, snagging her by the hair and shoving her to her knees on the concrete.

"Lyric, would be good for you to take little Bella back to Rycks's room. I'll come for you later."

"What are you going to do?" I didn't really care. I just wanted to see Topaz's reaction.

"I'm taking out trash," she said as she bent down to put her face next to the other woman's. Venus licked a long line from Topaz's jaw to her ear, then nipped the lobe sharply. "Too bad, really. You taste good. I'd have loved to find out if you're as good at eating pussy as you seem to be at sucking cock."

Topaz whimpered, looking up at Venus with a healthy dose of fear in her eyes. "If you don't tell Thorn, maybe we could work out something."

"Oh, baby," Venus tsked. "Far too late for that. I

suppose I'll just have to stick to men since you won't be here any longer."

"You can't throw me out. Only Thorn can do that."

There was a long silence while Venus contemplated those words. "I suppose… you're right." Topaz gave her a victorious grin, one filled with superior glee. "We'll just go talk to Thorn now."

"What?" Topaz's smile faded and her face paled. "You can't --"

"Now, this I can. Actually, I could toss you out on my own, but I prefer to have Thorn's blessing. I owe him more than this. Is small price to pay, letting him make decision about you."

She pulled Topaz up by her hair and shoved her forward, never letting go of her hair. Venus looked back over her shoulder. "Go to Rycks's room. Shut and lock door. I'll be back soon."

I looked back at Bella, who had a look of satisfaction on her face. She looked up at me. "I hope she has to go away," Bella said. "She was mean."

"Yeah, baby. She was." I held out my hand to her, smiling. "Come on. We'll go wait for Rycks upstairs."

"Will he come back, Mommy?"

"Of course, baby. He'll come back."

"You sure he won't go away and leave us here like she said?"

I knelt down in front of Bella. "Now, you listen to me," I said, gripping her shoulders firmly. "Rycks is a good man. He risked his life to come after you and to protect me. He won't leave us here to fend for ourselves. He will take us back to his home, and we'll work everything out from there."

"You promise?"

Did I? Did I really believe what I'd just told my daughter, or was it all bullshit to soothe her feelings? I thought back to everything that had happened. If Rycks had wanted rid of us, Fury would have said we were staying here. Instead, he'd made Bella aware she could come to him any time she needed. Surely that meant he thought we'd be with Rycks at the Black Reign compound. Besides. I trusted Rycks with my life. More importantly, I trusted him with my daughter's life.

"Yes, baby. I promise."

Chapter Nine
Rycks

Some places in the United States were still pretty much wilderness. The Dakotas, for example. While there were bustling cities, there was also peaceful emptiness. Only the wolves and God could find a man in some of those places. Just so happened, I knew of one such area. A friend from long ago owned it. I didn't know his real name. Hell, I doubt there were many left on the face of the earth who did. All I knew him as was Chief.

The trip took us about six hours. During that time, I got to know Rat Man on a personal level. Basically, I beat the fuck out of him, all the while questioning him on everything except his involvement in the Brotherhood. That was for later. This session was all about power dynamics. Once he cracked and gave me a little information, I could get anything I wanted from him.

I'll give him credit, though. He lasted longer than most men I've interrogated. By the time we landed, I had him singing like a canary. When he wasn't squealing like a girl. He was also minus every fingernail and toenail he had, his hair and most of his scalp, and his hands were basically useless pieces of meat. I mean, I had a lot more body surface to work with, but it never took much. He'd spilled how he had thrown Lyric at me six years before with the intention of me getting her pregnant. They'd waited until she was at her most fertile, then sent her to me. Had it not worked the first time, they'd have sent her back until I rejected her, or until she finally got pregnant. Had she not conceived, they'd have thrown her into their rotation of women. Either fucked her until she was of no more use to them or sold her. Likely the latter since she was such a lovely find. It was enough to make my blood boil.

Justice had his hands full. He had to watch everything closely. Though the plane had been modified specifically for the messy business I put it through, Justice wasn't taking any chances. Probably because Blood would still be in charge of the cleanup. The jet was to head straight back to Palm Beach where Blood and his crew would clean the thing from top to bottom. With every drop of blood that went beyond the tarp layered over much of the floor and aft seating, Justice glared at me. He'd probably lecture me later. Maybe try to throw me a beating. Meh. I could take him.

Now, I stood in the wide yard that surrounded the meager shack where Chief resided. There was a lantern burning inside the house but no other sign of life. I knew better than to think Chief was unaware of our presence, though.

"Never thought I'd see you again, boy." Chief, an elderly Native American, approached from my left. As I'd expected, I hadn't heard him approach.

"Been a long time."

He looked at the beat-up Ford I'd brought my prisoner in. Rat Man was under a tarp in the back, too hurt and afraid to move. Just in case, however, Justice was under that tarp with him.

"Hear you have a rat problem."

It never ceased to amaze me how Chief knew everything he did. "You could say that."

"Best way to get rid of a rat is to burn him out."

"That's what I was taught." I wouldn't ask. It was up to Chief to offer. If he didn't, this whole trip would have been for nothing.

"Got a building couple miles away." He pointed in a seemingly random direction, but I knew exactly which building he was referring to. "It's been filled with rats in the past. Had to make a hot fire to get rid of them, but it worked."

"My rat has some brothers," I said. Again, I didn't outright say it. That wasn't Chief's way. But I needed to make sure he knew who this guy had for an employer.

"Pfft! He has no brothers. He's the poor twice-removed seventh cousin. They wouldn't claim him if their lives depended on it."

I raised an eyebrow. "Maybe all my effort at breaking this one was for naught?"

"Na. You probably learned something. Any knowledge is power if it's in the right hands. Should save you some time now, though. He knows nothing about the brothers."

If Chief said so, then I could bank on it. In all the years I'd known him, the man had never been wrong. He never made statements he wasn't sure of. "Thanks, Chief. I owe you."

"No. I think I still owe you more than one. Take this off my tab, eh?"

I grinned at the old man. "Your help is still very much appreciated."

"Give your woman my love. Someday, I expect to meet her."

I gave him a grin and a shake of my head. "Tell me where you get your information and I'll consider it."

Chief barked a laugh. "The spirits, my friend. Spend a few weeks in a spirit walk and maybe they'll grant you the gift of sight as well."

"I have no patience for it, old man. I think it's

why the spirits gave me you."

"Perhaps. One thing I will ask before you go, my friend."

"Anything, Chief."

"Take care of your daughter. She is special, that one. Intelligent. She sees things others can't and always will. Not a mystic, but she's perceptive. If she tells you something, don't ignore her."

"You knew about her?"

"I did."

"And you didn't think to tell me?" It was the first time I could ever remember being angry at the older man. But if he'd let Bella suffer when he could have told me and prevented it, I might have to kill him.

"You could try," he said, giving me a stern look. My expression must have given my thoughts away. Chief was a master at reading people, and I'm sure my anger was making it easy for him. "I might be old, but I have powerful allies."

"She lived in a kind of hell, Chief. How do you expect me to feel about this?"

"Suffice it to say I had someone watching over her until you were ready to meet her."

That took me aback. "I don't follow."

"You weren't ready to meet your daughter or her mother again until you'd lost the most important thing in your life. Not because you didn't have room for them, but because you could never have fully appreciated them and what they could mean to you."

I sucked in a breath. "You didn't..." I couldn't say it. If I did, it would make it real and I really would kill the old man. Right alongside Rat Man.

"Of course, I didn't," he snapped. He appeared just as angry as I felt. "You take me for a man who kills women for fun? Or even allows a woman to die just to make your sorry life better? No. I knew you weren't ready, and it wasn't until her death I realized why you weren't ready. The devil knew it, too, though he still tried to find them both. Even sought my help. I assured him I had my best man watching out for her."

El Diablo. He knew. Never had I doubted my mentor, but this might be the one time I took exception to the man's secrecy.

"I see in your eyes your doubt. Don't. What we did, we did to help you all. El Diablo acted on my advice. He trusts me like you do. Ask your girls. They can tell you there was always someone looking out for them. Your woman might not remember, but I guarantee you the girl will." He tapped his temple with a weathered finger. "Told you. That one is intelligent and perceptive."

I took a breath. "I've trusted you with my life on more than one occasion."

"That you have. It's a testament to how much these girls mean to you that you don't now." He clapped my shoulder. "Take care of them. And don't think badly of this old man."

"Perhaps you're right. Though you opened up some raw wounds."

"I know. It's something you need to tell your woman so she understands your need to keep her close. And why you'll have to continue to bring in women who can't protect themselves."

Much as I hated the thought, he was right. "I'll talk to her second thing when I get back."

Chief chuckled. "Of course. First things first, eh?" He gestured over his shoulder. "You know where to dispose of the mess when you're done." I did.

I grinned, feeling better about the situation, but needing to get back to my girls like I needed to breathe.

Since Chief didn't believe Rat Man could give me much on the Brotherhood, that left me needing significantly less time than I'd originally thought.

I said my goodbyes and headed back to the truck. Seconds later, we were headed to the middle of nowhere where I could burn my rat problem out.

Three hours later, the deed was done. Turns out, Chief had upgraded his incinerator. Oh, it was properly attired for garbage disposal, but burned considerably hotter than I remembered. Rat Man screamed. Blood-curdling screams. Had I been less of a bastard, they might have bothered me. Instead, I thought of what he'd probably had planned for little Bella and I grinned. Yeah. The man deserved what he got and more. Might should have videoed the whole event for when I got back to Salvation's Bane. That way, when we caught the rat inside -- and we would catch him -- I could give a preview of what was in store for their sorry ass.

The "garbage disposal" was a dump over land on the way home from our plane. This time, we were on a cargo plane landing at an ExFil base. From there, we took a helicopter to the open yard of the Salvation's Bane compound. It was afternoon when we landed. Justice grasped my shoulder once, then moved ahead of me to greet Mae. She kissed and hugged Justice before coming to me. When she wrapped her arms around my neck, I felt like, maybe by killing Rat Man the way I had, it had given some vindication to women everywhere who'd been tortured or bulled. Rat Man hadn't tortured Mae, but it had been the same fucking club.

She clung to me for long moments before kissing my cheek. "I'm glad you're home safe, Rycks."

"Me too, sweetheart."

"Lyric and Bella are inside in your room. And we have news. Seems that Topaz is one of the moles in Bane. Venus and Thorn had something to do with her confession. I think it has to do with the stripped video footage of Lyric."

I snorted. "Didn't see that coming. Should have."

"She had access to every man in this place. Well, except the ones who have ol' ladies now. But before... yeah. She's been in place for a very long while. Long before Rat Man."

"Bet Thorn's shitting himself."

Mae tapped her chin thoughtfully. "Not sure Thorn ever gets *that* upset, but yeah. He's not what I'd call a happy camper."

"I'll go see what's going on," Justice said. "You go to your woman and your daughter. Meet her properly."

My daughter...

"Yeah. Think I'll do that."

I found them in the room I'd been designated by Bane. Venus stood outside and welcomed me warmly, ushering me inside. "Don't worry about club girls. I got your back." That wasn't cryptic at all...

I stepped in to get my first look at them. Bella was in Lyric's lap. Both were engrossed in a book Lyric was reading. Only, sometimes Bella would read. Apparently, they took a page at a time reading to each other. They were so engrossed, they didn't hear me enter. Which was fine by me. It gave me a chance to simply watch and listen.

They were reading *Charlotte's Web*. Bella seemed to love the rat, Templeton, and giggled at his antics. Much as I hated to disturb the moment, I wanted to be part of it.

Quietly as I could, I moved next to the loveseat

where they were curled up under a blanket. Lyric read softly, making different voices for the characters -- which Bella clearly loved -- until it came time to turn the page. The Bella took over and I slowly moved in beside the two.

At first, Bella stopped, her eyes going wide and her mouth dropping open. I smiled at her and nodded. "Go on." She gave me the biggest, most beautiful smile I'd ever beheld before starting again.

Carefully, I sat next to Lyric and pulled both my girls onto my lap. Lyric adjusted her hold on Bella and shifted until they were both resting comfortably against my chest. A funny pressure built in my chest, as if it were too full. As I looked down at my woman and my daughter, I knew that was exactly what the sensation was. My heart was full. There might have been a leak in the ceiling, because I was sure that drop of moisture on my face absolutely did not come from my eye. I cleared my throat and brushed it aside before anyone could notice.

Bella read the rest of her page, then looked up at me. "I think it's Daddy's turn."

Well, fuck. There went that stupid ceiling leak again. Lyric smiled and leaned up to kiss the spot where the offending moisture had landed. Clearing my throat, I began my page.

* * *

Lyric

I'm not sure I'd ever expected to see Rycks in this kind of setting. As hard a man as he was, he was right at home sitting on a loveseat with me and Bella both in his lap, reading a children's book. We could have been in some midwestern subdivision in a house with a white picket fence. It was that... *normal*. He slipped into the role of suburban dad with ease. Honestly? I wasn't sure which man I liked better. My rough biker was thrilling and a demon in bed, but the dad reading to my daughter stole my heart. Not to mention, everyone knows a man taking care of a child is sexy as all get out.

Rycks read to the end of the book. By that time, Bella was sound asleep. Like, *snoring* asleep. I couldn't help but giggle. "I'm not sure she's ever slept that soundly."

"'Bout fucking time, then." Rycks's deep, rumbling voice was right by my ear, sending shivers through my body. "You got her?"

"Yeah." I started to get up, but Rycks just pulled me closer and stood with both of us in his arms. Really, no man should be that strong. And yeah, it sent a thrill through me.

"She sleep with you?" His question was matter of fact, but I could see it was important to him.

"Sometimes. She did last night because she had questions about you. She did when we were with Kiss of Death, but she's already asking about getting her own room."

"Little independent thing, huh?"

"I think so. She'd probably come crawling into bed with me even if she did have her own room."

"Well, I see no reason for her to start now. But I have unfinished business with you. So, we'll put her in our bed, then get our own room for a little bit."

"I don't want to leave her." Much as I wanted time with Rycks, I was still terrified at the thought of letting Bella out of my sight for long.

"Don't worry, baby. Venus is right outside. I'm sure she wouldn't mind sitting with her until we come back."

He didn't really give me a chance to protest. Carrying me to the door, he buried his nose in my neck and inhaled as he walked. "Missed your smell."

I giggled. "That tickles!"

"Got more parts of you I want to tickle."

He opened the door and Venus glanced our way. "Everything OK?"

"Absolutely," Rycks said. "Bella is asleep in our bed. Would you mind sitting with her in case she wakes?"

"Not at all. She's... precious. Feisty kid, but very precious."

"That she is," Rycks agreed. "I owe you one, Venus."

She waved him off. "My pleasure. I hope you come over often when you leave for Black Reign. I'd like to get to know kid better." She grinned. "I can teach her to ride. We'll have matching Harleys."

"Not happening." Rycks shook his head.

"Absolutely not!" I protested. "She's too young for a bike of her own!"

"Huh?" Rycks looked down at me questioningly. "I mean, it's not happening that she gets a pink Harley. In fact, I'm going to petition Thorn to make Venus's illegal. I mean. A pink Harley is just all kinds of wrong."

The woman chuckled. "Good luck with that."

"You're both crazy," I declared.

"I am," Rycks agreed. "But you love me anyway."

With a sigh, I admitted, "Yeah. I guess I do."

Rycks took me upstairs where the officers typically stayed. "This is where Thorn was going to move us. Kind of a step up from the other room with an extra bedroom. You want to stay here?"

"Actually," I said as he opened the door and ushered me inside. "I was hoping we'd go back to Black Reign. That is, if they'll have me. I just… don't feel entirely safe here."

"I've already cleared it with El Diablo on my flight back. He's anxious to meet you and Bella."

"Everyone makes him out to be the boogieman. But you talk about him as if he's a proud father or something. Which is the real El Diablo?"

"Both." He shrugged. "Neither. Hell, I don't know. I know he's my mentor. He's the one guy I always want at my back and that I never want to cross. And before you ask, you should know that, if he didn't trust you, there's no way he'd let you into our clubhouse. Even with all the security and the fact that you'd be going into the proverbial lion's den, he'd never let you in if he thought you'd betray him in any way. He knew from the outset that you were innocent."

"No shit?"

He grinned at me. "Nope. He also knew about Bella and that she was my daughter. And why you were sent to me specifically. I wasn't too happy when I learned that, but he was right. And you and Bella were kept safe even if you didn't know it."

I frowned. "I don't understand."

"Apparently, there was someone in the club watching out for you. He kept Rat Man from going too far and kept him diverted when he might have otherwise fixated on you or Bella."

"Wait a minute." I thought back really hard. "Bella always talked about a man there. He was the only one she liked. She talked about him sometimes like they'd had real conversations. Always when I was at work in the city at the DA's office. It was like he was her babysitter or something. He'd come to her after I'd left, then leave her right before I got back. What did she call him?" I searched my memory. "Loki? Maybe?"

"Hum," he said, his brows drawn in concentration. "Could be. There was a Loki loosely associated with a friend of mine. Chief. I've known him almost as long as I've known El Diablo. Chief's the one who decided I wasn't ready for you and Bella."

Wasn't ready? "What does that mean?"

He sighed and sat on the bed. For the first time since I'd known him, Rycks looked vulnerable. "It's a long story. Short of it is, I about a year after you and I met, I lost my sister."

"Oh, Rycks! I'm so sorry!"

"I've come to terms with it. For the longest time, I blamed myself because I didn't take time out of my life to help her. We both left home at early ages. Me because I hated my dad. Sara because she killed our dad. She was nineteen."

"Oh, Lord," I gasped. "Do I need to ask why?"

"No. Dad was the lowest of the low. Sara was older than me by four years. I was fifteen the last time he beat me. Sara took matters into her own hands after that. As mean as I am, Sara was even more scary. I'm not sure exactly what happened, but she literally shoved me out of the door one night. Told me to go to Mexico City. Said someone would find me. It's where I met El Diablo." He shook his head. "Anyway, about a year after I met you, I'd gotten word that Sara had killed our father, then killed herself. Didn't seem like something she'd do, but El Diablo seemed to think the information was sound. He told me she'd want me to put it behind me and make a life for myself." He shrugged at me. "I mean, I couldn't deny he was right. She'd sent me straight to El Diablo. Besides, Sara was always one to make up her own mind. It didn't seem like her, but, if she decided that was the best course of action, she'd do it without hesitation."

"I'm so sorry, Rycks."

"For the longest time, I blamed myself. I mean, I should have tracked her down once I was working for El Diablo. He'd have helped me. We could have helped her somehow. At least, that's what I thought. In reality, I think something more sinister happened. I'm just not sure what."

"You think she was killed?"

"Actually, no. If she's dead, it happened just like I heard. She killed the old man, then killed herself. Only, I'm not so sure she's dead." He waved that off like it was unimportant. "The point is, I had to lose someone I loved. Someone I thought I could have helped before I was ready to find out about Bella. El Diablo and another friend pointed that out to me. It's why I take in girls I feel can't fend for themselves. Who are in impossible situations. Sara was a strong woman so it doesn't really fit, but in my mind, she needed my help and I wasn't there for her."

"And now you're paying your penance?"

"Maybe. I don't know. It started with Serilda and Winter. Then Mae. Had I met you after Sara died, I'd have recognized your plea for me to take you with me for what it was. A cry for help."

"I don't want you to feel sorry for me, Rycks." It was the last thing I wanted. I wanted him to want me for who I was. Because he loved me. Not out of some sense of obligation.

"Believe me, honey, I don't. I feel possessive. Territorial. Like I'll fucking die if you try to leave me again." I could see the truth of that on his face as he looked at me. "If I feel sorry for anyone, it's myself.

Because I'm just as big a pussy as I accuse Justice of being with his woman." He tried to grin at me, but failed. Instead, his eyes had the sheen of tears in them. He swallowed them back, looking disgruntled and uncomfortable. "You deserve better than me, but I'm too selfish to let you go, Lyric. I…" He cleared his throat and looked off to the side. "I love you."

My whole being settled. "I love you, too, Rycks."

"You and Bella will come back to Lake Worth with me tomorrow. I'll introduce you to El Diablo and we'll get settled." Finally, he looked at me and smiled. "I think you'll like the place. We have a suite all our own. The compound is huge and sprawling. Like a country club. Best of all, it's surrounded by armed guards. No one can get in or out without me knowing."

"As long as you're with us, we'll be happy."

"I will, baby. Always."

He leaned in to kiss me. One thing led to another and the next thing I knew, I was naked with Rycks's head buried between my legs. After that, there was really no point in trying to hold a conversation. I could barely focus on anything other than the sensation he created in my body with just his lips, teeth, and tongue.

Once he crawled up my body and tucked his cock against my entrance, all I could do was scream. And boy, did I scream. Rycks surged into me over and over, the sensations building until I thought I'd go mad with the need to come. I remembered him doing the same thing the first night we met. He did it so effortlessly back then. Same as now. Our bodies seemed to be in tune with each other. He gave me exactly what I needed and took what he needed from me. All I could do was cling to him and take what he gave me.

"So fucking perfect," he whispered in my ear. "You're absolutely… perfect."

"Rycks," I sighed. "I love you so much!"

"I love you, too, baby. I fuckin' love you, too! AHH!"

He erupted inside me, triggering my own orgasm. I screamed his name long and loud, glad he'd taken us away from Bella. Last thing I wanted to do was wake her. Not now. I needed Rycks all to myself. Later, we'd shore up our family unit.

"Nothing and no one will ever tear us apart, Lyric. You. Bella. Me. We're in this together."

"Yes," I sighed happily.

"You'll like Black Reign. We're like a regular MC in many ways. Some of the members of the original club are still there. But most came with El Diablo, El Segador, and myself. Any who are left have proven themselves loyal to El Diablo many times over."

"Anywhere you take us, we'll be happy. As long as you're with us."

"Always, baby. Always."

We lay for long moments, Rycks over me, his semi-hard cock still inside me. He kissed me over and over, our sweat-soaked bodies slick against each other. Finally, Rycks groaned and got to his feet. He padded into the bathroom. I could hear water running for a few moments. When he returned, he cleaned me gently before tossing the cloth back into the bathroom and drawing on a pair of drawstring sleep pants and a shirt.

"I'll have Venus bring you back something to sleep in. I'll bring Bella."

"All right." I sighed happily as he left. Maybe I'd get my happily ever after.

A few minutes later, Rycks entered with a sleeping Bella in his arms. "Not sure the kid's moved an inch," he said. "Venus put you a change of clothes on the couch."

"I'll get dressed. Give me a minute." It wasn't long before I was back in the bedroom, dressed for sleep. I crawled into the bed beside Bella. She mumbled something and turned her head in my direction. Rycks looked down at us, a satisfied little smile on his face. When he turned to leave, I called out softly. "There's plenty of room, Rycks. Stay."

He turned, hesitating when I knew he wasn't a man to hesitate. "You sure?"

"Absolutely."

He crawled in beside me, wrapping his arms around me and Bella both. The child put her tiny hand on top of his huge one in her sleep. I placed mine on top of hers. Behind me, Rycks sighed contentedly.

Yes. I was definitely getting my happily ever after.

Wrath (Black Reign MC 2)
Marteeka Karland

Wrath: When El Diablo sends me to infiltrate the DA's office and find out who's involved in the corruption there, I'm all over it. Then I meet a sexy little platinum-haired escort and all bets are off. If I can't pull myself together enough to complete this job, I'll fail my club and, more importantly, my mentor, the club president, El Diablo. That's something even this unholy attraction can't cause. But what's a man to do when all that stands in the way of the happiness of a sexy single mom and her feisty but vulnerable daughter is club business, and a few Saint Bernard puppies?

Celeste: I'm in a financial jam of the worst kind. I need to make enough money to pay for my daughter Holly's medical bills. Out of options, I accept an offer to be an escort. Not only that, but I soon find myself working for a motorcycle club as a "cam girl," doing live sex shows. Glamorous? Not at all. But it's more money than I can make working three jobs. Imagine my surprise when the man who paid for my services as an escort turns up in the control room of my first cam show. He's sexy as sin, and much more than he appears to be. He's also got me completely under his spell. Which sucks because he's quite possibly the rudest jackass I've ever had the displeasure of meeting.

Chapter One
Wrath

"I think you'll like corporate law, Vincent." The man currently schmoozing up to me was a weasel. If I could have my way, I'd've tossed the fucker off the balcony of the huge suite the firm of Lawson, Hughsman, and Gray had procured. The firm was having a little romancing session at the Four Seasons Resort in Palm Springs for several lawyers they were considering bringing into their fold. Including me. I was supposed to be scoping out Nathaniel Lawson, the son of the founding member of the firm. He was the personal attorney of the new District Attorney in the city. He was the man responsible for keeping away lawsuits and criminal investigations into anything Harold Collins might be threatened with so the DA's office at looked clean and untarnished. This guy, Stewart Gray, was a pompous windbag and as big a scumbag as everyone else in that fucking firm. And the fucking DA's office. I hated all of them. But I couldn't show it.

"Perhaps," I replied vaguely. "As long as it makes me money."

"Oh, there's plenty of money to be had," Gray chuckled. "Join us. We heard about your work taking down the former DA, William Barrison. Who knew the son of a bitch was so corrupt? Hid it for more than a decade, but you brought him out into the open. Thanks to you, the city is a much safer place."

"I live to serve." I grinned slightly. "As long as it makes me money."

We both laughed.

This was a bust. Nathaniel Lawson was on his best behavior, other than the high-end call girls and even higher-end drugs at the party. They were considering five other prospective partners. Only one of them would get the spot in the firm, and I was beginning to think this whole angle was a bust. I just wanted to get out, get with Black Reign, and rethink this whole setup. We needed a different approach.

"Well, my friend," Gray continued. "If you want to make money, I guarantee you, you've come to the right place. Lawson, Hughsman, and Gray can make you *a lot* of money." He emphasized "a lot" and gave me a knowing look. "With money comes power. With power comes perks." He gestured toward a long table with pretty much any kind of quality drug or liquor a man could want. There were Cuban cigars, Legacy rum, some kind of expensive absinthe, and, of course, heroin, cocaine, and various other mind-altering substances.

As if that whole line had been a setup, a door opened just beyond the well-stocked table and several very beautiful, very sophisticated women entered. "See what I mean?" Gray looked positively gleeful, actually rubbing his hands together as he eyed each woman like a kid in a candy store. "Yours to enjoy, Vincent. Take your pick. There's nothing they won't do. Live out your nastiest fantasies with as many of them as you like for as long as you like." He clapped my shoulder. "These are just a very few of the perks you can enjoy as one of us."

Normally, I'd have smiled politely and passed, but one woman caught my eye in a huge way. She was ethereal in her beauty. Long, platinum-blonde hair, flawlessly pale skin. She'd dressed in red, naturally. Some skimpy little number I couldn't even register. All I saw was the woman. Short and slight, she had rounded hips but was very slender. Her legs were perfectly formed. Just the right amount of muscle to grip a man tight during sex. She looked out of place among the other women. It wasn't something I could put my finger on, but she just didn't fit.

Nervous. She looked nervous. Where the other women smiled and sought out a partner, this girl seemed unsure of herself. She smiled politely when she had to, but she didn't have that shark-like quality the others did. If she was looking for the wealthiest man of the bunch -- and when did an escort not do that? -- she wasn't doing a good job. In fact, she seemed to avoid eye contact whenever she could. Lord knew more than one of the men in the room tried to get her attention. She was easily the most beautiful woman in that room. Instead, she wandered around, looking at the artwork on the walls. She avoided the table with the alcohol and drugs.

My very first thought the second I could see her from head to toe was that if I fucked her the way I wanted, I might break her delicate frame. My next thought was, "I can be gentle." It was a Goddamned lie, but I told myself that anyway.

"Ahh, I see one of them has caught your eye? Which one?"

I glanced at Gray, standing next to me. He leaned forward in anticipation. Did he have his eye on the little blonde, too? "Where do you get these girls?" I knew, of course, but I wanted to hear what he had to say.

He shrugged. "Most are from a high-end escort service out of Miami. One or two are local, I think. All of them were vetted and screened medically. All disease-free and with an IUD, verified by our physician."

I gulped down the rest of the scotch in the

lowball glass I held. Without saying anything else to Gray, I approached the young woman before anyone else had a chance.

"Come with me." I wasn't big on words and, really, if she was a paid escort there was no need for them.

Her eyes widened, and there was the slightest quiver to her bottom lip before she lowered her eyes and ducked her head slightly. Hmm... A little more demure than I'd like, but I could work with it. I took her hand, and I'll be Goddamned if she didn't tremble. My gaze snapped to hers.

"You OK?" I was a bastard, and I wanted this girl, but the farther away we got from the other women with their cloying perfumes and the more her unique clean, fresh scent wrapped itself around me, the more she wrapped herself around my insides. It was like discovering a new life form. I was eager, excited, and just plain in awe of her. She looked like a fuckin' angel.

"Of course," she said softly. "Where are we going?"

"To be alone," I said gruffly, my grip on her hand tightening. She went willingly, but the trembling didn't stop, and her palm became damp with sweat. She was nervous? What high-end escort got nervous? That wasn't an act. You can't fake a physical response. I shook it off, trying not to think about why she'd be nervous. I knew these lawyers weren't good people, but even though they put up smoke and mirrors for the DA's office and other high-power clients, we'd found nothing on human trafficking or child pornography. Well, other than the last DA. Which I'd exposed. His... business partners had taken care of the rest. The Brotherhood wasn't known for its gentleness. No one had found the body.

She followed me, having to nearly run to keep up with my long strides. I led her to the hotel room the firm had secured for me. I'd had no intention of using it, but I'd had it swept for bugs and anything that might compromise me in any way. Even the drugs and booze had been replaced by my brothers in Black Reign. Not that I'd intended on using anything. It was all there for appearances. Control was something I maintained at all times.

The room was spacious, with a sitting room that opened onto the balcony overlooking the ocean. I'd spent that morning watching the sunrise. It had been one of the most peaceful times I could remember. I watched her face closely as we crossed the room. As I expected, her gaze was drawn to the open balcony doors and the sound of the sea crashing against the beach. She glanced at me but immediately ducked her head.

"We can sit outside a while if you like." I'd brought the girl here for sex. Normally, I'd have simply taken what I wanted, but I found I also wanted to see what she'd do. What her reaction would be.

Those clear blue eyes widened, and she nodded, a faint smile parting her lips. She grinned slowly, the smile growing slightly when a breeze wafted in from the open doors.

Fuck. Me.

By all that's holy, the girl was... stunning! The transformation from shy to happy was so profound, I nearly fell to my knees. This time, it was she who led me. Never letting go of my hand, she walked outside and to the railing. She closed her eyes and inhaled.

"It smells so nice," she said softly. "The air coming off the ocean. It doesn't smell the same on the ground, but up here..." Fuck. Her voice was musical.

A little high-pitched, but sexy as fuck.

"Yeah," I said, suddenly unable to say much of anything. All I could do was stare at her. "Beautiful."

She glanced up at me, and her smile faded slightly before settling into something a little nervous but not unwelcoming. "I'm at your service. Would you like to stay here or go back inside?" How the fuck could she make my cock pound with the need to release with only that sexy little voice of hers? I'd fucked more women than I could count in my years, but never had I willingly made conversation with a woman I intended to fuck. Now, I found myself wanting to engage her in more just so I could listen to her sweet voice.

I motioned to the comfortable furniture next to us. "We can sit here, if you like."

"I think that would be wonderful."

As she sat, I noticed the slinky little red number she had on rode high up her thighs. Until now, I'd noticed the color but not really the dress, which revealed more than it concealed. That had never happened with a woman before. Always I'd notice her body, but this one had me captivated with the seeming innocence and elfin looks contrasted with the sexual being she was.

She was a puzzle. I didn't like puzzles. Rather, I didn't like unsolved puzzles.

"How did you end up here tonight?" I figured it was best to just dispense with the pretense. We both knew what was expected to happen, but I wanted information first.

One delicate, pale shoulder rose and fell. "It's fast money."

"And you needed money?"

"Why else would a person…" She trailed off,

unable to say she was prostituting herself out.

"A number of reasons, I imagine. Money might be first on the list. But some women do it for the power. Others for the thrill. I guess I just wanted to know where you fall."

"Definitely the money," she murmured, looking back out at the ocean. Her face softened and relaxed a little when she did. The serene expression on her face nearly made my chest ache.

"You like the ocean?"

She turned her head back to me. "It always seems so peaceful. I love the sound of the sea crashing against the rocks and shore, and the scent is so clean." She looked back. "At least, from up here. Up close, it smells a little funny."

I grinned. It was nearly like talking to a child. Which did nothing to break my interest in her. Just meant I'd card her ass before I fucked her. "I suppose it does." I reached over and took her hand. She let me, but her palm was sweaty with nerves. That alone had me proceeding carefully. "What's your name, sweetheart?"

"Celeste." When I didn't say anything, she sighed. "Celeste Pleasant."

"Beautiful name. Why do you need money, beautiful Celeste?"

Surprisingly, she met my gaze now. It wasn't a bold stare or even defiant. It simply… was. "My reasons are my own. Besides, anything I say you wouldn't believe, and I wouldn't blame you."

Intelligent girl. And perhaps not as naive as I'd thought. "Well, Celeste Pleasant. My name is Vincent Black. You already know I'm here with the firm of Lawson, Hughsman, and Gray. I'm not part of them, but they're courting me, so to speak." I'd hoped that if

I gave her a little of myself, maybe she would relax a bit. I had nothing to hide on that front. Anything I had to hide was more to do with Black Reign and my association with them.

"You're not like the others," she said. "You seem more... I don't know. Real?"

"I don't know about that. But I'm less drunk and much less high."

That got her to smile. I thought a little giggle almost escaped. "Yes. You are. Why is that?"

"I like to be in control. If I'm under the influence, I have no control."

"I understand. I feel the same."

"Are you still here to have sex with me?"

She took a deep breath. "I'm here to do whatever you ask. If that's sex, then yes."

"But you don't want to have sex with me." I made it a statement, trying to be gentle but wanting to feel her out. Normally, I could give two shits, but I thought Rycks had more of an influence on me than I wanted him to because I didn't want to scare this girl. I wanted her to be eager for this experience. Not just willing.

"I didn't say that." She shook her head vigorously, her eyes going wide. "I'm looking forward to it, actually." She slid from the plush couch to kneel at my feet, pushing my knees farther apart so she could fit between them. Her fingers went to the fly of my pants, and she deftly unbuttoned them and slid the zipper down. "I'll make it good for you," she whispered as she took my cock out.

I reached for a decanter of scotch sitting on the table beside us. There was also an assortment of high-end narcotics in different dishes, all prepackaged and ready for consumption. I couldn't do the drugs, but I was sure I needed the scotch. I poured two fingers full and brought the glass to my lips. Normally, I'd sip until I started to feel the warmth rising in my chest. When Celeste sank her lovely, plump, ruby-red lips down over my cock, I turned the glass up and downed its contents.

Biting back a groan, I looked down at Celeste. She looked back up at me with wide, clear blue eyes framed by those dark blonde lashes. Could a woman be more beguiling? Or sexy?

"Mmmm," she hummed around me as if sucking her favorite treat. She moved her hand gently up and down my shaft as I sat there unable to take my eyes from that wonderful sight. She was sex and sin rolled into a sweet package I had trouble understanding.

"Indeed." I sighed softly, petting the top of her silky head. I delved my fingers into her hair and let them slide through all those soft tresses. The length draped over my thighs, and I found I wanted my pants down so I could feel it against my skin. I sat still, though, just letting her work my cock. I'd intended to study her movements, needing to see if she was enjoying what she was doing or if it was forced.

"Sexy," I growled. "So fuckin' sexy." My head fell back briefly, and I groaned. When I looked back her eyes were wide. She took me deeper, running one hand up and down the lower half of my shaft. Her hand was tight, but so small her fingers and thumb didn't meet as she gripped me. The encouragement seemed to bolster her. Her movements became more confident, and she seemed to concentrate more on sucking my cock than my reaction to what she did. She definitely wasn't practiced. Damned, if that thought didn't make me harder.

I flexed my hips, testing how she'd do if I took

control. My thrusting into her mouth surprised her, but she didn't balk. She relaxed her throat, taking the extra length I gave to her. A little whimper escaped, and she moved closer, continuing to take what I gave her and making it easier for herself to do it.

"That's it, my beauty. You suck me so good. Take me deep." She tried, but gagged slightly. Instead of pulling back, however, she did it again. This time she relaxed her throat and took me for several seconds before she gagged again. Tears leaked from her eyes, and she gasped when she pulled back. The look on her face said she was afraid she'd disappointed me. "Good girl," I said, praising her. I needed her to want to please me. "Keep going. Your mouth feels wonderful on me."

God, it did! I was very close to coming. Which wouldn't do. I wasn't about to come until I was deep inside her. Looking at her now, between my legs, on her knees, her ass so rounded and firm under that red silk, all I could think about was how good it would be to spank her bare ass while she sucked me. Would it jiggle? I'd just bet it would for all of a heart-stopping second. Then it would turn pink from my smack. How would that look if I turned her around and fucked her while I spanked her? To see my handprint rising on her creamy white skin…

I groaned. Fuck! I had to get myself under control. It was obvious she was inexperienced as hookers went. But even that drew me to her. I knew she wasn't too innocent, or she wouldn't be here. But I found myself believing that this wasn't a full-time thing for her. She needed money quickly, and this was it.

She continued sucking me, using a rhythm where she sucked me comfortably for several seconds before taking me as deep as she could until she either gagged or had to come up for air. Each time she did it, she took more of me for a longer time. God, the girl wanted to please!

I poured another measure of scotch into my glass and took a drink. I was feeling the first shot slightly now and didn't want to go too far. I just needed to dull the effects of her talented mouth before I lost myself and had to start over. She deserved more than that for the fucking blowjob alone.

"Stop," I commanded. She let my cock slip out of her mouth and wiped saliva from her chin with the back of her hand discreetly. Yeah. Hadn't given many blowjobs. I could tell she wanted to ask me what the matter was, but I couldn't let her. "Stand and take off your dress for me. Let me see your body."

Her eyes widened a little, as if she understood we were moving to the next phase of the evening. In the dim lighting around the balcony, I could see sweat gleaming off her pale skin. Her palms were still a little sweaty, but she seemed to have calmed down a little.

"You good?" I had to ask her. She looked so out of her element.

"I'm good," she confirmed in a soft voice with a little smile.

"You sure? Because we don't have to go any further."

"No." She shook her head several times. "Really. I'm good with this."

"You just seem a little... tense." I spoke gently, trying to make sure my words didn't have a bite to them. Last thing I wanted to do was make her feel bad. On the contrary. I wanted to see what this girl was like when she loosened up.

"Just nervous," she smiled. "I'm fine."

Uh-oh. I might have been an asshole and closed off emotionally, but I knew when a woman said she was fine, she was anything but. I groaned. Looked like it was going to take some coaxing. If I hadn't had such a case of blue balls, I might have laughed at the situation. Who has to treat an escort with kid gloves? If my internal bullshit detector had given me even the slightest hint that she was playing me, I'd have just taken what I wanted. But I knew without a doubt that this girl was as inexperienced as she seemed. She might be doing this now, but she wasn't a professional.

"How much are you getting paid?"

Chapter Two
Wrath

"I -- uh, well. Five hundred by the firm and whatever you decide to tip me."

"Five hundred. For the night?" When she nodded, I wanted to swear. I knew the agency the firm used for escorts, and they made at least three times that amount.

"Yes."

"Do you work for the Miami agency?"

She shook her head. "I'm freelance."

"You know, with your beauty, you could charge them a lot more."

A startled look came across her face before she looked away. "I'm not very good at this."

If I'd had doubts before, they were removed. This girl wasn't a prostitute. At least, not in this league. "Have you ever done this before?"

She gave a little chuckle. "Of course. I guess I underpriced myself because I'm new in Palm Springs. I didn't realize I should have raised my fee."

I sighed, letting my hand fall casually to my groin to circle my cock. The lazy stroke seemed to draw her attention, and I grinned a little. "You like?"

"I think you're beautiful," she whispered. "I like watching you stroke yourself."

Oh, she was a little vixen! Demure she might be, but she wasn't opposed to what we were doing. I took another glass from the tray where the decanter sat and poured a small amount of the amber liquid. "Here." I lifted the glass to her. "Drink. It will help you loosen up." She leaned down, took the glass from my hand and sniffed delicately. Then she sipped, making a little face. I chuckled. "Not used to hard liquor?"

"I don't drink much."

"You know, I promise you'll enjoy this. You don't have to do anything you don't want to, and I'll make sure you get as much pleasure as you give me." I patted the space next to me. "Sit here and turn around so you can lie back."

She took a deep breath. It was as if she were saying to herself, *"This is it."* She sat down beside me and lay down like I'd asked her to. Her knees were bent and her legs together, her hands on her belly.

"Put your arms over your head, Celeste." When she did, I patted her knee and turned to face her more fully. "Now, drape one leg on the back of the couch and put the other foot on the floor." She did, but didn't spread her legs as widely as I'd hoped. Moving slowly so I didn't startle her, I put my hands on her thighs and gently pushed them wider apart. She gave a little whimper but didn't resist. "Relax for me, sweetheart. Can you do that?" When she nodded, I kissed her inner thigh. She jumped a little. "I'm not going to hurt you, Celeste. Just pleasure you."

"I -- OK. Yeah." She laughed nervously. "I'm just being silly."

"How about this?" I turned and looked at the assortment of pills and powders on the end table. Everything in here was from Black Reign. They'd replaced everything from the law firm with our own shit. Why? Just in case I wanted to indulge myself, I had no intention of getting hold of bad shit or shit that had been tampered with. I trusted every single thing in this room from the alcohol to the cocaine. Neither of which would work for Celeste. I picked up a Molly, turned to her and broke it in half. "This will help you relax. You're welcome to half."

"What is it?"

"Molly. Ecstasy." I took half and popped it in my mouth, swallowing. Then I offered her the other half. "You don't have to, but you're more than a little uptight. This will help you enjoy yourself and take away some of that anxiety I see on your lovely face."

"It's probably not a good idea."

I shrugged, laying the half-pill on the coffee table in front of us by itself. "If you change your mind, it's there. You can't get it mixed up with anything else."

She nodded, then opened her mouth before closing it again and taking a deep breath. I waited patiently. She had something to say, and I wanted to hear it. "Thank you."

"Oh?"

"Yeah. For trying to help me enjoy myself. Most guys wouldn't. The firm is paying for a service for you. You don't need me to be comfortable."

"No. But I'll have a better time if you have a good time." I winked at her. "Besides, sex is way more fun when you're into it. Give me a chance to prove it to you?"

She giggled. "How can a girl say no to that?"

"That's what I wanted to hear. Now, it's your turn."

I lowered myself to her sex and inhaled deeply. Sweet as a fresh breeze. She was clean-shaven. Smooth and silky. Despite her nerves, she was already wet, her pussy dripping with her honey. I took a long lick around the edge, licking up either side of her glistening lips to the hood of her clit. She gasped, and one hand went reflexively to my head. I had to grin. This was going to be so much fun. As responsive as she was, I couldn't wait to get her wound so tight she was ready to snap.

"See? And I haven't even started yet."

"Oh, my God," she whispered. "Oh, God!"

Covering her little pussy with my mouth, I lapped at her, licking up every drop of cream she had while coaxing more. She was sweet. Savory. Addictive. Yeah, no way this first time would last long, no matter what I wanted. I just had to last long enough to get her to the very edge and hold her there awhile. If I could do that, then coming wouldn't be that much of a problem because she'd come with me.

Little whimpers came from Celeste in increasing frequency. Especially when I inserted two fingers into her. Her back arched off the couch and she gave a sharp little gasp.

I chuckled. "Liked that, did you? There's more to come, sweet. Much, much more."

"OK," she said, her voice quivering. "It feels so good."

I continued to play with her, flicking my tongue over her clit but never lingering long enough for her to get off. Her little pussy was soaked, dripping wet. I wet my fingers in all that honey, stroking her over and over. She was silky smooth, and scorching hot. With every cry she gave me, I was rewarded with more moisture until her inner thighs were damp where she had moved and I was playing.

"Oh, God! Vincent! Please!"

Her use of my given name instead of my road name brought me up short. That was right. She didn't know who I was. Or that I belonged to Black Reign. She only knew me as Vincent Black. An attorney the law firm who'd hired her was trying to hire. Apparently, the Molly I'd taken was starting to take effect. Likely, the mix of the drug with the scotch was going to hit me harder than just the drug alone.

"That's what I want to hear," I purred next to her

clit. "Cry my name. Beg me to fuck you."

When one finger strayed to her ass, she gave a sharp cry and jerked her head up. "Fuck," she gasped. "Omigod!"

I chuckled and probed her ass with that one finger. "Someone likes having her ass played with. I wonder if I could get you worked up enough for me to fuck you there?"

"What?" Her eyes widened and her wide, shocked gaze found mine. "You'd want to..."

"Fuck your ass?" I grinned. "Oh, yeah, baby. I'd slide my cock in there and fuck you until you screamed."

She whimpered. I wasn't sure if it was with shock or fear or if she was just plain turned-on. I'd have to be careful. I was beginning to regret taking that Molly. It never did much for me before other than make me slightly dizzy. I'd only taken it this time to prove to her it was safe if she decided she wanted one. The alcohol was definitely working against me.

I gave a final lick to her clit, then raised myself above her. I moved my body between her legs, draping the one dangling over the side of the couch over my thigh. "Gonna fuck you now, Celeste. Are you ready for me?"

"Yes," she whimpered. "Please."

In the back of my mind, I knew there was something I was forgetting, but my brain was shutting down. The drugs, the alcohol, and the mind-numbing lust were all taking its toll on me. In a few minutes, I'd be lucky to remember my own fucking name. Right now, all I could think about was that all-consuming need to get my dick inside her pussy.

I lay on top of her as I guided my cock to her entrance, then shoved. We both cried out. Thankfully, she dug her heels into my ass and pulled me closer, so I was pretty sure she wasn't hurting. Her cunt squeezed me like she meant to strangle my dick, rhythmic spasms that told me she'd come as I entered her. That was my permission.

The hard, steady rhythm I settled into wasn't gentle. My body rolled over hers, thrusting over and over as hard as I could. I could hear myself grunting with every surge forward and Celeste whimpering, but all I could process was the tremendous pleasure wrapping around me and pulling me down into oblivion.

"So fucking tight. Hot. *Fuck!*"

"Vincent!" Her scream pierced my brain. She came around me in a wet rush I felt over my balls and inner thighs.

"Fuck yeah!" I yelled. "Fuck! Fuck!"

I hooked one arm around her back to clamp onto her shoulder, pulling her down to me with every thrust I made. When she raised her head, my other hand shot to her throat, and I held her still. Submissive.

"Never had it this good," I bit out between clenched teeth. "Gonna fuck you all fuckin' night."

"Yes," she breathed. "Please. Fuck me."

With her whispered plea, I felt my balls tighten, readying for release. "Gonna come! Gonna come so fuckin' hard! Fuckin' come in your fuckin' pussy so God… damned… *HARD!*"

With a brutal yell, I emptied myself inside Celeste. My dick pulsed over and over as my cum erupted like a geyser. Celeste screamed her own orgasm, clutching my back, digging in her nails and scoring my flesh. Her heels dug into my ass, holding me tight against her. My hand was still around her throat, but she just arched her neck to give me better access. Both of us were panting like we'd run a marathon, sweat soaking our bodies.

I sighed, the sound as content as I felt. For some reason, I felt the insane urge to kiss Celeste. She'd given me more pleasure in less than an hour than I could remember ever receiving from sex in my entire life. When I bent my head to take her mouth, she stiffened but allowed my kiss. Her mouth parted, and I slipped my tongue inside to lap at hers. Celeste sighed, relaxing once again, her moan filling me with satisfaction.

Kissing Celeste was a revelation in itself. She followed my lead but wasn't afraid to let me know what she wanted. When I tried to pull back, she nipped my lower lip. I chuckled and continued to kiss her. Over and over, I thrust my tongue into her mouth. My dick was still inside her, and it gave a very interested jerk. She moaned and whimpered, finally winding her arms around my neck, her fingers playing at the hairline at the back of my neck.

With a groan, I ended the kiss so I could trail my lips down her neck. I needed to taste every inch of her. When she gasped, I realized it probably stung when I left a hickey on her neck. Which I hadn't meant to do, but seeing the mark was satisfying. So I moved to her breast and did it again.

God, it felt good being inside her! Just being skin to skin with her was a pleasure I'd never expected to find. I gave a little thrust of my cock. Immediately, I was hard again. Ready to go another round. Celeste's hair was fanned over the couch in silky waves. The glazed look in her eyes told me she'd enjoyed herself nearly as much as I had. Her lips were kiss-swollen and ruby-red from where I'd sucked at her mouth. Was there ever a more beautiful, satisfying sight?

Without a word, I began to move inside her again. She gave a contented sigh and smiled up at me. Neither of us spoke, a spell weaving us together in the moment.

Carefully, I slid behind her, turning her so her back was to my front and I was partially under her. One arm cradled her head, reaching around her to cup the weight of her breast. My cock never left her wet pussy. I hooked the leg she had draped over the back of the couch on my arm, pulling her open even more. Then I started a gentle rocking motion, fucking her at my leisure.

I slid my hand to the place where we joined, rubbing at her clit with my finger. Celeste arched back against me, turning her head so she could see me. I leaned in to take her mouth, and she immediately cradled my head, opening her mouth to receive me. God, the woman was perfect! She fit perfectly against me. She kissed me perfectly. Her fucking pussy was fucking perfect! How had I lived without this my entire adult life?

Steadily, I increased my pace as she encouraged me. Though I listened to what she wanted, I was firmly in control of the situation. I chose what to do. I chose when to make her come. When I would come myself. It wasn't long before she needed more than I could give her in this position. And, quite frankly, I wanted to pound into her when I came. I needed that edge to my fucking. Just shy of pain. I always had.

Then she did something I didn't expect. She stopped, whimpering, her body once again slickening with sweat. She reached behind her to grasp my cock with her tiny hand. We were both wet with the combination of her juices and my cum. So, when she tucked my cock against her little asshole, I groaned out loud.

"God, baby. Are you sure? I may not be able to be gentle."

"Will you stop if it hurts?" Her voice was still that sweet, melodic soprano I'd grown to love hearing.

"I'll never hurt you intentionally. I'm just telling you that you'll need to talk to me. If it hurts, tell me at the first sign so I stop immediately."

She nodded even as she pushed back onto my cock. Her ass enveloped the head. She stiffened but didn't push away. Instead, she took a deep breath and sank back even farther. I stayed as still as I could, but my hips thrust occasionally in reflex as she worked herself back on my cock. It wasn't long before her cheeks came against my abdomen.

I let her adjust for several seconds, watching as she breathed through the invasion. "You good?"

She nodded. "Yes. It's not as difficult as I thought it might be."

I chuckled. "You're turned-on. Lust makes a lot of things easier." As I spoke the words, I knew they were true. Lust had let her submit her body for me to use. Lust was making it easier for her to accept my cock in her ass. "You'll be sore tomorrow so you have to make sure to tell me if you hurt so I can stop."

Her fingers found the back of my thigh and she sank her nails deep. "Don't you dare stop."

Giving a few experimental thrusts, I watched her face for discomfort. When there was none, I slid my hand up to her other breast, plucking at her nipples as I slid in and out of her slowly. "Play with your clit, Celeste. Finger yourself."

She obeyed me without question. I could feel her little fingers dipping inside her where we were separated by a thin barrier.

"I feel you," she gasped, then stuffed another finger inside her. Then another. With four fingers sliding in and out of her pussy, I could easily pick up her rhythm and the frantic need she seemed to have as she picked up the pace.

"That's it, baby. Fuck your little pussy. Stretch it for me."

With a cry, she did. Her body moved up and down with the force of my thrusts. Each time I slammed into her, the breath exploded from her lungs. Sometimes, a little cry came with it. Her fingers slid as deep as she could get them. She still pumped them in and out.

"You're a hot-blooded little thing," I said as I picked up the pace. "So fuckin' sexy. So fuckin' dirty."

"This is so good," she gasped. "Oh, God!"

"You gonna come on my cock, dirty little girl?"

"Yes, Vincent!"

"Tell me what you're gonna do. Say it!"

"I'm gonna come," she gasped.

"Where?" I needed this dirty talk from her. I had no idea why. I never had before. Hell, if anyone talked dirty during sex, it was me. But I wanted to hear the filthy words coming from this angel's mouth. And that was what she looked like. She was an angel with a demon's appetites.

"On your cock. Gonna come on your cock with it deep inside my ass!" Though her words were needy and frenzied, she spoke softly. The need there still came through, but she wasn't at all in her comfort zone. Hell, she had my dick up her ass when I was certain anal play hadn't been something she'd indulged in before.

"That's it! Fuck yeah! You come on me and I'm comin' in you. You want it?"

"Yes! Come inside my ass," she gasped, the words barely above a whisper. "Please, Vincent! Please!"

Two strokes later, I did. For the second time that night, I came inside the little vixen I'd been given for the evening. It was like I was staking my claim on her when I'd never felt the need to keep a woman for my own. Why would I? I could have any woman I wanted at the clubhouse who knew the score and knew I didn't want a woman clinging to me. I wanted to fuck any woman I chose, and that was exactly what I did. But with this woman, there was something different going on. I wanted everyone who saw her after she left me to know she'd been with someone else and know she was taken.

Only she wasn't. Was all of this the fucking Molly talking? Molly and the fucking whiskey?

Fuck. I had no clue. I knew I wanted this woman again. I hadn't even rebounded from our second session and I wanted her again.

Sleep. We needed to rest. Both of us but me most especially. I kissed the side of her neck before I rose. I'd intended to simply go to the bathroom and clean up, but I found myself scooping Celeste up and taking her with me.

Then we took a shower. And had sex. I came deep inside her pussy once again. Then she sank to her knees and sucked me like I'd never been sucked before. I'm pretty sure she drank my cum that time, but things started to get blurry after that. All I know was that, the next morning, I woke up in that same hotel suite. With Celeste in my arms.

Fuck.

Fucking fuck.

She had her head on my shoulder, all that white-blonde hair tangling us together. That had never happened before. I never actually slept with a woman. Which meant I needed to get rid of this one. I glanced at the heavily draped window. A sliver of bright sunshine peeked through. I looked at the bedside clock. One in the afternoon? Holy shit!

Gently, I slid from under Celeste, careful not to wake her yet. I needed to get myself together before that happened. I wasn't meeting her this morning until that possessiveness I'd felt last night was long departed.

Making my way to the shower, I shook off the last remaining effects of that fucking Molly. This was why I hated losing control. The whole situation had gotten wildly out of control. What the hell had I done to her last night? I was pretty sure she'd agreed to anything I did, but I couldn't be sure. I just hope that, if I'd hurt her, she'd enjoyed the pain.

No matter. I could fix this. Celeste was a call girl. She made a sum of money just by showing up. I'd tip her big so she wouldn't complain. I doubted the firm would give a fuck and, honestly, it didn't really matter at this point. I might be able to get the information I wanted from inside the institution, but I wasn't sure we couldn't get what we wanted another way.

Whatever. I just needed some cash, then to pay Celeste. Once that was done, I'd see her out and be on my fucking way.

Fuck.

Chapter Three
Celeste

I stretched as wakefulness tried to intrude on my perfect dream. My body was sore all over, but it wasn't unpleasant. It only served to remind me of the incredible time I'd enjoyed with Vincent Black, the enigmatic lawyer from the firm who'd paid all those escorts to schmoose their recruits or whatever they called them. Colleagues? I didn't know. Didn't care. All I cared about was the incredible man who'd been so gentle with me until it was time to not be gentle.

Vincent had rocked my world. I wasn't an inexperienced woman, but nothing could have prepared me for his sexual appetites. I'd enjoyed every blissful second. Even the anal sex. Again, I wasn't a virgin, but I'd never enjoyed it. I had last night.

The shower shut off. I hadn't even realized it was going until the noise was no longer there. Vincent stepped out of the bathroom, a white terry towel wrapped around his narrow hips. Muscle rippled over his body like an Adonis. Curiously, he had several tattoos over his chest and shoulders as well as down his arms in "sleeves." None would be in sight if he wore one of the expensive suits he'd worn last night. I'm sure I saw them last night, but I was focused on other things. Like the fact that I had to please him if I wanted a nice tip, and I really needed the tip. After that, he kind of made me forget about anything but the way he played with my body.

He didn't say a word to me, but made his way to the closet. He dropped the towel as he stepped inside, presumably to dress. This was the really awkward part. What was I supposed to do now? I had absolutely no idea where my clothes were. Probably out on the balcony. I'd just stood to hurry to the bathroom when he stepped out of the closet, fastening his cufflinks.

He gave me a passing glance before looking at his watch. "You're welcome to stay here tonight if you need to. Room's paid through checkout tomorrow morning."

I snagged a towel and wrapped it around me. "I'm good. I just need to get my clothes."

He raised one arrogant eyebrow. "Why don't you run through the shower. I'll get your clothes and order lunch for you. Anything you'd like?"

"Uh, no. I'm fine. Thank you."

He nodded, then left the room. This was a different side of Vincent than I'd seen last night. Maybe it was just the fun of it all that had opened him up, but now he was closed off. Unreadable.

As I let the water pour over me in the shower, all the aches and soreness of my body became known. I needed a long soak in a hot bath. I could do it here, but I had the feeling it would be better to leave when he did. Things weren't as cordial as they had been last night, and I wasn't sure why.

By the time I stepped out of the bathroom, he'd retrieved my clothing. All but my panties.

"Not sure where your underwear is." Again, there was no expression on his face.

I looked at the skimpy dress I'd worn last night. "This is gonna be fun," I muttered.

"Didn't you have a coat or something you wore over your dress when you arrived?"

"Yes. We left the other suite so fast I didn't have a chance to get it." I felt stupid. This is what I get for prostituting myself. Oh, well. I didn't regret it. Hopefully it got me enough money for one more treatment for Holly. After that, I'd figure out how to get enough money for one more. And one more after that until Holly was well.

"I see." He nodded to the dress. "Put it on. You can wear my jacket out of the hotel."

"It's so big, it will swallow me whole, but it will definitely cover me. I appreciate your generosity."

He shrugged. "Get dressed. We'll settle up, and I'll take you through the lobby."

I hesitated. When he raised an eyebrow at me I blurted out my question. "Will I see you again?"

Vincent gave me an irritated look, shaking his head. "Why would we do that?"

"Well... I --"

"We had a pleasant night. You were my entertainment, and you did well. But I don't make a habit of paying for sex, and I don't do relationships. So, no. We won't see each other again."

I felt like he'd just slapped me. I knew this was nothing more than a transaction, but I had to go and enjoy myself. I'd been prepared for him to take his pleasure and send me on my way. I hadn't been prepared for anything as intense as last night had been.

Tears stung my eyes, but I cleared my throat and blinked them away. "Sorry. Not sure why I said that. Give me five minutes and I'll be ready to go."

I snagged my dress and shoes and hurried into the bathroom. As I looked into the mirror, one tear tracked down my cheek, and I dashed it away. Crying over this guy wasn't an option. It never was. I was there to fuck for money and that was what I'd done. I'd get my money and get out. With any luck, I'd forget about this whole experience because, certainly, I was never going to repeat it.

When I exited the bathroom, he had his jacket waiting for me on the bed. I heard him talking quietly in the other room. I slipped into his jacket and immediately his scent washed over me. It was a mixture of leather, sandalwood… and motor oil? Odd, but it was decidedly masculine and heady as hell. I tried to block it out, to ignore how comforting the scent was. I remembered being surrounded by it last night as he'd taken me over and over again. Last night, he couldn't seem to get enough of me. Now… Well. What was done was done.

I stepped into the outer suite and found Vincent waiting by the door. When I approached, he ended his call. "Ready?"

"Yes." I tried to sound confident and not as shaken as I felt. My makeup had long since been washed away and I felt exposed. At least, if I'd had my makeup and had time to fix my hair, I wouldn't look so ridiculous in this stupid dress. His jacket did, indeed, swallow me, coming past mid-thigh. You could just see the hemline of my dress. Otherwise, it probably looked like I had nothing on underneath.

Once we got to the lobby, Vincent took my elbow and steered me to a waiting cab. He opened the door for me. Once inside, I shrugged out of his jacket and handed it to him.

"Wait," he said. "Front right breast pocket. The envelope is yours." I retrieved the envelope and handed him his jacket once again. He took it, then handed the cabbie two one-hundred-dollar bills. "Take the lady wherever she wants to go and keep the change." He gave me one more glance before turning and walking away.

Thankfully, the cabbie said nothing. He just sat there until I was ready. I gave him my address. "On the way, ma'am. And good afternoon."

As he pulled away from the hotel, I looked back.

I'd just had the best sex of my life with the hottest man I'd ever seen. I made a few hundred dollars from the firm and more from my tip. Tempting as it was to check that envelope, I knew better. I'd open it after I got home.

The little apartment in Lake Worth I rented wasn't much, but it was in a safe, sturdy, and relatively nice part of town close to the ocean. The owners were wonderful. Mrs. McDonald had helped me so much with Holly, especially since the leukemia diagnosis. When I had to work extra hours, Mrs. McDonald stayed with Holly. She also helped when Holly was sick from the chemo and made sure we had food in the house, even when I had food for Holly but none for myself. If I needed an extension on the rent, she gave it. She seemed to never keep a running tab and just let me pay what I could when I could. I, however, knew exactly how much I owed Mrs. McDonald. To the penny. For rent, food, babysitting services… everything. Somehow, someday, I'd find a way to pay her back.

I unlocked the door and stepped inside. And, of course, Mrs. McDonald had cleaned. And bought groceries. There was fresh fruit and a loaf of bread on the counter. Holly's favorite kind of peanut butter was sitting next to the refrigerator over the silverware drawer. The older woman and her husband lived in the house adjacent to the garage my apartment was above, so she'd know when I got home. Hopefully, she'd give me a few minutes to change clothes because I didn't want to have to explain the outfit.

I glanced out the window and saw Holly playing on the swing set in the backyard of the McDonalds'. She laughed as Mrs. McDonald pushed from the front. The older woman glanced in my direction and waved, continuing to push Holly so she squealed with glee. I waved back, then went to change.

The Florida sun was hot, but the breeze coming off the ocean was refreshing. I dressed in shorts and a tank before sitting on the bed to open the envelope. I gasped at what I found there. After counting and recounting, I discovered Vincent Black had paid me well for my night with him. Five *thousand* dollars. With the money the firm paid me, I'd expected maybe to make a thousand. And that was if the client tipped well. I never thought I'd have this much.

It meant at least two more treatments for Holly. Any extra I could use to pay on the massive hospital debt we'd accrued during the first few months after her diagnosis. We were nearing the end of her treatment. She was so close to being done. So close. The doctors just wanted a few more treatments to make sure she had the best shot of staying in remission. I wanted a healthy child, but I'd also be glad to have my baby grow some hair. This money would help. If I was a touch humiliated, so what? Anything was worth helping my baby get better.

I put the money in a little locked box with the cash I saved for Holly's doctor visits and treatments. Once done, I headed outside to play with my daughter.

Holly giggled and squealed as she pleaded with Mrs. McDonald to push her higher. The older woman swore she would, but it was obvious she just kept the same steady motion. I approached them and waved to Holly.

"Everything all right, dear?" Mrs. McDonald smiled at me but looked genuinely interested.

"Yes. All's well." I smiled, but I could tell Mrs. McDonald knew I was still raw from my experience. Though she had no idea what was going on, I'd never been able to hide much from her. She was worse than my mom ever thought about being.

"I see." She looked back to Holly and pushed again. "You know, keeping that little girl healthy has been your number one priority since I met the two of you. I don't expect that's changed at all."

"No," I said softly. "It hasn't."

"I know women who've drawn the line at what they're willing to do for their child." She shook her head. "Never known you to say there was something you wouldn't do to help Holly. Might not be something you want to do, but you do whatever you have to for that child. She's lucky to have a mother as selfless as you."

I wanted to cry. "You're too kind to me, Mrs. McDonald. Much too kind."

"Pfft! If I'd had children, I'd hope they would be as wonderful as you are. Your family must be proud of you."

"My mom probably would be. My dad?" I shrugged. "I doubt it. At least not this time." I added softly.

"I doubt it's as bad as all that. I'm not saying you shouldn't ask for help." She gave me the side eye. "But as a mother, you're doing what you can to help your child."

I had no idea if the older woman suspected I'd sold my body for sex, but I wasn't about to enlighten her. "If my parents were still alive, they'd help without question."

"You know, Gerald and I could help. We've got more than enough in savings to --"

"No." I cut her off softly. "As much as I appreciate it, I'm not there yet. The doctor is kind in letting me pay as I can, and I'm making the payments to the hospital. With what I got last night I'll be close to the end of her treatments, and all I'll have left is the hospital payment."

"Just keep us in mind, dear. We're more than willing to help."

"You help me more than you let on. Don't think I didn't see the apartment cleaned and the groceries you bought. I'll add that to the tally."

She laughed and waved me away. "Like you can prove it was me. You might want to check and make sure a thief didn't break in."

"A thief. Who cleaned the house, bought Holly her favorite brand of peanut butter, and made it past Mr. McDonald's security system? Right."

She shrugged. "It could happen." She gave Holly another push. "Now, you run along. Rest. Me and little Holly are doing fine."

I sighed. That was the trouble with Mrs. McDonald. She took me in like I was her daughter. She treated Holly like a beloved grandchild. While I loved it, it also made me feel guilty for intruding on the couple. "You and Mr. McDonald are too good to me."

"We might stop if you called us Gerald and Glinda."

"If I do that, you'll convince yourselves I'm your long-lost daughter, and the next thing I know you'll take over everything." I tried to sound put out, but I was sure my grin belied me.

"Oh, rubbish!" She laughed. "We're working on a plan already on how to accomplish that. Give us time. We'll have you firmly under our wing."

I had no doubt she would. If I had any conscience whatsoever, I'd move. But I just couldn't. Not only did Holly love the couple, but I loved them, too.

I made my way back to my apartment and collapsed on the couch. I left the door open so Mrs. McDonald could bring Holly back with little trouble. I didn't realize how tired I was until I lay down. It was two in the afternoon, and I was exhausted. To be fair, Vincent had kept me up all night with bouts of sex. I'd loved every single second of it and wouldn't trade it for anything. Which was part of my problem. I couldn't work up the shame I should. I wasn't sorry, and I would definitely do it again if I had to. At least, if it were with Vincent.

I sighed. This is exactly the reason I knew better than to do take an escort job. A friend I'd met, Mercedes, had told me how much money I could make, and I hadn't asked too many questions. Once faced with the prospect of actually having to make good on my decision, I'd balked a little, but it was mostly because I had never been a woman to have casual sex. In fact, I'd had exactly one sexual partner, and he was Holly's biological father. We'd had a lot of sex, but I'd only had sex with him.

Once my head hit the pillow on the couch, I took a breath and sighed. Then, I was out.

* * *

"Celeste..." Vincent growled my name as he took my mouth. His weight was heavy atop me, and I sank deeper into my couch. "So fucking sweet."

I moaned as I kissed him, needing him to stoke that fire in me no other man ever had. My clit was on fire at the mere thought of him sinking his cock into my pussy. I could feel him throbbing against my clit even now.

"Need you," I panted. "Need you inside me. To fuck me."

He smiled against my lips. "Oh, I'm gonna fuck you all right. Gonna fuck you long and hard, and then I'll pay for all Holly's treatments. All you have to do is keep letting me fuck you."

"You'll help Holly?"

"No, baby. I'll help you. All that matters to me is fucking your sweet little cunt and ass. And I definitely want your ass again. Want my cum deep in both. When I get tired of that, I'll get Mercedes to help us. Maybe, by that time, Holly won't need the treatments any longer."

I sobbed. This wasn't what I wanted. Was it? Vincent had been a means to an end. Like I'd been the same to him. His end was getting off. I'd done that and he'd paid me.

"But you said you didn't do relationships?"

He laughed cruelly even as he sank his cock deep into my channel. "Honey, this isn't a relationship. I'm just fucking you."

"I thought you didn't pay for sex either?"

He shrugged. "The pussy was good. I'm willing to pay for the best. If I find another woman better than you, our arrangement will end, as will the money to help Holly." He chuckled. "I suggest you find new and shocking ways to please me."

Before I could protest, he started to move. I wanted to cry. I was crying. I was also on the verge of coming.

"That's it, my little Celeste. Come for me. Milk my cock so I can empty my cum inside your sweet pussy."

I cried out, unable to hold back that scream. Then Vincent shuddered above me, his own groan loud in my tiny apartment.

"We can't be loud," I whispered. "Holly…"

"Will be fine. Besides. I think I'm bored." He stood up and waved someone forward. Mercedes. How'd she get in here? "Eat my cum out of her hot little pussy, Mercedes. Make her come, and you get her share of the money I'm paying."

I cried out in denial, shaking my head. But it was already too late. Mercedes's blonde head covered my pussy and she sucked.

I woke with a gasp, my body covered in sweat. The sun was still bright, but it had moved, no longer shining through the kitchen window. I looked out at the ocean on the horizon and sighed. I was so fucked. I'd almost let myself believe in a fairytale that didn't exist. Still thought about it.

A quick glance at the clock said it was just after five in the evening. Not late, but later than I'd intended on napping. Of course, Mrs. McDonald hadn't brought Holly back yet. The woman would wait until after she'd fed her. I had no idea what I'd do without the older couple.

I went to the bathroom to brush my teeth and freshen up. As I returned, Mr. McDonald opened the door. He looked worried which made my stomach drop.

"Holly has a nosebleed. Nothing too bad, but it isn't stopping. You might want to come take a look."

I nodded even as I grabbed my purse from the bar. I raced down the stairs to find Holly sitting on the bottom step of the McDonalds' back deck, next to the swing set. She was calm, but pale, though she looked a little scared. Mrs. McDonald had an ice pack to the bridge of her nose and a tissue at her nose.

"It started about ten minutes ago," she said. "I know it's happened before and we've dealt with it, but it's not stopping this time."

"Doesn't look too heavy," I said as I glanced at the few discarded tissues in the wastebasket beside the pair. "Is it just a steady stream?"

"Yes. But my little Holly is brave, isn't she?" The girl nodded her agreement but kept silent. "Do you think you should call her doctor?"

I pulled out my phone. "Yes. I can do that now.

He gave me a number that should go directly to him if I had an emergency. Do you think this qualifies?" My heart was racing, but this was also my child. What seemed like an emergency to me might be nothing more than regular side effects of her most recent chemo treatment.

"Honey, have you ever used that number? Have you ever bothered the man?" Mr. McDonald asked the question gently, but I could tell he was a little irritated.

"Well, no, but --"

"Call him. If he doesn't like it, he shouldn't have offered the number."

With a sigh, I did. Dr. Donovan Muse answered on the second ring. After a brief question-and-answer session he instructed us to bring her to JFK Memorial Hospital emergency room and he'd take it from there.

"I need to take her to the ER," I said. "He said to go to JFK."

"I'll get her GI and Frog," Mr. McDonald said. "Do you think you'll need the diaper bag? I know when she gets sick she sometimes has accidents." At four, Holly was mostly potty trained, but her illness had sometimes made things difficult.

"Please. And her blanket. She likes to wrap up in it sometimes."

"I'll be right back. You and Glinda get in the car."

"You don't have to go with me."

"Not hearing a word of that, young lady. And before you say we don't have to, we know that. We're doing it because we love Holly." He looked me in the eyes. "And you."

There was no way to stop the tears. "I appreciate all you've done, Mr. McDonald. Thank you." He nodded and mumbled something under his breath gruffly, then left to get the items we needed.

The ride to the hospital seemed like the longest of my life. Holly didn't make a sound, but the blood continued to trickle. She held onto her frog and had the pacifier she called a GI in her mouth. She only used it when she was stressed, and Lord knew, the child had reason enough to stress.

Once we go inside the ER, a nurse brought us straight back to a small treatment room. I was surprised no one asked for insurance or anything. I always dreaded that because I had nothing for Holly. I was trying for all I was worth to not think about how much this was going to cost.

"Dr. Collins said to give him a couple of minutes. He'll be in to see you shortly."

I thought about asking for the paperwork, but figured there wasn't much point. Wasn't like I could pay them today anyway. They'd send a bill. True to his word, Dr. Collins came to us in less than ten minutes.

"Sorry about that," he said, pulling up a stool in front of Holly. "Now. Dr. Donovan said you weren't feeling well." He spoke directly to Holly. I still held tissue to her nose, but had lost the ice pack. It hadn't seemed to be helping anyway. "What seems to be the problem?"

Holly pushed at my hand and lifted up her little face. "My nose is bleedin'," she said before pulling the tissue back to her nose.

"That's not good, is it?" He gently pulled away the tissue and studied the little girl. "Just a very slow flow. How long?" He looked at me.

"Maybe forty-five minutes now?" I glanced at Mrs. McDonald who nodded.

"Stronger than this?"

"At first, I think. But not much."

"How've you been feeling, Holly? Felt like playing?"

She nodded. "Played on my swing set today. For a really long time."

He sat back and studied the child a while. "I've got something I think might work." He grinned. "I'll be right back."

A few minutes later, he came with nasal spray and more tissues. He squirted two sprays up Holly's nose, then gently pinched her nose together. While they waited, he talked to her about her frog. He asked its name. When she said, "His name's Frog. Duh!" he looked appropriately put out, but was as gentle with her as a person could be. After several minutes, he changed tissues. When he changed again, it was clean.

"There," he said with a grin. "All better."

Holly touched her nose, then grinned. "All better." Surprisingly, she wiggled out of my lap and went to Dr. Collins, giving him a shy hug. "Thanks for making my nose be better."

"You're quite welcome."

"Is this from the chemo?" I asked, knowing that was the likely culprit.

"Most likely, since she had no other trauma. I could do blood work today, but Dr. Muse said Holly was due in the office in a couple of days. Just make sure you keep her appointment. He'll take it from there. In the meantime, if this happens again tonight, I'm here until seven in the morning. Come back and ask for me. I'll take care of her."

Mr. McDonald nodded briskly, not saying a word while his wife smiled. "Thank you so much, Dr. Collins."

"Please, call me Doc."

Mr. McDonald raised an eyebrow. "You know

who we are, then?"

"Pops called me right before Blade did."

"Good." Mr. McDonald stood, offering Doc his hand. "Figured he would want to know."

"You were right. He's been involved from afar, but..."

"No worries. He's got it all covered."

"Not all," Mrs. McDonald said. She sounded almost angry. "He should be here to --"

"Glinda," Mr. McDonald admonished. "Not here or now. Doc will pass on the message."

Holly had climbed up in my lap and was demanding my attention, so I hadn't actively engaged in the conversation. Now, I needed to.

"What are you guys talking about? Who's Pops?"

"Never you mind, dear," Mrs. McDonald said. "We need to get Holly home. She's had a long day and it's getting late. Are we good to go, Doc, or do you need to watch Holly for a while?"

"I think you're good. Just keep an eye on her tonight. Maybe she could sleep with you?" He glanced at me.

"Of course," I said. "She does when she doesn't feel well."

"Or anytime I want to," Holly said with a grin. "Mommy holds me and sings me to sleep sometimes."

"That sounds like the perfect medicine," Doc said. He handed me the nasal spray. "If it starts bleeding again but isn't any worse than it was this time, do two sprays up each nostril. Then hold pressure just above the nares opening." He demonstrated, squeezing Holly's nose briefly with two fingers. "If it doesn't stop in ten minutes or so, come back to see me." He handed me a card. "My cell number. If you can't get ahold of Blade, call me."

"Blade? You mentioned him before, but I don't know who that is."

He shrugged. "Dr. Muse. We've been friends since before med school. Always known him as Blade." I got the feeling there was more to it, but let it go. Not my business.

As we were walking out of the hospital, something caught my eye. Normally, I'd just have ignored it, since I had more important things on my mind, but something just wouldn't let me. I turned my head to find Vincent getting out of a sleek little red Porsche. He glanced my way and did a double take. Frowning at me, he started to go into the hospital, then seemed to notice something. He looked at me again, his gaze shifting from me to Holly. He frowned and stopped, turning to stalk toward me.

Oh God. This was the worst possible scenario. I absolutely couldn't let him make a scene in front of Mr. and Mrs. McDonald.

"Take her," I said to Mrs. McDonald "I'll be right back."

"But I want to go with you, Mommy," Holly whined.

"Hush, sweetie. Won't take me a moment. Be good for Mrs. McDonald."

I hurried to meet Vincent before he could get too close. "Hi," I said by way of greeting.

"What the fuck are you doing here?"

The question and its gruff tone took me aback. "Holly had a small issue that needed dealing with. Dr. Collins helped us."

"Dr. Collins, huh? You see him often?" I ignored the sneer he put into his voice.

"This is the first time. Dr. Muse told us to come here. He must have called Dr. Collins ahead of us."

"I see." He looked around me to see Mrs. McDonald putting Holly in the booster seat in the back of the car. "She the reason you needed money?"

"That's not your business," I said automatically.

"Is if she's hurt. Why did you have to bring her to the emergency room?"

I stiffened. "I said, it's none of your business. And she's not hurt. Even if she was it still wouldn't be your business."

"So she is the reason you need money." He looked over my shoulder again. "Someone hurt her?"

"What do you want, Vincent? We've already established we weren't seeing each other again. And no. No one hurt her. She's not injured."

He flashed a charming smile, one I'd have fallen for with a wave and a giggle a few hours ago. Now, it didn't affect me at all. Really!

"Just the answer to that simple question. Is that girl the reason you need money?"

"No," I said immediately. It wasn't entirely a lie. Holly wasn't the reason I needed money. It was her cancer. "She's not the reason I need money. Satisfied?"

He shrugged. "Like you said. None of my business." He pulled a card from his jacket pocket and handed it to me. "My address is on the back. Come visit me if you decide to let me know why you need money so badly you were willing to sell your body to me for a night. We'll see what we can arrange."

I felt like he'd slapped me in the face. I wanted to turn around and leave him standing there. I wanted to kick him in the balls. Instead, I snatched the fucking card from his hands, knowing it might be a necessary evil. I wouldn't revisit this unless it was absolutely the only alternative I had, but I couldn't make myself close any door willingly.

On the verge of tears, I headed back to the car where Mrs. McDonald gave me a look filled with concern. "Everything all right, dear?"

"It's fine."

Mr. McDonald snorted. "If I had a nickel for every time a woman said that word meaning exactly the opposite…"

"Hush, Gerald," Mrs. McDonald said.

"I'm just saying, Glinda. I always know when I've screwed up because you say that word in that tone of voice every single time."

All the way home, I stewed, growing more and more angry with every passing second. How dare he treat me like that! Ugh! No matter. It wasn't like I had to see the infuriating man again. He might be sex and sin on a stick, but he was a complete asshole. How in the world had I ever thought he was anything but a cad?

As I readied an exhausted Holly for bed, I decided I'd throw away the little business card. I could find a different way to get money than selling my body to Vincent Black. I admitted to myself, however, that if he'd continued to be the man I'd met the night before, I'd have willingly given myself to him for free.

Chapter Four
Celeste

The next few weeks proved to be an exercise in frustration and heartache. Holly didn't have any more nosebleeds, but the last round of chemo made her so sick it broke my heart. I was up night and day with her after the treatment for several days. Dr. Muse was more than helpful, even coming to the house to check on Holly. He gave us medication for the nausea and such, but some things we had to get at the pharmacy or through her regular pediatrician. If Dr. Muse got word from the pediatrician what was going on, he would show up with medicine in hand and make sure I knew how to give it or that Holly could actually take it, then I'd get a lecture about not coming to him first. Which was decidedly odd. I knew he couldn't do this for all his patients, so why us?

Even with the help with Holly's medications, I was still in a financial pickle. I couldn't work, though Mr. and Mrs. McDonald certainly helped more than they should have. I just didn't feel like I should leave Holly alone. As a result, the diner and the dry cleaners where I was working had to let me go. Not their fault. With the increasing demand for services as places opened back up after the pandemic, they needed more reliable help. The owner of the diner still let me pick up available slots when I could, but it wasn't steady income. After paying my monthly payment at the hospital, and the extras for Holly's medicine, I barely had enough money to fill my car up with gas. I was definitely at a point where I was seriously looking at that card Vincent had given me.

With a sigh, I picked it up and stared at the plain black card with gold-embossed writing. It had his name, address, and phone number. That was it. No *Attorney at Law* or whatever or anything to indicate what his profession was. Just the simple black card.

I was supposed to be resting. Mrs. McDonald had finally set her foot down and told me she was keeping Holly tonight and most of the day tomorrow. I was welcomed to come visit, but I had to leave after supper and couldn't come back before supper the next day. That left me time to think. Which was how I found myself at the entrance to an upscale apartment building in Lake Worth. I'd dressed conservatively, knowing I'd have to do this on my own and not through the back entrance surrounded by a dozen more women.

I tried the elevator, but the floor I needed was restricted. I almost lost my nerve but a gentleman in an expensive-looking suit approached me and I was trapped.

"Good afternoon, ma'am," he said, pleasantly. "Is there something I can help you with?"

On reflex, I held out my card. "I-I'm here to see Mr. Black," I stammered. "I'm not expected, but he said any time."

The man smiled at me. It wasn't a smirk or anything, simply a friendly gesture. "Not a problem. Mr. Black often has guests he's not expecting. This card is all you need." He indicated for me to step into the elevator. Once I did, he entered a code and stepped off. "Good day, ma'am. Please pass on my salutations to Mr. Black." It occurred to me to tip the man, but when I reached for my purse he held up his hands. "No, thank you. Mr. Black pays us well enough." Then he backed away and was gone as the doors slid shut.

I'd never been so nervous in my life! Even the night of the party when I'd first met Vincent wasn't this awful. When the doors opened, I stepped into the small foyer. I walked to the door a few feet away and knocked. It seemed to take forever before someone opened the door. When it opened, it wasn't who I expected.

"Can I help you?" A tall redhead in a micro-thong bikini stood with one hand braced on the door, the other on the frame. I definitely wasn't getting past her without physical force.

"I'm here to see Mr. Black," I said, holding out the card. Not that there was really any point. Vincent Black had obviously moved on. Not like he hadn't warned me.

The redhead glanced at the card but didn't take it. "Wrath, baby. There's a little mouse here to see you." She gave me a superior grin, then turned and sashayed away. "Wrath" walked by her and swatted her ass playfully, leaving a pink flush on her left butt cheek. And, yeah, Wrath was Vincent Black.

"What?" he said, still looking back at the redhead.

"I -- uh," I had to swallow every ounce of my pride. I took a breath and tried again. "I was hoping we could negotiate something. Maybe a schedule of sorts."

That got his attention and he turned, a look of irritation on his face. "I don't nego --" He stopped when he turned to face me, recognizing me. "You."

I raised my chin but couldn't quite meet his gaze. "I know you said you didn't pay for sex, but you also gave me the card. I wanted to know what you had in mind."

He leaned casually against the door frame. Dressed in cotton lounge pants and nothing else, he was sculpted perfection. All that ink on his body was sexy as sin and on fine display. "What are you offering?"

"More of what I offered the last time."

He shrugged. "I can get that here." He jerked his head back in the direction the redhead went. "For free." The smirk on his face was cruel.

"Did you give me this just to humiliate me?" I asked the question softly, but it felt like a dagger had just been plunged into my heart and twisted. Not because I liked the bastard or anything. Because I'd willingly *let* him humiliate me.

"Tell me why you need money so badly and I'll see what I can do."

I stiffened. He could have asked anything, could have said anything other than that one simple demand and I'd have given it to him. I was willing to do anything for my daughter, but I didn't want to use her illness to elicit charity from this man. I'd figure it out. I might have to sink even lower than I already had, but I'd do it.

"I can see this was a bigger mistake than I thought," I muttered. "I'm sorry to have bothered you, Mr. Black." I turned to leave. Thank goodness the elevator opened right away. When I turned to press the "L" for lobby, he was still standing there, looking at me with an intensity I hadn't seen from him before. I looked away and sagged against the elevator wall as the doors closed. I was going to be sick. No doubt about it.

When the doors opened, I made my way as quickly as I could to the lobby lavatory. Inside was a fresh-faced woman with brown hair in a tight bun. She smiled at me when I entered, but soon gave me a look of alarm. Probably because I was sweating profusely and was likely pale as a sheet.

"Sick," I managed to gasp out. She immediately helped me to an open stall and locked the door. I vomited over and over, sobbing as I did so. I was startled when I felt a gentle hand on my shoulder, pulling my hair out of the way. She must have fastened a hair tie loosely around it because it stayed out of my face while I was repeatedly sick.

When I was done, I sat back on my ass, leaning against the wall. The girl handed me a damp towel and brushed stray tendrils out of my face.

"Better?" she asked.

I nodded weakly.

"You don't have track marks, so I'm guessing this isn't a drug thing. You don't smell like alcohol, so nothing there." She gave me an assessing look. "Escort," she finally said. "An unwilling one. Freelance?"

Again, I nodded.

"I understand," she said, sitting beside me. "Was this your first time?"

"Second," I said, my voice gruff. "Only I didn't do anything this time. I think the guy set me up to humiliate me. Must get off on it or something." I shook my head. "Just wish he'd paid me for it."

"No offense, but how old are you?" She looked curious, not judgmental.

"Twenty," I said. "But this isn't for me. I just... need money."

"Hm..." she said, tapping her chin with her finger. "If you've already slept with a guy for sex, why not take a step back?"

I glanced up at her tiredly. "I don't understand." And I doubted I would. My befuddled brain had had all it could take today.

"How would you feel about doing webcams?"

"Not sure what you mean."

"You know. Live sex shows and chats."

I blinked up at her. "I couldn't do that. I have no idea how to even go about it."

Her smile was encouraging. "Honey, it's nothing like having sex with a stranger. Look," she said, pulling out her phone. "Give me your number and I'll send you a text. If you decide you want more information, text or call."

"Do you do it?"

She grinned. "Sometimes. I work here because my brother thinks I need a respectable job. Personally, I'd rather do the cam thing all the time. It's loads more money and fun to boot."

"What do I have to buy to set myself up?"

"If you do it on your own, not much. A computer with a camera, though I recommend one that's adjustable so you can get the best angles. Or, you could work for someone who already has the equipment. You split the earnings and you'll still come away with more money than a crappy minimum-wage job."

I pushed myself off the wall and the girl helped me stand. "I'll think about it." She helped me too my feet. "Either do it on your own or come to me. The people I know are good peeps. They take a percentage, but they're fair and they'll protect you. A couple of the girls had stalkers and the guys took care of him."

"Great," I muttered. "A stalker is all I need."

I washed my hands and leaned against the sink for long moments, the girl -- her text said "this is Eden" -- stood with me, rubbing my back gently.

"I don't know what brought you to this point," she said softly, "but there's always hope. Just let me know if you want my help. Not just with this, but with anything. I know some people who are great at fixing problems." Her smile was genuine.

"I appreciate it. I may take you up on some of this."

"Good. Now. Go to a shooting range somewhere and put a bullet in that motherfucker's head who made you cry."

I barked a laugh. "Good plan."

* * *

I lasted all of a week before I sent off a text to Eden. Holly was better, but she was weak and listless most of the time. We'd done a trial of a medication that changed all that, but it was over five hundred dollars for a month's supply. Dr. Muse estimated she'd need at least two months, and I simply had nothing else to pull money from. Dr. Muse offered to pay for it and add it to our bill, but I didn't want to be any more indebted to him than I already was because, really, he'd been more than generous to us.

Thankfully, Eden called me almost immediately after I fired off the text. "What's up? Everything OK?" She actually sounded worried about me. I must really be lonely and in need of adult companionship if I was hearing sympathy in a stranger's voice.

"How long does it take me to get my money?" I asked the question expecting it to be a couple of weeks. I mean, I'd only ever had legitimate jobs. This was completely new territory.

"Oh, you'll get paid when you go home. Work as many sessions as you want. Typically, a session lasts thirty minutes. The guys can help pace you if you like so you hit that window." She giggled. "It's actually more fun that way. It helps get -- and keep -- you worked up. At least, it does for me."

"Well, OK, then," I said. I was nervous, but it sounded kind of fun. "Just... what's the catch? Will these guys expect me to sleep with them?"

"Honey, any of the guys decide they want you in their bed, sleep will not be involved. But no. They're very professional. None of them would ever hit on you just because of this. Rycks would kick their asses if they tried." She sounded happy, like just talking about all this was the highlight of her day.

"Who's Rycks?"

"He's in charge of security. Well, one of the men in charge of security. He does stuff that deals with outside women. He's very protective and would never want a woman to feel like she had to do something she didn't want to. In fact, he'll be the one to interview you."

"Well, I guess I'll give it a try. What do I need to do?"

"I'll talk to Rycks and see when he can talk to you. Give me a few and I'll call you back."

It took less than fifteen minutes. I was on pins and needles the whole time. I actually jumped when my phone rang.

"Do you know a place called Tito's Diner just outside Palm Beach?"

"Yeah. It's maybe fifteen minutes away."

"Rycks said to have you meet him there. I'll be with him. If you decide you want to try this, all he needs is the email you use on PayPal, and you'll be paid immediately after each session, no matter how many sessions you decide to do."

"When? Does he want to meet?"

"Well, you said it's fifteen minutes away, so say, thirty minutes?"

"Wow. That's fast."

"They're always looking for new girls to have some variety."

"OK, then. I'll be there as quick as I can."

The meet wasn't as creepy as I thought it would be. The atmosphere helped. I didn't frequent the place much because of my lack of funds, but everyone who lived in the Palm Springs area knew Tito's was the best place to eat.

Rycks was surprisingly easy to talk to and was very careful to stay out of my personal space. "You never have to do anything you're not comfortable with," he said. We'll start out with recorded shows where we'll pay you a flat fee. Once those shows air, you'll receive seventy-five percent of the tips on top of what you've already been paid." He explained everything as simply as he could. "After everyone gets a feel for what you're comfortable with and you get a feel for what the whole thing's like, we'll go to truly live shows. Those tend to make more because you can interact with the audience. Hopefully, you'll have gained a following by that time and the tips will be better. You'll still be paid the same for the actual work, but the tip split will go down to fifty-fifty."

"So it's in my best interest to… mingle outside of the cam sessions? Garner a following?"

He shrugged. "Strictly optional. We generally limit your sessions to eight thirty-minute sessions a week but that can increase or decrease depending on how popular you are."

"I'm not in this long term. I hope you understand that," I said, not wanting to commit to something for the foreseeable future. "I need some fast money. Assuming I can save myself a good padding in case I get into a bind again, that's it. I don't intend to do this very long."

"That's perfectly fine. There is no commitment on your part and no contract on our part. You get paid by the show. If at any time we don't fulfill that requirement, you're free to leave. If you decide you want to do this, talk to the girls before you actually do the first show. Every single one of them will tell you they've been paid on time every time. I take that very seriously."

I sighed. I didn't really have much of a choice. He was offering a hundred per half-hour show and I could do as many or as few as I liked. I had no idea how much I should make hourly from this type of work, but if it was instant money, I was ready to take that plunge. It wasn't my lowest, but it was pretty low.

"I'll do it," I said softly.

Rycks hesitated, waiting until I looked up before responding. "Are you sure, sweetheart? You don't look like you're at all excited about this. Most girls do it for the excitement. They enjoy it. At least, the ones we hire do. If it's about the money, I'll find something else for you to do."

"Is there anything that can make me two hundred dollars an hour?"

He shook his head. "Afraid not. Not outside of sex."

"Tried that, didn't work out so well," I muttered. I took a deep breath. "Guess I'll be your newest cam girl." I gave him a bright smile. I hoped it looked genuine, but it probably didn't.

"If you're sure."

"I am. When do I start?"

"Up to you. You're welcome to watch a few shows when you get there. See what it's like. Whoever you work with will give you direction, but it's really pretty simple. The key is to have a good time. You can look polished and have every move choreographed, but if you aren't enjoying the sex, no one else will either."

"What time should I be there?"

"Again, up to you. I have guys who prefer to work during the day, others who do better at night. We'll make your schedule work."

"Let me see what I need to do in the next few days, and I'll text Eden. Will that work?"

"Absolutely," Rycks said. When the busty redhead working the tables appeared with the bill, Rycks took it and handed her a few bills. "Keep the change, Marge." He grinned at the older woman, who returned his smile.

"He don't treat you right, honey, you come see me," she said. "That stuff ain't for me, but anyone who does it should be treated fairly. Rycks there is as square as they come."

It should have embarrassed me. I hadn't even thought anyone would be listening in on our conversation, but, if Marge thought ill of me, she certainly didn't act like it.

"Now, don't let me embarrass you, honey. We all gotta make a living. If you're gonna do something like this, it's best if you get honest, decent people to help you." She nodded to Rycks. "Those boys might look rough around the edges sometimes, but they're good people. Besides, if they ain't, all you have to do is tell me or Elena and we'll straighten them out."

"That's good to know." I tried to smile at her, but I felt like I'd just sold one more piece of my soul. Oh, well. I'd figure it out. That was what I did. I figured shit out. With my life after I realized I was going to be a single mom. When I found out Holly had leukemia. I'd figure this out, too. Besides, if it helped me give Holly a better quality of life during the last of her chemo treatments, it was worth any price I had to pay.

Chapter Five
Wrath

It had been weeks since that fucking party with Lawson, Hughsman, and fucking Gray. Not a word. I knew they'd want to delve deep into my background, but Black Reign had been prepared for that. Though I'd helped out Justice and Mae after that little debacle, I'd been careful to keep myself apart from Black Reign for months just in case someone put us all together. Nothing in my background check would lead to Black Reign. I just didn't expect it would take this long to get the call back. I knew I had the job locked up. No one in that room -- including the fucking partners -- could stay with me on the subject of law. I was a prodigy in that regard, remembering everything I was exposed to. The one thing I wasn't good at? Fucking waiting.

I finally said fuck it and went to the clubhouse, which was really a complex of large buildings and, well, mansions really. It was like a really large resort where there was a combination of sophistication and roughneck. One evening El Diablo could have over White-House-level guests, the next the most raunchy, raucous sex party could be happening. Sometimes, if the guests could be convinced the utmost discretion would be observed, both would happen at the same time. More than one daughter of a head of state had been fucked behind these walls. The Black Reign club girls had been known to make more than one stuffy national leader bellow to the rafters. Literally. Repeatedly. Yet, El Diablo managed to keep it all a secret. Nothing made the papers. No one said a word.

The estate sat on three hundred acres of prime real estate bordering the ocean. The compound took up more than half of that with all the buildings and outdoor recreational structures. It was less like a MC outfit than it was a private luxury residence.

The main building up front was where the majority of the members had their private residences. Any patched member was welcome there whether he had his own home or not. Some did, though most preferred to stay where club girls would clean and generally pamper them. The other buildings held various things, including test facilities for high-tech equipment like drones and ATV tanks to various types of new-aged fire power. All from the tech giant Argent Tech. Other buildings were for various high-end brothels or private sex clubs, from BDSM to age play to various online sex recordings. It was, understandably, a popular place with the club, as well as guests of the club officers. It was where Wrath headed now.

Being the middle of the week during the day, nothing much was happening except at the video studios. There was always fun to be had watching the cam girls live. If he enjoyed a particular woman's show, he could usually persuade her into a back room for an hour or so. If he paid her well.

Walking into one of the studios, he saw three men watching the screen intently. Not in itself unusual, but all three seemed to hardly breathe. It was almost like they were mesmerized. All three sported some serious wood and one, Hardcase, dropped his hand to his crotch and gave two hard scrubs with the heel of his hand down his length.

"Now, slowly, part your thighs. That's it. Not too wide. Just let us get a glimpse of what's beneath that thong. Good. Nice." Razor was chief of video production for Black Reign. Though El Diablo had more money than he knew what to do with, the club had to earn its own, and Razor had been known to bring down several million a year with online videos of all kinds. Cam girls were a big part of it, but he also did on-demand sex shows, film production, and personal video recordings of couples who wanted their fucking memorialized. Wrath tended to roll his eyes at the latter, but there was a waiting list for that shit. Normally, he just edited or cleaned up postproduction of cam-girl shows, but he was actually directing this one. It was a little beneath his paygrade, but who was Wrath to judge?

"Sit up on your knees. Frame your breasts with your -- yeah. Just like that. Unfasten your bra but don't remove it yet. Give me a flirty look. Remember these guys are going to be begging you to show them your tits. You don't want to give in too easily or you won't get tips. Hold your bra with one hand and dip into your thong with the other. That's it. Now, wet your finger and rub it over your nipple under your bra." Pause. "That's it. You're doing great, baby. Now, can you lift that tit up so you can lick... Awesome! Do it again while looking at the camera. Eyes open." He switched off the mic and spoke to the other men in the room. "She's gonna bring in the money like fuckin' crazy. Did you see her expressions?"

The two men in the control room with Razor, Iron and Tank, murmured their agreement.

"Put her on speaker," Iron said. "What's she sound like?"

"Gotta work on that," Razor said. "She's still a little shy but she'll come around. He reached over and flipped a switch. Immediately, little whimpers came over the speakers in the control room. It wasn't much, but the girl's little whimpers filtered through. And they sounded vaguely... familiar?

I stepped into the control room more fully, trying

to get a peek on the monitors. Iron and Razor were huddled around the biggest screen, with Tank standing in front of the one-way glass staring at the girl currently masturbating for the camera.

"That's it, baby. You're doing great. Drop your bra over the side of the bed and let us look. Arch your back and cup your tits from the side. Don't cover your nipples."

Again, those little whimpers sounded familiar. The girl... Fuck! I couldn't tell. Her hair was jet-black, but her skin milky white. Those pouty lips of hers were painted jet-black, like her hair, but she had no tattoos or piercings that might indicate a Goth or something similar. She definitely wasn't one of our club girls. Another club, then? No, that didn't fit either. With every sound she made, I got the feeling I knew this girl. But from where?

"You're lookin' hot as sin, baby," Razor encouraged her. "Fuckin' smokin'. Wonderful. That's good. Stretch your nipples a little. Lick them both if you feel the urge. Good. You can paint them with your pussy juice again, yes. Keep doing that for just a minute. Lick your nipples as much as you can."

"She's so fuckin' small I don't know how she's gettin' her tongue to her tit, but she's definitely managin'." Tank said. "New blood's always good to watch, but this chick's fuckin' hot."

"Agreed," Iron said. "She needs extra help, I'm in."

All three men chuckled.

They let her play with herself like that for a couple of minutes. Razor continued to direct and encourage her, but she was rapidly getting the hang of it. I watched raptly, but kept quiet in the background, not wanting to break the spell being woven around us all.

"You ready to lose the thong?" Razor's voice was more husky than usual. Yeah, the man was definitely getting into this girl. "First, I want you to slide the edge just over your pussy so we can see your clit. Don't worry about the rest of it just yet. We just want to see your clit. That's it. Now wet your finger. You can use your mouth or your pussy, I don't care. I just want to be able to see your finger gleaming. Can you do that? Good, baby. You're doing great. Now, rub your little clit for me." I didn't miss that Razor had gone from "us" and "we" to "me." That was rare with the big man. He always viewed the videos with a clinical eye, trying to make them more appealing to anyone watching. But he was enjoying the fuck outta this.

"So beautiful," he murmured. "OK. Now slide your thong off your hips, then sit back and pull it off your legs. You can just toss it over the bed. Keep your legs together for now. Sit back on your heels... that's it."

OK, there was something about seeing this girl on her knees like this. Visions of Celeste that night at the hotel floated through my mind. Her kneeling before me, her eyes wide as she enveloped my cock with her mouth. I'd been flush on Ecstasy and getting freer with the sex by that time. She hadn't taken any. Or drunk more than a sip. I, on the other hand, had more than a little to drink and that half a Molly.

Now my heart was racing. I had remembered a pleasant time with Celeste, but watching this cam girl was bringing it back to me. There was a lot the drugs and alcohol had dulled about that night. Sure, I'd had an awesome time. Hell, I'd lost every bit of good sense I'd had, I was so caught up in the pleasure. But it was hard to remember exactly what I'd done. When I'd seen Celeste outside the hospital that evening, I hadn't tried to remember. When she'd showed up at my apartment, I'd started to remember more, but had blocked it out. Why wouldn't I? I never had a reason to remember sex with a woman before. She was clean and had an IUD. There wasn't much else to worry about.

But then I remembered something. It came to me at the same time the cam girl through the one-way glass gave a soft gasp, her fingers disappearing into her pussy. Celeste was fucking me for money. She needed money. Why? She wouldn't tell me. Then at the hospital, I'd learned she was caring for a little girl. When Celeste showed up at my apartment she'd shut down and left when I'd asked her what she needed money for. Did she need it to leave a man? No, that didn't make sense. If so, she wouldn't be here or sleeping with a stranger for sex. That would be too risky for her. And why was watching this girl working it for the camera making me remember all this with complete and total clarity?

I never did anything without a reason. Hell, even fucking Celeste had been to convince the law firm I was all in with them. At least, right up until I took that fucking Molly. After that, I'm not sure what the fuck I was doing other than losing myself in the sweetest pussy I'd ever come across.

Looking up at the window again, the girl had spread her legs and was rubbing her clit with nimble fingers. The little sounds she made were maddening! And so fucking familiar...

Wait. "Is she wearing a wig?"

Tank didn't even look at me. His gaze was focused entirely on the sexy little thing finger-banging herself. "Yeah. I didn't want her to, but she insisted. And all the makeup. She's got all this platinum-blonde hair I'd love to wrap around my dick and jerk off with," he replied absently, but I was ready to lose my mind. No way. It couldn't be.

"What's her name?" I bit out the question more sharply than I'd intended, but I was so losing my shit.

"Don't know. Razor just calls her baby."

"Not good enough! What's her fuckin' name?"

Razor looked up at me from his spot at the monitor. "You can't keep it down, you need to leave. What are you doin' here, anyway? Aren't you supposed to be schmoozing rich people or some happy horseshit?"

"I want to know who that girl is."

"Oh, something like it's none of your goddamned business," Razor said, an annoyed look on his face. "I'm trying to get her to orgasm. She's a little new at this, and I'd like to teach her right so she can get the most buck for her bang."

Iron snorted. "Good one."

I wasn't amused. "You want her there? I'll get her there."

I shoved Razor aside and took his headphones. Taking a breath, I keyed the mic. "Did I tell you what a pretty little pussy you have?" She froze, her eyes going wide. "Don't stop. I want to see you flood your hand with your juice. Just for me. Can you do that?"

"This ain't fuckin' funny, Wrath," Razor bit out. "Don't you dare scare her off or I'll fuckin' rip out your fuckin' balls."

"I -- Vincent?" Sure enough, my little Celeste breathed my name on a little whimper. Instantly I heard Razor snap out a command.

"Zoom in on her pussy! Now!" They did. It was suddenly glistening with fluid.

"That's my girl," I praised. "You're all nice and

wet. Ready for my cock, aren't you?"

She whimpered but shook her head.

"Denying me? Oh, now that just won't do." I pressed my hand to the glass, as if she could see me there. "Spread your pussy lips. Show me how wet you are. I'll judge if you're ready for me or not."

Even as she shook her head, Celeste did as I asked. A little sob escaped and her body quivered.

"Hum..." I mused. "That has to be the juiciest, most beautiful little pussy in the whole world. I could eat you up."

"Yes," she whispered on a breath. "I need --" She cut herself off, shaking her head.

"You need what, honey? Need me to eat that little pussy? Need me to finger it until you come? Fuck it?"

"Ahh!" She cried out, arching her back. Two fingers plunged into her cunt, in and out at a furious rate.

"Use three," I growled. She did, writhing on the bed now, but still she didn't come. "Still can't come?"

"I -- I need... I... need..."

I yanked the headset off and stormed out of the control room. Behind me I heard Razor barking orders to the other two about changing the angle of the cameras or some shit. I didn't really care. All I knew was that Celeste needed me to make her come and that was exactly what I was going to do.

Throwing open the door to the little room they had set up, I stormed in, then kicked it shut. Celeste scooted back farther on the bed, a mixture of fear, lust, and hesitation on her face. She was understandably reluctant to let me do this after what had happened, but as far as I was concerned, things had changed. Along with the haze of lust-filled sex, I was also remembering the intelligent, funny, sensitive woman I'd had in my arms. I'd promised her pleasure, and I'd delivered. But at what cost to her later? This was exactly the reason I avoided drugs of any kind. I'd told myself I'd taken that half a pill to prove to her it was safe, but the real reason I'd done it was to blunt my need for her enough to last beyond the first five fucking seconds inside her pussy. Celeste affected me like no woman ever had. Part of it was her hesitant, shy nature. The other was that I knew she needed something desperately, and I wanted to be the one to give it to her. I'd only realized that when I'd watch her responding to Razor's voice.

I knew where the cameras were in that room. Same as they were in most of the webcam rooms. Snagging her ankle, I pulled her to the edge of the bed and bent to inhale her pussy. Sure enough, it was wet to the point of dripping down to wet her ass, and she smelled tangy sweet. Like a tart little berry not all the way ripe.

Without further preamble, I devoured her cunt. I growled and slurped while she writhed underneath me. Her cries now filled the air more completely. She sounded just like what she was. A woman in need. Her fingers tunneled in my hair, fisting there to cause a bite of pain. It only made me harder and all the more hungry for her.

Glancing to the side, I saw a pink dildo with a white handle. It had two heads to it, one smaller and shorter than the other. No doubt where that was supposed to go. I lifted my head and snagged the toy and the bottle of lube next to it.

"We don't need this," I said, referring to the lube, "but I won't take a chance on hurting you like…" I trailed off. I hadn't used lube with her when I'd taken her ass before. "I'm going to make sure you're needing this as much as I need to do it."

She spread her legs, catching each knee with a hand. Fuck! Shit!

"You're so Goddamned wet. So fuckin' lusty. This greedy little pussy needs to be filled, doesn't it?" When she nodded, biting her lip, I slapped the inside of her thigh. Hard. She cried out and jumped. "Words, baby. Give me words."

"Yes," she whispered.

"Yes what?"

"Yes! I need you to fill me up!"

"Want me to fuck you with this?" I lifted up the contraption, now gleaming with lubrication.

"I --"

I smacked her thigh again, then her upturned pussy. The slap to her pussy made her scream to the ceiling.

"Tell me!" The demand was hard. Unyielding.

"YES! GOD, YES!"

I aimed the dildos and guided them into both her holes. The second they were in, she came in a wet rush. "That's it, my girl," I purred. "You like havin' your holes full? Like showin' all those people what they'll never have? When we're done here, I'm gonna take you to my room and fuck the livin' shit outta you. Then I'm gonna plug your ass for the rest of the day with a remote-control vibrator plug and every time you fuck with me, I'm gonna turn it on and make you beg me to fuck you!"

Celeste screamed and screamed. Her pussy quivered around the dildo. I had to concentrate to keep in mind where the cameras were so Razor could get a good view. If she was doing this for money -- which there was no doubt she was -- she was going to get the most she could. Once I had her safely in my room, we were going to have a long talk.

Before I fucked her.

Or after.

It didn't matter. We were talking.

Chapter Six
Celeste

What had just happened? I was soaked in sweat, sticky where I'd come so much, and wrapped in a bed sheet from the bed I'd been wallering around on, coming my brains out. My head spun because I'd hyperventilated... *while I came*... I was a fucking mess!

Looking up, I saw Vincent's harsh expression as he hurried down the hall. He carried me outside and to his truck, a huge, black behemoth of a Ford, and put me inside. Without a word, he sped off to a big building farther back in the compound and skidded to a stop in the parking lot.

The building had a similar design and color as the others I'd seen, but this one was massive where the others were simply huge. How many buildings were in this place? Rycks had explained this was a motorcycle club, but weren't those run out of dirty garages with women hanging out in droves and illegal drugs everywhere? Or something. Hell, where were the dead bodies? Did this make me one of the women?

Ugh! I was so lust-stupid I couldn't think!

Somehow, we made it to what I could only assume was his room. Not the apartment I'd been to before, but a room here. The clubhouse. Err, compound. Something. How could they call this a clubhouse? It was more like a club *estate*, for Christ's sake!

"What MC has this kind of setup?"

"A very rich one," Vincent said.

"Let me down."

"Just hold still." He carried me to the bathroom and started the shower, never taking his arm from around me. The bathroom was as big as my apartment.

The shower was the frameless kind, big enough to wash a fucking car in. I found myself crashing hard. The endorphins from the orgasms and the stress and the orgasms... Yeah. I was weak as a newborn kitten. And I still had to get home tonight to get Holly from Mrs. McDonald.

"Holly," I managed to say. My stupid eyes were drooping. "I have to get home to Holly. Let me go."

"You can't go home like this," he said gently as he took the sheet from me and carried me into the shower with him. "You need rest. Tell me where she is, and I'll make sure she's safe for the night."

"Mr. and Mrs. McDonald have her. They've kept her so much lately. I can't ask them to keep her again."

"Gerald and Glinda McDonald? The couple with the two of you at the hospital?"

"Yes. I rent the apartment above their garage." I knew I was giving him too much, but I couldn't seem to stop myself. My brain just wouldn't pull itself together and shut the fuck up.

"You let me worry about it. Just for tonight. Can you give me that much?"

I looked up at him. I knew tears were swimming in my eyes but, again, I couldn't help it. "You'll hurt me. Like you did before."

Did I imagine he winced? No clue. But he pulled me tightly against his body and held me under the spray of water. I reached up to move the wig out of the way, but the jet-black thing was gone.

"Got rid of it before we left the studio. You're hair's up and out of the spray." He squirted something on my back and rubbed it gently into my skin, down between my cheeks to my pussy. I whimpered as he brushed his fingers all around, getting the mess of wetness clean from between my thighs and my ass cheeks. "Just let me take care of you tonight. Tomorrow you'll feel better and can do whatever you need to."

"If you can just take me home…"

"Not happening tonight, honey. Not until you've slept a few hours."

I sighed, too tired to fight. I was vaguely aware of Vincent rinsing me off before turning off the water and stepping out. He set me on the vanity counter and pulled out two big fluffy towels. One he slung around his hips, the other he used to dry me off.

"I must look bedraggled," I said in a sulking voice. "Like I've just been fucked hard and put up wet."

"Not yet. And I promise I'll clean you up just like I did this time."

I could see he was joking. At least partially, but I wasn't having it. "I mean it, Vincent. I don't want to sleep with you."

"No intention of sleeping, honey."

"No sex! God! What's wrong with you?" Though my wits were still muddled, a good mad would get my adrenaline pumping. Lord knew I'd need every ounce of brain power I possessed to spar with Vincent. "You treat me like shit, then step into the cam show I was trying to do to make me come my brains out? What the fuck?"

"Sex has little to do with whether or not we like each other, Celeste. We have explosive chemistry. That's more than some people have."

"Well, we don't have anything," I snapped. "I'm leaving. I need to get home to Holly. Where's my phone? I need to make sure they put money in my account." And to refill Holly's prescription at the pharmacy if I had enough.

Instead of answering me, Vincent scooped me up and carried me to the bed, putting me on my feet in front of it. Then he took the fucking towel.

"Give that back!" Instead, he tossed me a T-shirt from a nearby drawer. Wouldn't you know, it smelled just like him. The jerk. Then he tossed me my phone. Which should have been in my purse. "What'd you do with my bag?" He just pointed to the corner where it sat next to his dresser.

"Do what you have to do. Call the McDonalds and tell them you'll be back first thing in the morning.

"I'm going home now, Vincent."

"Not until we get some things straight." He pointed at my phone. "First thing in the morning." When I opened my mouth to protest, he added, "Or, I can go pick her up tonight. I'm sure Lyric would love to have her. Once we finish our discussion you can spend some time with her until bed, but you'll be staying with me tonight. I have a feeling our discussion is going to take a fuckin' long time."

"Who's Lyric?"

"Rycks's ol' lady. She's got a kid of her own about four. Might be a friend for Holly."

"I'm not pawning my kid off on a stranger, Vincent."

"Stop being difficult," he said, exasperation in his voice. "You don't want her to stay with Lyric, I'll get Doc or Blade over here to stay with her."

I had to think a minute. I remember those names... "Dr. Collins and Dr. Muse? You can't do that."

"The hell I can't." He whipped out his phone. "I take it she'd more comfortable with Dr. Muse?"

"Well, yeah, but --"

He silenced me with a kiss before putting the

phone to his ear. "It's Wrath. Need you to pick up Holly and bring her to the Reign compound. No, I'm sure she's fine. Celeste and I have some things to settle, and she doesn't want to put out the McDonalds by asking them to watch her tonight. She trusts you." There was a pause. Vincent glanced at me. "No. I didn't know that." His look grew darker. "Didn't know that either." Then, "Are you fucking kidding me? Just get over here. I'll have the girls make up a room for you close to us." He ended the call, sent off a text, then looked at me, his expression dark. "You're in so much trouble."

I sighed. "Fine. I'll be in trouble. I'm too exhausted to care much."

He sighed. "Lie down. I'll be back in a few minutes. Blade is bringing Holly here. I need to make sure they have a room close to us so she can come to you if she needs you."

"I still don't like this. I just want to go home."

"Not tonight, honey. Lie down. Rest. I'll be back and we can talk."

* * *

Sometime later, I woke. It was full dark outside, and everything was quiet. I was so warm and comfortable I didn't want to move, but my bladder had other ideas. I tried to get up, but there was a brawny arm around my middle holding me against an equally brawny chest. When I tried to get up again, Vincent grunted at me.

"Let me go."

"Where you goin'?"

"To take a piss! Let me up!"

His chuckle beside my ear told me he'd been goading me. Fuck. This was a fucking mess.

I stumbled to the bathroom and turned on the

light. I looked better than I had when I'd come here today. The dark circles were gone, at least. I felt better too. I wasn't sure what time it was, but it had to be late. I still had on Vincent's shirt. It still smelled like him, especially since he'd been wrapped around me.

I stood there looking in the mirror for a long time, the full impact of what I'd done hitting me. Yes, I'd had on a ton of makeup and a wig, but I'd masturbated on camera for strangers on the internet to watch. Then, I'd let Vincent use a dildo on me and make me come -- like for real come. I didn't even know how much money I'd made. They'd promised two hundred up-front, but I had no idea if they'd actually paid me.

The door opened and Vincent looked in on me. When he saw me standing there, his face softened and he stepped inside the room to stand behind me. His big hands went to my shoulders. I barely came up to his chin. All those muscles wrapped around me made me feel safe. And when he touched me... I lost my Goddamn mind. How I wished he was a different kind of person. If he were the kind of man to protect women and children, he'd be my dream man. Instead, he was self-absorbed and shallow. Kind of reminded me of Holly's father.

"Come back to bed, Celeste. You still need rest."

"I need to check to make sure I got paid."

"Why?"

"I think what I did was humiliating enough to deserve payment," I spat. Shrugging him off, I left the bathroom and snagged my phone. He'd put it on the nightstand next to my side of the bed. Sure enough, there was a deposit. Three times what we'd agreed on, but it was there. "There's more than there should be."

"Razor said he could make way more with that

video than he first thought. Said there would likely be more in a few days once he got it up and running. You gonna tell me what this is all about now?"

"Still not any of your business."

"Holly's sick. Isn't she?"

"Did Dr. Muse tell you?"

"He did."

"That's a breach of trust on his part." It hurt, but if the two men were friends, I knew Dr. Muse wouldn't miss any opportunity to get Holly any help she needed. If he thought Vincent could help her, he wouldn't hesitate to tell him what was wrong.

"Maybe. But he knows I can help with the financial part of your problem."

"No. Holly is my responsibility. I'll take care of her."

"How? By prostituting yourself? For letting Razor film you fucking yourself for the whole world to see?"

It wasn't anything I hadn't been beating myself up over already, but it still hurt to hear it from someone else. "You have no right to judge me!"

"I'm not. I'm just pointing out that you've got a ready resource right here. Use me instead of showing every man in the Goddamn world what's mi -- err -- what should be kept private."

"Look. I'm not proud of what I've done. But for that little girl to get the medical care she needs, I'll do it again. I'll do it as much as it takes until Dr. Muse tells me she's in remission. We're so close to the end of her treatment, and he says she's responded well. We had a minor setback with the last treatment making her sick and her nosebleed, but she's still doing well. Yes, I'm in a shit-ton of debt and I have to use every dime I have for her medication and hospital bills, but if I can make this much money on every show I do for a few weeks, I'll be in much better shape."

"No," he said.

"No what?"

"No, you're not doing that anymore. No more webcams."

"You can't dictate to me, Vincent. We're not a couple, and Holly is not your daughter."

"What kind of example do you think this sets for her, her mother fucking in front of an audience?"

That was my last straw. I stepped toward Vincent and slapped his too-handsome face. "Fuck you, Vincent! Fuck! You!"

"You could do that," he said, nodding as if I'd just come up with the most brilliant idea. "In fact, I could pay you, just like I did the night we met. You'll be my private escort, and I'll pay for Holly's medical expenses.

"Are you out of your mind?" I was feeling a little desperate now. Mainly because I wasn't as opposed to the idea as I should be.

"Why would you say that? You've already fucked me once for money. Twice if you count the cam show. You enjoyed yourself both times. If you're going to keep doing it, why not just do it with me?"

"Because you're a jerk! I hate you!"

"You don't have to love me, Celeste. Just fuck me." Though his words were crude, Vincent didn't sound unkind or cruel. Just matter-of-fact. "I'll pay you well and Holly's taken care of. If you'll calm down a little, we can discuss this and come up with an arrangement so it's more like a job and Holly's life isn't disrupted. She'll have the normal babysitting hours, and you don't have to worry about finding a sitter at odd hours. Problem solved all the way around."

He was really going to make me do this. It was so logical I wanted to scratch his eyeballs out. Mainly because he was right. I already knew I could enjoy myself while getting paid to fuck him. Was it ideal? Not in the least. But it was feasible. And I didn't have to worry about fucking someone I didn't know.

"I hate you."

"Yeah, you said that." Then he pulled me to him and kissed me. It was like he was sealing a deal I wasn't sure I wanted a part of, but he knew I couldn't resist. And he was right.

The longer he kissed me, the more I fought. Not to push him away, but for dominance. If I was going to do this, it was going to be on my own terms. He could kiss my ass.

Over and over we kissed, tongues tangling, teeth nipping. Vincent had my hair fisted hard in his hand, holding me still for him. Instead of complying, I bit him hard. He hissed and pulled my hair harder. He trailed his lips down my jaw to my neck and bit me just as hard as I'd bit him. I cried out, but the pain did little to tamp down my desire for the bastard.

"You're not getting your way, Celeste," he said at my ear. "I'm the dominant in this relationship. No matter what happens next, I'm the master. You're my pet."

"Go fuck yourself," I spat.

"Much rather have you fuck me."

"Why? You've got tons of woman out there willing to fuck you for free. Isn't that what you told me?"

"Not in so many words, no. But I don't want any of them. At least, not right now. I want you, Celeste."

"You're insane."

"Maybe. But I'm willing to bet that if I reach

down and run my fingers through your pussy, you'll be as wet as I am hard."

I was done. With a groan I surrendered to him, accepted his kiss and melted against his body for him to do with me as he pleased.

Chapter Seven
Wrath

Celeste was right. I was insane. Not only was I all but forcing her into an arrangement with me where I paid her for the use of her body, but I was doing it for all the wrong reasons. I was going to help with Holly's medical expenses regardless. That had already started while she slept. I was doing this because I couldn't stand the thought of other men looking at her. I knew that Razor, the bastard, was already planning on asking her to move to actual sex shows instead of just masturbation. The thought ate me alive.

While Celeste had been resting, Blade had arrived with Holly, and I'd had a chance to meet the girl. Naturally, the McDonalds had come with the child. They weren't going to let just anyone take Holly with them, not even her doctor. I'd spoken with the couple and Blade at length about Holly's condition and what they knew of Celeste's financial situation. Now, the hospital and the pharmacy had been paid off. Blade had picked up Holly's medicine, and the child was currently sleeping across the hall. The McDonalds had expressed their gratitude and brought me up to speed on who they were. And who Celeste was.

I didn't pretend to know who Mama and Pops were, but El Diablo held them in high esteem, even though they were closely affiliated with Bones MC. That pair was tight with the McDonalds, who were now haranguing El Diablo and me. Apparently, he knew more about both couples than even Bones did. Bottom line for me was the McDonalds expected me to take care of both Celeste and Holly because they needed a strong man in their lives. I agreed. Just to be fair, though, I tried to explain that I probably wasn't the right man for the job, but Gerald McDonald had seen straight to my fucking soul. He knew there was something about Celeste I couldn't let go, and the bastard pushed me.

If I were honest with myself, he didn't have to push hard. For the first time since I'd met El Diablo, I found my loyalties divided. OK, so not really divided, but expanded. I already thought of Celeste and Holly as my girls, and I had to see them safe and cared for. El Diablo would be able to appreciate that. He had his own demons in that regard. But making room for my girls in my life meant less time and energy to devote to furthering El Diablo's goals for the future.

And all that was moot anyway if Celeste wouldn't let me into her life. Fuck. I needed a fucking drink. More, I needed Celeste.

I'd made love to her for the better part of the night, letting her sleep in the next morning. I needed to get to know Holly. From experience watching Rycks and Lyric with Bella, the quickest way to get Celeste to let me into her life was to coax her daughter into mine.

"I like Doc and Blade better'n you." The little four-year-old brat, Holly, was Satan's spawn.

"Why would you say that? I brought you ice cream."

"You brought *vanilla* ice cream. Everyone knows the only real ice cream is chocolate ice cream." She put her little hands on her hips. "What kind of person gets vanilla?"

"How old did you say you were again?" Glinda McDonald had said she was four, but she talked like she was much older. And the kid was cutting me to fucking shreds.

"Old enough to know not to buy anyone vanilla ice cream unless they ask for it." She wrinkled her delicate nose, and Doc burst out laughing.

Blade shrugged and handed her a cup of chocolate ice cream with whipped cream and three cherries. "Kid's got a point. You some kinda dumbass?"

"Don't swear in front of the kid, you dipshit," I growled at Blade.

Holly looked up at Blade. "He's not very smart, is he?"

"Nope. Make sure to tell your mom. She needs a smart man takin' care of the two of you."

"Stay outta this, Blade. This is between me and Holly." If Holly didn't need his particular medical specialty, I'd've killed the motherfucker on the spot.

"Why should I stay out of it? With you outta the picture, me and Doc have a good chance with Celeste."

"Yeah," Holly agreed. "And either of them would be a thousand times better than you."

I sighed. How did I get myself into this fucking mess? Holly was the cutest thing I'd ever seen in my life, with more sass than any child had a right to. I loved her the first second I met her. Pretty sure she despised me on sight. She was really skinny, probably from her illness and the recent chemo treatment. She had no hair or eyebrows or lashes, but wore a lacy little elastic band with a big flower around her head. She also had little earrings in her ears that she changed with her outfit. They were usually either gold or silver, so a good quality that wouldn't hurt her delicate skin, but she seemed to have an endless variety of them.

"Fine. What's it gonna take for me to be the best pick for you and your mom?"

She looked me up and down like she was eyeing a piece of meat. I'd seen that look from women so many times in my life, it wasn't funny. Only difference was, this was one chick who definitely found me lacking. In every department. Finally, she shook her head.

"I'm not sure there's any way to save you. Maybe if you had a Saint Bernard puppy or something, but even that would be cutting it close."

"A Saint Bernard puppy? Are you fuckin' kiddin' me?"

"You really shouldn't swear in front of me. I'm a kid."

"Yeah," Blade said, draping an arm around Holly's shoulder like they were best buds. "You really are some kind of dumbass." Without looking at each other, Blade and Holly fist-bumped.

"A Saint Bernard puppy," I said, giving Blade a withering look. He simply grinned. "What about a goldfish?"

Holly rolled her eyes. "I'm done," she said, holding up her hand in a talk-to-the-hand gesture. "Just when I thought you couldn't be any lamer."

Doc laughed so hard he nearly fell out of his chair. "On that note, I'm outta here." He reached out his hand to Holly. "Wonderful to meet you again, Maddog."

"Maddog? You named her Maddog?" This wasn't going as well as I'd thought it would.

"Noooo," Holly drew out the word like she was rapidly losing her patience with me. "I picked my own name. 'Cause I'm mean like a mad dog."

Again, she and Blade fist-bumped without looking at each other. Holly crossed her arms over her chest and cocked her hip to one side and her head to the other.

"Fuck," I muttered.

"Might want to go find that Saint Bernard

puppy," Blade said. "Kid is prepared to wait until she gets what she wants before she endorses you with her mother."

I looked at Holly for confirmation.

"Yup," she said, pursing her lips and looking like a spoiled teenager.

"What's going on here?"

Celeste looked adorably sleepy. Her hair wasn't the sleek, sophisticated work of art I'd seen the first day I met her. In fact, she had it up in a messy bun. Several strands had escaped and tangled together. She still wore my T-shirt but had put on a pair of gym shorts too. They swallowed her whole, coming to her knees. If they hadn't had a drawstring, they'd have fallen off her hips to pool at her feet on the floor. Odds said she wasn't wearing panties.

"Wrath here was just getting to know Holly. They were negotiating for a puppy." Blade supplied that information almost gleefully. Well, except that he looked stern and surly, just like he always did. Why in the world Holly preferred him to me I'd never know.

"No puppy," Celeste said, all traces of sleep vanishing in an instant. "We don't have a place for a puppy."

"If Wrath here comes up with a Saint Bernard puppy, I'll fence in the backyard for him to live," Gerald McDonald volunteered happily.

Celeste's eyes got wide. "Oh, no, young lady! Not happening."

Holly shrugged. "I didn't expect it would. Wrath's too much of a lame-o to even know where to get a Saint Bernard puppy." Oh, the little brat was laying it on thick. That was a double-dog dare if ever I heard one.

I expected Celeste to scold her daughter, and I

was prepared to defend the child. Instead, she looked me up and down. "You're right, baby. He is a lame-o."

"All right," I said. "That's it." I turned and scooped Celeste up, draping her over one shoulder. Holly let out a peal of giggles as I walked out with her mother. "I'll be back for you later, you little brat." I growled and Holly giggled even more. God help me, I was getting that little girl the puppy she wanted if it killed me.

I took Celeste back to my room with her protesting all the way. More than once, I swatted her ass, earning a squeal from her.

"We've got things to discuss, woman," I said.

"We were supposed to do that last night, but you couldn't keep your dick in your pants."

"I seem to remember waking up more than once with your mouth devouring my dick like your favorite treat."

"That was a wet dream, you prick!"

"Oh, it was definitely a dream come true. What man wouldn't love wakin' up to a beautiful woman blowin' him?" I tossed her onto the bed, then followed her down. When she was pinned beneath me, I worked my hips so they were between her legs, mashing my cock against her pussy. "You sore? We've been going at it pretty hard."

She sighed. "I'm fine."

I winced. "There's that word."

"Look. This isn't a good idea to continue. I shouldn't have led you on last night."

"You seemed to enjoy yourself. I see no reason for that to stop."

"Why do they call you Wrath?"

The question took me off guard. She was deflecting, but she needed to know as much as I could tell her. "Because it never ends well for anyone who crosses me. I'm ruthless in a courtroom. Most of my opponents prefer to settle out of court because, once I get before a judge, there's no give in me. I go to trial, I take it all the way. No plea. Same way once I make up my mind about something I want. I go after it."

She stared at me a long time, studying me. Maybe trying to decide what she was going to say next. One thing I had in abundance in my life was patience. I stroked her cheek with my thumb and just waited.

"I'm not going to deny I enjoy sex with you, Vincent. But it's precisely because I enjoy it so much that I can't do this with you. You're not the kind of man to be with one woman, and, if this continues, I couldn't bear it when you did go to another woman." She shook her head. "I just can't do that."

"I still want you. What if I promise that I'll only be with you while we're together?"

"I'm pretty sure I told you no last night. I haven't changed my mind."

"Bet I can make you tell me yes today."

She blinked up at me, her mouth parting as if to say something, then she shook her head. "No. I can't. You don't respect me, and if I do this with you, I won't respect myself."

"I respect you, Celeste. No one can meet Holly, see what she's living through, and not respect how you've taken care of that girl." I brushed my thumb across her lower lip. "If you believe nothing else I tell you, believe this. I respect you more than any woman I've ever met."

She shook her head, but before she could say anything my phone buzzed in my pocket. The vibration pattern said it was the phone call I'd been waiting on.

"Fuck," I swore as I fished it out and looked at the screen. "I've got to take this."

"What is it?"

"Club business. Give me a minute and we'll finish this discussion."

She nodded, but scooted out from under me as I pushed up off the bed. I walked into the sitting room before answering.

"Vincent Black," I said crisply with a purposeful slant of annoyance in my voice.

"Vincent! It's Stewart. I have some news for you."

"Stewart…" I said, trying to make it seem like I'd forgotten the man. It had been over a month. Not unreasonable I'd have forgotten who he was if I'd been busy.

There was a pause. Yeah. I'd taken the wind out of his sails. The more off-balance I could keep someone, the better my advantage was. "Stewart Gray." When I still said nothing, he continued in a clipped voice. "Lawson, Hughsman, and Gray?" As I suspected, he hated having his name at the end of that trio. I could tell it in his voice. He was the one who did the menial tasks. I'd also bet he was a slimeball, but a slimeball who knew nothing about the real shit going down in the firm.

"Oh, yes. It's been more than a month since we last talked. I figured your firm's interests had changed."

"With your versatility, there's no way we could change direction so far you wouldn't be an asset."

"Not much of one or it wouldn't have taken you a month to decide."

"Well, this isn't so much about the firm as it is

about one of our clients. He wants to bring you in with him."

That caught me off guard. "Not following."

"Harold Collins is interested in bringing you into an assistant district attorney roll. We've spent the last month putting together a portfolio on you."

"I have no interest in ADA pay, Stewart. If I was, I'd be the DA."

Gray chuckled at that. Giovanni had said he'd get me into the DA's office if I was patient. But honestly, I hadn't expected it to come this way. "Mr. Collins is one of our most important clients," Gray explained. "We wanted you with us, but he believes you will be a better asset working for him." Giovanni had put just enough shady shit in my background portfolio to make me enticing to a man like Collins without seeming like it was too good to be true.

"Again, I didn't become a lawyer to work for public-servant pay. Not interested.

"Ah, but you don't know all the benefits."

"It's a city job. I'd say the benefits were pretty much standard."

"Meet with him. Tonight. What can it cost you but a couple of hours?

I was silent for a moment, making it seem like I was indecisive. "Fine. What time?"

"Tonight. Eight p.m. Saldis on the Pier."

This was what I'd been waiting for. If I could get close enough to Collins, or Nathanial Lawson and Richard Hughsman, there was every possibility I could clone their phones. Once we had that information, Giovanni Romano at Argent Tech could hack their world, and we'd have what we needed to take down the key people in the firm helping the DA avoid prosecution. It might go a long way toward putting this whole mess to rest. This wasn't El Diablo's end game, but it brought him one step closer. This was my project, and I was singularly suited for it.

"Do you want an escort? I can have one waiting for you when you get there. You can celebrate after the deal is done."

"No. I made an exception last time, but I don't mix business with pleasure."

"A beautiful woman on your arm can be a huge asset." This was a play on the firm's part. Get me suckered in with drugs or sex, or both, and I'd be solidly in their pocket. Collins probably thought so as well.

"Agreed. But only after I've had time to know what she's capable of and what her agenda is."

"Oh, I assure you, any escort we'd pick for you would be completely loyal to the firm. And there are benefits afterward, as you know." If I could see Stewart Gray's face right now, I'm sure he'd be leering.

"I'm sure there are, but I'm not interested, Stewart." I hung up the phone. The timing was piss poor, but at least all the prep work hadn't been for nothing.

Tapping Shotgun's number, I waited for the other man to pick up. "Giovanni was right," I said when he answered on the second ring. "I think I'm in. Gray has set up a meeting with Collins tonight. Apparently, Collins wants me as an ADA."

"Good. Data said he and Suzy are onto something. Not sure how big it is, but if you can clone their phones, we might be getting somewhere. Especially Collins, but that's like the Holy Grail of information, so aim high, but don't expect it."

"If it's possible with the equipment you give me, I'll get it."

"Good."

I hesitated, not wanting to give too much away… or seem like too much of a pussy. "Do me a favor."

"Yeah?"

"Have someone keep an eye on Celeste. Razor's gonna try to get her to do more."

"Yeah. Heard he had a little hottie on cam. Celeste wasn't bad either."

"Suck my dick, Shotgun. I'm being serious."

"I don't swing that way, but I can probably pass on to the club girls you're interested."

"I'm not. So don't."

"Oh? You finally got you a woman willin' to be your ol' lady?"

"No. And I don't need a fuckin' ol' lady. But Celeste is a little touchy about it, and I want to keep her in my bed a while longer."

"Sure thing. Only…"

"Just say what's on your mind."

"Have you considered she ain't the kinda woman you're lookin' for?"

"Why not? She's one damned hot fuck. Besides, she needs my help. I meet her needs. She meets mine. I don't see the problem." I totally saw the problem, but if the brothers smelled blood in the water, they'd push me toward Celeste until I had no choice but to marry the girl, and I wasn't ready for that.

"If you can't see that girl has 'forever' written all over her, you really are a lame-o."

I sighed. "That's not going away any time soon, is it?"

"Not if I can help it. Or Blade. Or Doc. They might be Bane, but they're all right. Doin' right by the kid too. And her mama."

"You sayin' I ain't?"

"I'm sayin' you better really think about what you're doin' here. That one's special. Like Rycks's Lyric."

"You think I don't know that? I'm just not ready to lead her into believing I'm ready to settle down and have a fuckin' family." I glanced over my shoulder, hoping like shit Celeste wasn't trying to listen in. Truth was, I might just be ready to settle down and have a fucking family, but I wasn't ready to admit that to anyone. Hell, I wasn't even sure. I was too consumed with the sex.

"Just think about what you're doing before you do it. I doubt you'll get a second chance with that one. She's got too much responsibility to waste her time on a man who's not serious about her."

"Am I hearing this right? You? Giving me relationship advice? Exactly how many relationships have you had, Shotgun?"

The man didn't hesitate. "One. Exactly one. Which is why I know what I'm fuckin' talkin' about." He ended the call.

Shotgun was right. I knew it. I just wasn't ready to admit I needed her so much I was willing to surrender my soul for her. I tried to keep telling myself it was all about sex, but it wasn't. It was her smile. Her sighs. The way she did anything she had to in order to protect her daughter. Didn't I want those same traits in a woman I intended to keep? So, why was I so reluctant to make a commitment to Celeste?

Control. It all came down to fucking control. If I let her know how I really felt, she'd have control over me. And I couldn't live like that. I had to be in control.

I walked back into the bedroom. "I'm sorry, Celeste. I've been called to a meeting I can't miss."

She cocked her head to the side. "What's going

on? Your whole demeanor has changed."

Had it? I was probably in business mode. My brothers in Black Reign said when I did that I could be a little scary. Judging by the way she hugged the pillow to herself, I'd say they were right.

I smiled, trying to soften my expression. "Club business, sweetheart. I won't be back until late. There may be a party tonight in the main house. I only tell you because it gets pretty wild out there. They'll take over the pool. If you and Holly want to swim, I suggest you do it before dark."

"Just go do your thing. I'll spend the evening with Holly."

Nodding, I reached out a hand for her. "Come shower with me."

She sighed. "I'm not your paid live-in girlfriend, Vincent."

"No. But you love sex with me as much as I love it with you. Give me this for free, hum?"

That got a little smile out of her. "You're such a cad."

"Maybe." I winked at her as I pulled her into my arms. "But I think you like me anyway."

Chapter Eight
Celeste

One thing I would have sworn I'd never do in my whole entire life was be anywhere near something like a motorcycle club. Now, not only was I working for one as a cam girl, but I was living in a clubhouse. Except it was more like a luxury resort than a clubhouse. It was the only way I could reconcile what I was doing with what I thought I should be doing. Masturbating, or letting Vincent use a dildo and perform oral sex on me, wasn't exactly what I thought I should be doing. Yet here I was.

I never considered myself judgmental, but apparently I was. I'd decided to get to know my surroundings. In the process, I'd met some really nice people. Men and women both. The club girls, while not all looking to be my best friend, were mostly nice. A few looked at me with some venom but were usually distracted by one of the men quickly enough. One thing I learned really quick was that they were territorial of the unattached men. If he hadn't claimed an ol' lady, the club girls considered him theirs. And, no. I wasn't a club girl just because I worked for the club. I was still an outsider. One with a kid who was monopolizing Vincent -- Wrath's -- time.

"You know, I'll give you credit for one thing. You must have some serious vajayjay magic goin' on in that pussy of yours. You've kept Wrath away from us longer than any woman he's fucked on the regular since I've been here."

The woman was tall, busty, and very curvy. She wasn't fat by any means, just voluptuous. Tiny waist, rounded ass, and perfect, high breasts. She moved like sin with every step she took. She had tattoos in all the right places and piercings she wasn't afraid to show. Her thighs were thick but supple with just the right amount of give to them without being excessive. In short, she was everything I was not. She was even sexier than the women I'd met with the escort agency.

"I'm not stopping him, if that's what you're getting at. He's free to do whatever he wants." I wasn't sure if I was trying to defend myself or let them know I wasn't trying to encroach on their territory. And it pained me how absurdly pleased I was by the woman's statement.

"Oh, don't worry. He promised me the next time he came to a party, he was all mine." She grinned like a Cheshire cat. "And I promise you, sweet darlin', I've got way more to keep a man like Wrath occupied than you do."

"Back off, Lolita. You know she's not to be harassed." A younger, slight woman pushed between me and Lolita. She wasn't aggressive, but inserted herself in a position to defuse the situation. "Go find Tank. He always puts you in a good mood."

Lolita looked down at me from her superior height and snorted at me. "You don't have a claim on Wrath, so why don't you just move back to wherever you came from?"

I didn't answer, but kept my eyes on the other woman until she finally turned and sauntered off with a group of club girls around her.

"Don't mind Lolita. She's getting older and is a little insecure in her place here. She'll move on to someone else soon." The woman grinned at me. "I'm Red," she said, indicating her hair, which was flame red with kinky curls. She reminded me somewhat of Orphan Annie.

"I'm Celeste," I said softly. "She wants Vinc...

err, Wrath?"

"She's been with him a few times. Mostly during parties. He never takes her anywhere but in the great room when everyone's partying. Probably because he gets horny and she's always throwing herself at him." Red shrugged as if it were no big deal. Little did she know she'd just stabbed a dagger into my heart.

"I guess I shouldn't be here. I just wanted to see what it was really like. You know. In the clubhouse? At a party?"

Red grinned at me. "The party hasn't started yet. Won't until later. They get pretty rowdy, especially Lolita's crew. If you're averse to public sex, you might want to be out of here before dark." She hesitated a moment, then said, "Might want to ask before you drink something. They usually lace the beer with Ecstasy unless you tell them not to. Everyone knows it so it's not like it's a secret. The girls just like to feel good when they fuck." She giggled.

"Are you kidding me?" I was horrified, yet strangely titillated. What would it be like to have sex with Vincent while high? Scratch that. If I had sex with Vincent while I was high, it wouldn't be sex. It would be straight-up nasty fucking, and it would be with Wrath.

She laughed. "No. It's all in good fun. Just make sure to tell them you want the plain beer. No Molly."

"This is almost more than I can take in," I said with a sigh. "I've been drunk before, but drugs aren't something I'd ever contemplated. I guess when Holly came along when I was so young, I just never experimented like a lot of young women do."

"It's not for everyone. Everyone here knows and respects it. No one would ever force you or anything." She hiked a thumb over her shoulder. "Lolita's group might, but they're just trying to run you off. The guys aren't like her and shut her down when they see it happening."

"Thanks for the advice, Red."

"No problem." She gave me a bright smile, then stepped a little closer to me to speak in a soft voice. "I saw the video Razor made of you. You're a natural as a cam girl. Who was the guy? He cut it so it never showed his face."

"Uh, I don't know if I'm supposed to say anything. If he cut his face out…"

"I get you." She giggled. "No worries. He just looked like he lit your world up."

"Can't deny that," I said with a sigh and a grin. "I was having trouble getting off, and he helped."

Red nodded. "Most of the time, we don't actually have an orgasm when we do those," she said. "Now I know why Razor wants us to. You looked really hot. You gonna do more?" Red asked me the question in a curious kind of way, not as if she looked down on me or anything. It was encouraging. Also, it gave me a little more courage about this place. If I was going to do this, I had to stop struggling with my comfort zone.

"I don't know. Maybe? I intended to, but Vincent is trying to shut it down. To tell the truth, even as much fun as I had at the end, I'm not sure it's for me."

"You know, no one is going to judge you here for that video. In fact, I suspect there will be more than one cam girl trying to duplicate your performance. You really rocked it! Even before the guy came in. Don't be ashamed if you enjoyed parts of it. Sure, it's about money, but if you don't enjoy it, they'll find something else for you to do. Not all ways to bring in money for Black Reign involve sex. They're good at finding your skill set and making use of it. Just talk to Rycks. He's good at that kind of thing."

"He's the one who helped me get in."

"Have you met his ol' lady? Lyric is so wonderful. She's put more than one club girl on her ass. It was awesome to watch."

"Yes. She brought Bella to play with Holly. I think the two are going to be great friends. Well, that is, as long as Holly stops teaching Bella "'tude," as Bella calls it. Yesterday she told Rycks that if he didn't buy her a pony he was a lame-o. And she got a no-look fist bump from Holly."

Red threw her head back and laughed. "I would have loved to have seen the look on Rycks's face! I bet Lyric would've as well."

"I got a dirty look, but he winked at me so I guess it was OK."

Red pulled me in for a hug. It surprised me so much I hugged her back before I thought. "You're going to be fine here. Just don't let the club girls like Lolita get to you. They will test you. Kick their asses. No one will stop you, and you might find it turns your guy on."

"I don't have a guy."

That got me a "yeah, right" look. "I think you underestimate the attention you're getting from Wrath. That man wants you."

"Oh, yeah. He wants me all right. I want him, too." I laughed when I didn't really feel like it. In truth, the conversation turn was breaking my heart again. "He's not exactly what I'd call a one-woman man."

She gave me a funny look, then waved it off with a smile. "Just keep your eyes and your mind open. He might surprise you."

Red left me and I continued to wander around. I noticed that, as the sun went down, the clothes came off. I saw people I'd already met, but I didn't recognize most of the men who came rolling in later. They all wore Black Reign jackets or vests. I saw Rycks with Lyric from across the room. Rycks didn't wear "colors," as I'd learned the jackets and vests were called, and neither did Lyric. In fact, I noticed that only a select few men didn't wear colors. All of them seemed to be deferred to by others. Almost reverently in some cases. Especially the one they called El Diablo. He looked more like a wealthy businessman than a biker. He was polite, but I saw more than one roughneck biker back down from him when he gave them a stern look. Every single club girl not engaged actively in sex with a partner flocked to him. The most dominant ones stayed with him. Though he petted or kissed the women, he never seemed to actually acknowledge them. It was like they were accessories to him. Part of his outfit.

Red had been right. Once darkness descended on the Black Reign compound, inhibitions got flung into the ocean breeze. I didn't see a single woman with clothes on. Anywhere. They did indeed take over the pool area. Not a single swimsuit in sight. Everywhere I walked in the vast campus-like area of the compound people were partying. I had no idea if everyone here was affiliated with Black Reign, but I figured they probably were in some way. Even if they weren't exactly members. Some talked business, like they owned businesses who paid a percentage to Black Reign or sold a product for the club. Drugs, maybe? I heard talk of things from Cuban cigars and some kind of expensive caviar illegal in the U.S. to exotic alcohols and prostitution. It was obvious this club had ties all over Lake Worth and Palm Springs.

Mr. and Mrs. McDonald had refused to leave me

while I was here with Holly, though I'd assured them they could go home. I really didn't intend on being here that long. Especially not with Holly. The last thing I wanted was for her to find out what was going on with me and Vincent. How could I possibly explain that to a four-year-old?

Honey, I'm living with Vincent, having sex with him and selling myself in order to pay for your medical care because I wasn't smart enough to not get knocked up with you when I was just sixteen so I could go to college and make something of myself. Yeah. No.

I was just about to head back to Holly when there was a commotion. Several of the men hollered out a welcoming greeting. At first I didn't understand who they were calling out to, then I heard, "Wrath! You motherfucker! Get in here!"

I turned to see several men approach the open door where Vincent entered. He was dressed in that immaculate suit he'd dressed in before leaving me that afternoon. His tie was askew, and the top button of his shirt was undone, but he looked so breathtakingly handsome I nearly dropped to my knees.

Vincent greeted the men stoically enough until the one they called Shotgun approached him. The two men stared at each other for a long moment. It was hard to tell if they were angry with each other or not, but the tension seemed to draw out to a breaking point. Then Vincent pulled out his phone and handed it to Shotgun. A slow grin spread across Vincent's face as Shotgun scrolled through the phone. Then Shotgun broke into a wide grin and clapped Vincent's shoulder hard in apparent celebration. The men surrounding them whooped and congratulated Vincent with hard slaps to his back and arms. Vincent didn't seemed fazed by the big, strong men whaling away on him. He simply took it like he might if Holly had hit him. The man was freakishly strong.

There was no way I could deny it any longer. I wanted Vincent Black for my own. Whatever that meant. Even if it was only for a short time. I simply couldn't stay away from him.

As I was having my epiphany, I was bumped hard by a gaggle of club girls. One of them, a redhead, turned to look at me over her shoulder. She smirked as if she knew something I didn't. I thought I recognized her, but all I could think about in that moment was Vincent. What he looked like when he made love to me. What he smelled like. *What he tasted like...*

I grinned as I lifted my hand to try to get his attention. If that didn't work, I'd brave shoving my way through the throng of naked women and mostly naked men to get to him. It was obvious he was fresh from some kind of win and, if he were like most men, he'd want to celebrate. I intended to be the one he celebrated with.

I was about to call out to him when a woman in a teal-colored thong and nothing else appeared at his side. She waited until he looked down at her, then she jumped into his arms, fusing her mouth to his. And wouldn't you know it, it was the same bimbo from his apartment the day I'd gone to him to offer myself to him so I could pay for Holly's treatments. The same bimbo who'd just bumped into me.

For the second time in less than a minute, my knees got weak. This time, I sat down on the floor by the wall where I stood. Hard. I lost sight of them then, thank God. I'm not sure I could have stood to see that continue. By the sounds of the laughter all around, they were definitely continuing.

Stumbling to my feet, I managed to shove my

way through the few people in the back of the room. I got stopped a time or two by couples or the occasional man I couldn't easily get around, but I finally made it to the back door. Once outside, I hurried toward the building where I had stayed with Wrath. I needed to get my shit and Holly and get out before Wrath made his way back to me. And that was the really fucked-up part. I just *knew* he'd come back to me. He wouldn't stay gone and tell me to move in with Holly, or to get out of the compound altogether. No. He'd come back to our suite and seduce me again. And he wouldn't let me go until he was good and Goddamned ready.

* * *

Wrath

I'd done it. I'd tiptoed around that fucking prick, Harold Collins and his bastards at Lawson, Hughsman, and fucking Gray and gotten exactly what I'd wanted. I got clones of two of the three I'd wanted. I got Collins's ten minutes after I'd gotten there and managed to get Lawson's as well. I'd already gotten fucking Stewart Gray's so the only one left out was Richard Hughsman. With any luck, we'd get enough with what we had for El Diablo to do whatever he had planned. I knew my mission was nothing more than a small cog in a big wheel, but I was here to do whatever El Diablo required of me. Needless to say, I'd come back from this run on an adrenaline high like no other. The only thing in the world I wanted in that moment was to find Celeste and fuck the living shit out of her.

I gave my phone with the little device attached to it to Shotgun for conformation I'd gotten what he wanted. He fumbled with it for a second, then grinned at me. Whoops sounded all around me as my brothers congratulated me. Fucking-A, because it had taken a stroke of luck to get the shit Shotgun wanted.

Before I realized she was on me, a woman jumped into my arms smelling of perfume, sweat, and sex wrapping herself around me like she was a boa constrictor. It was automatic for me to catch her flying form but took every ounce of discipline I had not to fling her across the room when she mashed her lips to mine. Naturally, the guys loved it. Even some of the club girls cheered us on.

When I felt another woman at my back, snaking her hand down my ass and around my thigh to my crotch, then another hand go into my pocket to find my fucking dick, I'd had enough. Not caring if I physically hurt someone, I started shoving women away from me. I'm sure I elbowed someone in the mouth, and if someone hadn't realized the rage pouring off me and gotten that bitch untangled from my body, I'd have probably punched a woman intentionally for the first time in my fucking life.

The second I was free, I glanced around to see a platinum blonde stumble through the crowd to the back exit of the clubhouse. *Celeste.* And I'd just bet she'd seen the whole fucking thing.

I shoved someone out of my way and followed Celeste, determined to catch her and make her understand what had happened. Somewhere in the haze of lust-filled adrenaline high, I knew this was in no way her fault, and she had every right to be angry and hurt. At the same time, I felt she should have given me the benefit of the doubt and at least waited to see what would happen. My anger only made me need to get to her that much worse. Also, I knew that, like any woman in her position would, she was going to try to take Holly and run. If she did, I doubted she'd ever willingly come back to me.

Well, at least the problem of how to make her quit web-camming was fixed.

As I exited the clubhouse, I saw her hurrying straight to the building where my suite was. Good. I followed her retreating form, gaining ground on her as we neared the building. The second she opened the door, I snagged her upper arm. She gasped as she whirled around. The second she realized who had her, she lashed out, slapping me hard full on the face.

"Let me go, you bastard!"

"Not until we get to our room."

"I'm not going anywhere with you! I'm getting Holly and the McDonalds and getting the hell outta here!"

"No. You're not," I said as calmly as I could. "You're going to go to our suite with me, and we're going to fucking talk about this."

"What's there to talk about?" she screamed, tears springing to her eyes and spilling down her cheeks. "I saw that woman jump into your arms and kiss you. It was the same woman at your apartment that day I came to sell myself to you!"

I cocked my head. "Was it? I had no idea who it was. You should have stuck around for the exciting conclusion. Might have been worth your time."

"I don't fucking care anymore, Vincent. No!" She shook her head, trying to twist her arm free of my grasp. "You're Wrath. It suits you much better."

"Honey," I said, finally losing my patience with her. "You have no fucking idea." I scooped her up over my shoulder and carried her upstairs to our suite. All the while, she pounded on my back and tried to wiggle free. More than once I swatted her ass, but she didn't seem to notice. She was all wildcat and fierce. It just turned me more the fuck on.

Once inside our rooms, I set her down. The instant I did, Celeste flew at me, screaming and swinging punches like a banshee. She kicked out, landing a hit to my shin before letting go another furious scream and launching herself at me.

I caught her, wrapping my arms tightly around her. It was the second time in less than ten minutes I'd had a woman in my arms, and I could honestly say, this time, with Celeste doing all she could to really hurt me, was the sexiest thing I'd ever witnessed. Instead of trying to stop her, I let Celeste have free rein to take out her frustration on me. Mainly because, once she was done, it would be my turn. It didn't take long for the fight to go out of Celeste, and she simply clung to me, sobbing her heart out.

"I trusted you, Vincent! I thought that, as long as we were together, you would be only with me. Why did I let you convince me you were even capable of that? I trusted you, and you stabbed me in the heart!"

I fisted her hair in my hand and made her look up at me. Her eyes were swollen from her crying, and tears continued to flow freely from her eyes. As much as it tore me up inside seeing her like this, knowing I was the cause of it, it also meant that she cared for me. Hell, with this reaction, I'd bet my last fucking dollar she loved me. Even if she didn't want to, I knew Celeste loved me.

"Listen to me, Celeste, and you really fuckin' listen to what I say now." I waited until she stilled enough to follow my directions. "I have not, nor have I planned on, being with another woman since I brought you kicking and screaming into my life here at the club. Only you, Celeste."

"What do you call that woman wrapped around you when you came back tonight? Because it sure looked like she expected more than to climb your body like a jungle gym. That was the same woman in your apartment that day I came to you. Have you been fucking her this entire time? Because, let me tell you, club girls count if you put your dick in their pussy, Vincent!"

"Weren't you listening? I haven't fucked another woman at all! You missed what happened after she threw herself at me. There were three club girls around me, Celeste. Three! I could have had all three of them if I'd wanted. Instead, I may have injured more than one of them. I didn't mean to, but in trying to get them all off of me, I connected with someone. Dima, the woman from my apartment, got thrown off me in the struggle. I'm not sure if anyone caught her or not. All I knew was I had to get to you. I completed the job I was sent to do, and all I could think about was getting back to you so I could fuck your brains out in celebration."

As I'd hoped, Celeste was shocked into silence. I took full advantage, slanting my mouth over hers in a hard kiss. Instead of fighting against my kiss, she fisted her hands in both sides of my hair and fought for dominance. Challenge issued? Challenge fucking accepted.

I let her cling to me while I shrugged out of my jacket. Celeste unwound herself from my body and shoved at the jacket before moving to the buttons on my shirt. When they proved too time-consuming, she simply yanked it apart, sending buttons flying. Her shirt was next and, thankfully, she wasn't wearing a bra. She whipped the shirt over her head, then shoved her shorts and panties down her generous hips and perfect, perfect thighs. My hands were already unbuttoning my trousers when hers flew to my zipper. When her fingers brushed my hard cock, I groaned aloud.

"Get these fuckin' things off me, Celeste!'

She did, shoving my pants along with my boxer briefs down my legs so I could step out of them. Instead of pulling me to the bed so I could cram my dick inside her that instant, Celeste dropped to her knees when she tugged down my pants and took me into her mouth.

The shock was almost enough to send me over the edge. I gripped her hair in two tight fists to keep her from moving. If she went to work on me with the force she was using now, I'd last about two seconds before I blew my wad down her fucking throat.

"AHH!" I gasped, throwing my head back. My body erupted in sweat and my knees went weak. I held her still so that my cock was half in her mouth. I could feel the back of her throat but she didn't gag. She took me like a champ and held me. "Don't fuckin' move, Celeste! Don't you fuckin' move!"

She never took her eyes off me, narrowing her gaze as she slid her hands around to my ass and dug in her nails. When she pulled back, I was afraid she was gagging so I let her. My mistake. She slid even farther down my length, sucking for all she was worth. My cock throbbed and jerked in her mouth and she did the same thing again. I clenched my teeth, trying to hold it together, but the more she moved, the less power I had.

Once again, I pulled at her hair, trying to gain the upper hand. If I could get on top of the situation for just a few seconds, I could get my body back under my own control instead of surrendering it to her. When she pushed back this time, I didn't let her up, instead baring my teeth at her. She moved a hand around to cup my sac, tugging and massaging my heavy balls. I gasped, my cock throbbing and twitching inside her mouth. Then, my little, innocent-looking Celeste did something I wasn't expecting. The little wench used her other hand to delve between my cheeks to find my back entrance.

I'd played with a lot of women this way. More than I cared to think about. Hell, I'd fucked Celeste's ass the first night we'd met. But never, *never*, had I even contemplated that I might let a woman do this to me.

At first, she just circled my hole, rubbing back and forth between it and the path leading to my balls. Then, she penetrated me with just the tip of her finger. I gasped, my grip tightening in her hair. She had to be hurting from how tight I was holding her, but she persisted on keeping my cock in her mouth the way she wanted it. The little vixen even used her fucking teeth when I got too tight, so I'd loosen my hold in case she got the idea she'd do some real damage. It just turned me on more.

"You fuckin' little bitch," I swore. "You'll pay for this."

She just grunted at me, as if to say, "Go for it, buddy. But right now, I've got you where I fuckin' want you."

My cock disappeared even deeper into her mouth as her finger slid deeper into my asshole. She must have hit the spot she was looking for because my cock absolutely *pounded* inside her mouth. It throbbed and ached with the need to just fucking come already! She slid it out, then back in, deeper than before. How she managed it, I had no idea. Looking down at Celeste, I saw her lips were stretched wide, my cock filling her mouth completely, I was certain she was more of a demon than an angel. And I wouldn't have it any other fucking way. Her eyes watered and saliva coated my dick as well as her chin, dripping down to land on her breasts. Her finger was busy working inside my ass as she continued to take me deeper and deeper, her throat bulging with the effort to take me all the way down.

Sensations burst through and around me. The messy, erotic sight she made, the feeling of her fucking me the same way I'd once fucked her. My dick about to explode down her fucking throat. All of it overwhelmed me. Finally, I just thought, *Fuck it*, and let her work that fucking magic with her mouth and finger.

"You fuckin' asked for this, baby. Now you swallow me all the fuck down!" With a brutal roar, I emptied my load deep down her throat. I could feel her swallowing as I came, her throat working my dick like her pussy would if she were coming around me. My body seemed to seize up. I was unable to do anything other than watch helplessly as I came and came for my greedy little girl. My woman who'd turned into the perfect woman for an outlaw biker. She could be sweet and nurturing, shy yet eager, or she could be the woman who wouldn't stand for her man touching another woman. The woman willing to punish as well as pleasure. And so fucking hot I couldn't process what was actually happening.

My orgasm seemed to go on forever. Each pulse of my dick spurted more cum down her throat. And my little Celeste didn't lose a fucking drop.

When at last my body relaxed, I thought I might crumple to the floor in a heap in front of her. But in this power struggle, surrendering that much wasn't an option. Not even to Celeste.

I pulled her to her feet, fusing my mouth to hers

once more, tasting myself on her lips and tongue. She didn't pull back, giving me what I demanded of her even as her fingers slid around my still-hard cock and stroked.

Without a word, I turned her around, pulling her back against my front. My cock pulsed against her lower back just above the seam of her ass. I fastened my mouth on her neck and sucked. Hard.

"Gonna mark your body all over, woman. You insist on doing those fuckin' cam shows, you're gonna do it with my fuckin' marks all over you."

"Razor might have something to say about that." She tried to make that a threat, but we both knew it wasn't.

"Razor don't get a say. His job is to see you perform your best and to record it to make money."

"I'll just cover it with makeup."

"You'll go in to that fuckin' room and show everyone in the Goddamned world you've been marked," I growled. "You belong to me. I'll even get my fuckin' name tattooed on your fuckin' skin if you keep it up." I sucked again, harder this time, making another hickey just below the first one. "But, when you're near the end of your show, when you're begging to come and can't, it will be me who pushes you over the edge. Just like last time. I'll stick my dick in whatever hole I decide to and fuck you until I'm satisfied. If you do me good, I might let you come. If you do, it will be screaming my name at the top of your fuckin' lungs." I know I sounded harsh, but Goddammit if she wasn't responding to me.

I had no idea where all this was coming from. Yes, it was in my head, but I'd never had any intention of actually voicing it. The woman was making me crazy. If I wasn't careful I was going to scare her off. Or repulse her with my deviance.

"Just so long as you know, I'll do my best to hold you on the edge until you're screaming my fucking name as well, Wrath." It was the first time she'd used my road name in a sexual situation. The only other time had been when we argued, and she'd basically indicated she hated the difference between Wrath and Vincent. Was I reading her wrong?

"My name is Vincent!"

"No," she said, turning her head to look at me over her shoulder. She didn't look like she was repulsed or disgusted, or even angry. She looked like she was ready to eat me alive if I didn't make the first move. "Vincent is kind and loving. Wrath is raw. Carnal. Right now, you're all Wrath."

I moved my hand to her throat, gripping it none too gently. "You sayin' you prefer that soft side of me?"

She shook her head as much as she could, her eyes devouring me. "I'm saying you better put up or shut up. Wrath won't stand for a woman besting him. Right now?" She gripped my ass with one hand and squeezed, digging her nails into my flesh so there'd probably be little crescents from the rounded tips. If not blood. "I've got the upper hand. *I* own *you!*" She bared her little teeth at me. "Prove me wrong."

I roared, my hand clamping down tight on her throat in what had to be a punishing grip. Then I tucked my cock beneath her ass and found her pussy. She was so slick, sliding into her was easy. When she gasped, I could feel her sucking in air through my grip on her throat. But I wasn't finished. She'd thrown down the challenge. It was time to prove I was worthy of the name Wrath.

* * *

Celeste

Yeah. I'd thrown down the gauntlet. Now I had to accept the consequences. My anger had gotten the best of me. Anger and hurt. That woman... She'd been so smug when I'd seen her at his apartment. Then to see her wrapped around him so tightly? All the things Vincent and I had done together flashed through my mind in a flurry. He'd known that woman far longer than he had me. How much more had she done with him? How many memories did he have of her? Probably way more than he had of me. It was depressing and frustrating all at once.

"Oh, no," he said, biting down on my neck. "You don't get to think about anything but me and you together. Here. Now."

"Kind of hard when I got an eyeful of your redhead with her tits all up in your face. She probably knows how to fuck you better. I think you need to just go find her and do your thing."

His grip on my neck tightened, cutting off my air for a split second before he relaxed slightly. "Never!" His voice was almost a snarl. "Not one bitch in this place could ever take your place in my bed, Celeste. Not one. Not twenty. You're the only woman who makes me this crazy! Motherfuck!"

Wrath started to fuck. His cock drove in and out of me in a hard, driving rhythm. He rode me hard even though the position wasn't ideal. He had one hand at my throat while the other one was clamped around my chest. He gave me one hard squeeze, then let go and pushed my upper body down while one hand clapped around my hip.

"Spread your fuckin' legs," he snarled. "Bend the fuck over." With a heavy hand on my back, he pushed me forward until gravity finally took over and my hands were on the floor. He stepped farther between my legs, keeping me off-balance. I'd have fallen if not for his punishing grip on my hips.

"Gonna fuck you, Celeste." For emphasis, he found my pussy again and pulled me back against him. His cock sank deep until his balls clapped my clit with every surge forward his body made. "When I come next, it's gonna be deep inside your cunt. You think any of those bitches got that from me?"

"How would I know?" My words were broken by the brutal way his body slammed into mine. "For all I know you've come inside every single one of them! They seem to want you to. I bet there's not one of them who wouldn't let you do whatever you wanted to her."

"I've already got a woman like that. Why would I want any of them?"

The pain of those words sliced through me like nothing else could. I tried to stand, but he just stepped forward, keeping me off balance. At this point, he was taking most of my weight except what my hands supported. "You fucking bastard!"

"Yeah. I am," he agreed.

"Get off me!"

"Now, why would I do that? Fuckin' you *is* what I want. When I put my cum in you, I'm gonna make sure it stays so you might as well get used to being upside down." He swatted my ass. Hard. I yelped and lost my balance. Wrath simply shifted his grip to a firmer hold and kept fucking me in a rapid, hard drive.

"Let me up. I'm gonna fall."

"I won't let you fall," he grunted back. When I slipped again, crying out and flailing a little, he paused his fucking to adjust his grip. Lifting me off the ground, he said, "Wrap your legs around my waist.

Lock them if you can."

At first, I struggled to find the right way to go about it. When I found the right angle, I managed to lock my ankles around his hips to hold myself up. Somehow, Wrath got me into a semi-upright position. My back was arched but I was still impaled on his cock. I steadied myself as best I could by holding on to his arms where they'd locked around me tightly.

He walked with me to a wooden rack that had his leathers and helmet. A huge mirror hung on the wall behind it. I could see myself. The lust-stupid look on my face. The way this unfamiliar position looked as complicated as it felt. I had no idea how I managed to concentrate enough on what I was doing not to fall, but then, I didn't protest because, somewhere in deep recesses of my mind, I trusted Wrath to do what he said. Did that mean I trusted him to tell me the truth? Had he really not fucked that woman or any other woman since he decided to bring me into his life?

"Put your hands on the rack," he ordered. "Brace yourself as hard as you can."

"Won't it break? What are you --" I looked over my shoulder just in time to see his face harden as he brought his hand down on my ass. "AHH!! What the fuck, Wrath?"

I started to unwrap my legs from his waist, but he smacked my ass again before thrusting his hips several times, fucking me even as he punished me. "Don't let your legs down. You stay where I put you." He growled the command, setting his stance before giving me the ride of my fucking life.

I had no choice but to do as he said. Once he started fucking me again, there was no give to it. Thank God that rack was solid.

"Look at us," he growled at my ear. I did, finding

his gaze in the mirror. He increased his speed and intensity, his cock slamming into my cunt with brutal force. "We. Belong. You're mine. I'm yours. You get me?"

"Wrath, I --"

Again, he snarled, gripping my throat in a tight hold. Tears flooded my eyes and spilled down my cheeks. Not from emotion, but from the physical punishment I was taking. The really stupid part was, I was enjoying the fuck out of it.

"Shut up! Listen! Turn off that fuckin' intelligent brain of yours and fuckin' listen to me!" I let loose a little sob I hadn't realized I was holding back. "You're mine, Celeste. I'm yours. There is no one else for either of us. Not club girls. Not Razor and his horny-ass cam crew. It's just you. And me." He'd slowed down a little as he spoke, but he was still banging my body with sharp thrusts. I realized then that he'd insisted on this position because it made me completely vulnerable to him. He was keeping me from falling. I was just along for the ride. In his own way, he was proving to me he could take care of me. He was making promises to me he intended to keep and intended me to reciprocate. I knew I could. But could he?

I looked at him, his eyes intently focused on mine, his body working mine. "I'm not letting you go, Celeste. And I'm not asking you to let me go. We hold on to each other. As tight as we can. We make a home for Holly. Then, together, we'll figure it all out."

"You swear. No women. I can't... When I saw her..."

"No!" He slapped my ass again. I cried out even as my sex dripped for him. "She's not ever a part of the equation. Just me and you. No other women for me. No other men for you. Get me?" I nodded, but he just smacked my ass again. I was going to have a permanent handprint on my ass when we got done. "Words, Celeste."

"Yes. I understand."

"Good. Now. You still want to cam for Razor?"

"I -- I don't know." Did I? It was fun but... "It's good money."

"Do you want to or not? It's a yes or no question."

I thought about it. Did I? "I kind of enjoyed parts of it."

For a long moment he just stared at me. Then a slow smile spread across his lips. Cocky and seductive, this was a side of Vincent -- Wrath -- I couldn't resist. "You liked me making you come. Didn't you?"

I gave him a haughty look. Didn't want to make it easy for him. "Maybe."

"Fine. You want to do that, we'll do it. I can work your body from the other side of the glass. If you can't come, I'll come in and fuck you until we both scream."

He let my legs down, then pulled out of me. I whimpered with the loss. Turning me around, he framed my face with his big hands. "Do we understand each other?"

"I hope so. Because I love being with you. Not just the sex either, though that seems to be most of what we do." I giggled a little. He grinned, then stepped closer to me, his dick hitting my belly wetly. He bent his knees until the head of his dick slid through my folds to find my entrance. As he straightened slowly, he slipped inside me. I gasped, and clung to his shoulders. His cock was buried deep while we both stood there. I leaned back just a little to give him room to move. He did. Just a gentle slide in and out of my wet pussy.

"Fuck," he said, looking at the place where we joined. Then his face hardened, and he lifted me. Automatically, my legs went around his waist. While he carried me back to the bed, I moved my body, fucking him while he walked. By the time he fell on the bed with me, I was humping his cock for all I was worth. "You're not makin' me come before I'm ready, little wench. So forget about it." He swatted my ass. *Again*!

"Owe! What is it with you and spanking my ass?"

He smirked as he put us in the center of the bed, his weight settling on me. "Sometimes, it just has to happen."

Then I didn't care, because Wrath was back. Fucking me. Making me his…

Chapter Nine
Celeste

I was getting addicted to camming. At least, when Wrath was around to help me. Over the weeks since I started doing it regularly, I hadn't once done it without Wrath with me. Every single time, after we'd finished a session, Wrath would take me back to our suite and fuck me into oblivion. And there was a distinct personality difference between Vincent and Wrath. Wrath, while a little rough and explosively passionate with me during sex, was devoid of emotion most of the time. Yet he always made sure I was satisfied no matter what we did. Vincent was gentle and funny. Rough sometimes, but his affection for us was in everything he did with me and Holly. He played as hard as he did anything else, but he was unfailingly gentle with the two of us. I'd seen it many times, especially when Rycks or El Diablo spoke with him.

We were playing with Holly in the pool when El Diablo showed up. For once, he didn't have his usual club girls hanging on to him.

"Vincent," he called cheerfully. "So glad to see you taking time to be with your girls." El Diablo's smooth British accent was easy to listen to. He looked Hispanic, with his dark good looks and jet-black hair, but his accent told a different story and shrouded him in mystery. No one knew much about him except maybe El Segador and Rycks. If Vincent knew much, he wasn't saying anything. And I was good with that. Club business was club business, and I didn't want to know anything about it.

"Holly insisted," Vincent said, glancing at the little girl. Every time he looked at her, he grinned.

Holly pretended to be making up her mind about him, but he was the first person she asked about when I got her up in the mornings. Though I slept in Vincent's room most of the time, I always made a point to get Holly up and fix her breakfast. Mr. and Mrs. McDonald stayed at night but went home during the day most of the time.

El Diablo frowned. "I was expecting a Saint Bernard puppy, but have yet to see one. Did I misunderstand the deal?"

Holly, though she'd been playing with Vincent for the better part of two hours, turned to him in an exasperated huff. "Yeah, I've been waiting for that, too." She turned back to El Diablo. "You know, if you can come up with the puppy, I'll make sure Mommy picks you."

The other man winked at her. "Don't tempt me, sweetness. The place will be filled with puppies. All for you."

Holly turned to look at Vincent. "You need to take lessons. That guy is *smooth*."

I giggled before ducking my head.

"But you said no puppies," Vincent said, looking at me with his hands on his hips. "A guy can't win for losing around this place." He winked at Holly, who giggled before he moved to the edge of the pool and El Diablo. "I'll just be over here, planning the puppy takeover of the year." He gave me a withering look, like I'd just gotten him into deep trouble on purpose, before giving Holly another conspiratorial wink.

I loved the way he interacted with my daughter. She tried to pretend she was still put out with him, but I could tell they were forming a bond of sorts. One Holly desperately needed. Vincent was turning into the father figure she'd never had, and I was too busy to realize she was missing that. She wasn't there yet, but I could all but see their bond growing, tying them to each other.

The two men conversed in low tones for several minutes before Vincent came back to us. As usual, when he discussed club business with one of his brothers, his mood changed. Wrath was back, even if just for a little while.

"Everything OK?" Sometimes I asked just to let him know he needed to pull himself back for Holly's sake. He'd never scared the child, but I didn't want him to inadvertently hurt her feelings. I didn't really think he would, but I guess part of me was having trouble accepting he meant what he said about wanting us in his life. About wanting to be in ours.

"It is. I have a meeting tonight, so I'll be home late." He raised an eyebrow at me. "You good with that?"

I shrugged. "Club business?"

"Yep."

"Just no women, or I'll forgo the Saint Bernard puppy and get her an attack wildcat."

Holly burst into giggles. "That'll get him, Mommy!"

Vincent shook his head. "I'm going to be forever outnumbered." He pulled me into his arms, whispering in my ear, "Unless I can put a son in your sexy little belly." I gasped and shivered at the same time.

"Vincent!"

His warm laughter surrounded me as he took my mouth in a soft, sweet kiss. "I'll be back later. Have to get ready."

Once Vincent had left, Holly fizzled out. Her excitement at playing in the pool with Vincent had been the only thing keeping her upright, I knew. I should have put her down for a nap a couple of hours ago, but she'd been having so much fun, I decided to let her play herself out. Lord knew she'd had too few days like this.

Inside, I got her bathed and in clean clothes, then lay with her until she fell asleep. Mrs. McDonald sat on a rocking chair, reading. She grinned up at me.

"I'm happy you're finding a place here, Celeste. They may seem like rough men, but they all have good hearts. Did you know that El Diablo started a fund for Holly? All the men have contributed. Even a few of the women, though that doesn't seem to be their thing. She's charmed her way into their lives. They'll help her and protect you both."

"You seem pretty certain." I trusted the older woman's judgment implicitly, but I'd never thought a biker gang, or whatever, could have such compassion for a child like Holly. Her father certainly hadn't.

"I am, dear. I've talked to my sister-in-law. She runs the house of a group of men who work with this club from time to time. Ruth says El Diablo is somewhat of a mystery, but that Giovanni has checked out every single member of Black Reign. He says they have shady pasts, but each follow their own code. Much like Giovanni, Alex, and Azriel. They own Argent Tech. Have you heard of it?"

"I have. Not sure what they do, but aren't they big in weapons or something?"

"Not exactly. The technology that goes into smart weapons is what they deal with. Anything else, Ruth doesn't say, but they also do a lot of medical research. From what I hear, El Diablo reached out to Giovanni as well. Suffice it to say, I don't think you'll need to do much of the things that brought you here anymore.

Holly will be well taken care of."

"By strangers? I'm not sure I want that."

"By men with big hearts, Celeste." Mrs. McDonald gave her a stern look. "You need to learn to accept help when it's given. I admire all you were willing to do to help your daughter, but this is another of those things you've got to be willing to swallow your pride for. Accept what they offer you. Be grateful. They'll feel good about themselves, and you can tell Holly how they all pitched in to help her. She'll form bonds with them and have an army of strong, capable men willing to lay down their lives to protect that little girl."

I sighed, knowing she was right. "As long as they don't fill the suite with puppies, I suppose I can accept that."

Mrs. McDonald grinned proudly. "That's my girl. Now. You go. See your man before he leaves. I'll keep watch over Holly."

I smiled as I entered our suite. Any time alone with Vincent I treasured. Holly was doing so much better, but it meant that she demanded our attention. I loved that she at least somewhat accepted Vincent into her life. After it being just the two of us for so long before the McDonalds came into our life, I was grateful she was forming attachments and accepting others. Like the whole club of big, gruff bikers. True, some of them appeared more refined on the surface, like El Diablo, but at heart, they were all drawn to a long ribbon of highway where it was just the man, a machine, the wind, and the sea air. But to a man, every single one of them had been unfailingly attentive to my little girl. For that, I loved them all.

The second I shut and locked the door behind me, I knew something was different. A change in the atmosphere. When Vincent walked out of the closet wearing an immaculate tuxedo, my breath caught.

In the suit he'd worn when he'd been called out on the last secret meeting, he'd been so handsome my chest hurt looking at him. In this tux, he was absolutely devastating. The obviously tailored jacket accented his broad shoulders. The pants, his narrow hips. His thighs filled out the slacks to perfection. He wore gold cufflinks at his wrists and a gold lapel pin on the jacket collar.

"Wow," I said, looking him up and down like I'd wanted to devour him. Not surprising because he had that effect on me, but there was just something about a powerful man in an expensive suit. "You look incredible."

He glanced at me over his shoulder. "Thanks. I thought you were with Holly?" His tone was mild and there was no expression on his face, but I could tell he didn't really want me there. Instantly, I was on full alert.

"She's out cold. All the playing and swimming today wore her out. Mrs. McDonald is sitting with her." I waited for him to speak. When he didn't, I asked, "What's going on, Vincent?"

"Just a dinner."

"Seems like a rather fancy dinner to me. I'm no fashion mogul, but that's an expensive-looking tux."

He shrugged. "I suppose." Again there was silence while he finished tying his tie. When he turned around, his eyes were glacial cold. "Don't wait up for me, Celeste. I'm not sure how long I'll be." This was Wrath. Not Vincent. Only instead of the intense lover bent on pushing me to my limits, this man was a stone-cold killer. Whatever was going on, he'd turned into someone else.

He started to leave, to walk around me. He hadn't once looked me in the eyes.

I stepped in front of him. "Where're you going, Vincent?"

"Club business, Celeste. Excuse me." Again, he tried to step around me. Again, I blocked him. He gave an exasperated sigh. "I don't have time for this, honey."

"Make time. What's going on?"

"A dinner with a... business partner. It's formal." Why did he sound so evasive?

"Yeah, I can see that. What kind of business partner?"

This time he did look at me, but only for a moment before averting his gaze. "The kind that has business with the club, Celeste." His voice was clipped, almost cruel. "You know I don't talk about club business. Now, if you'll excuse me."

This time, I let him go. Something was off. He'd slipped completely into the persona his club demanded of him. While I knew he had an important position, I didn't like that he was so thoroughly submerged before he left me. It just seemed... wrong. I had no idea what was going on, but when a man dresses up that fine, it's not a simple dinner.

Once he left, I sat in my favorite chair in front of the window overlooking the ocean. I tried to think, to figure out what I'd missed. Why he was going to a formal dinner and why he wasn't he taking me with him? Weren't all events like that expected to be attended by a couple, if possible? Maybe not. But it sounded reasonable. Even if I had no idea what was going on, having a date for dinner was normal, especially in a business setting.

Wait. Didn't I remember seeing on the news

something major going on in the city? I turned on the TV. The local news would have something if I remembered correctly. After the current show completed, the local news started. Sure enough, there was a charity event happening at the Four Seasons in Palm Springs. It included several prominent businesses and municipal offices.

Apparently, it was a big event. A reporter was on scene in front of the hotel, watching with other reporters and photographers as the guests exited expensive cars and limos to walk up the red carpet and into the hotel.

I was just about to turn it off when something caught my eye. Out of a limo, two men emerged. One of them had a shark's smile. He waved to the crowd arrogantly before moving on into the hotel. The other walked stoically, not waving or acknowledging anyone around him. He gave off an arrogant air, as if he were better than anyone around him and didn't dare to acknowledge anyone. As he turned to hold the door and allow a woman to enter the building ahead of him, I heard the reporter speak.

"District Attorney Harold Collins and Assistant District Attorney Vincent Black are among the local celebrities and officials here today. Mr. Black is a recent appointee to the DA's office and expected to oversee much of the current casework. Mr. Black's reputation as a shark attorney is expected to follow him into the DA's office. Sources tell me that, while Mr. Black has, historically, refused to negotiate once a case has gone to trial, he also has a reputation of trying to reach fair and reasonable plea agreements before going in front of a judge and jury, saving the taxpayers money."

Whatever else the man said was lost to me. Why did they say Vincent was the new ADA? Why had he gone to a charity event without a date? Why hadn't that date been me?

It took me a long, long time to process all this. I just stood there in front of the TV, unable to move or turn it off. My body started to tremble, and I broke out in a sweat. All this time. Every day we went to the studio to film a show for the club's porn website, had Vincent been... ashamed of me? Had this been why he'd wanted me to stop doing shows? So he didn't have to worry someone at his work would find out I masturbated and got fucked on camera for money? He'd asked me to quit and I'd refused, not wanting to take the club's money to help my daughter unless I contributed my own money to her care. I thought I was being responsible. But had I been embarrassing him instead?

The thought was humiliating. Utterly humiliating.

I went back to my suite. Mrs. McDonald was still sitting in her chair, reading. Holly was still asleep. What did I do? Gather everyone up and leave? I could, but then what would happen to Holly? I didn't know what to do. As if sensing my disquiet, Mrs. McDonald looked up from her reading.

"What's the matter, child?"

I tried to hold it together, I really did. But the concern in the older woman's face was my undoing. I dissolved into tears right there. She put her arms around me and tried her best to console me, but there was nothing she could do. Eventually, I just sobbed and sobbed until I made myself sick. Mrs. McDonald held my hair out of the way while I vomited over and over. She tried to soothe me, but I could barely hear what she said. My mind could not get past everything I'd done over the last few weeks. All the sex on camera.

Off camera. The club parties I'd witnessed and had enjoyed watching. Thank God, Vincent hadn't tried to fuck me in front of everyone like some of the women did. I'd never be able to look at anyone here ever again if I did. It didn't matter that the club girls did it. And, yes, I guess I was a little prejudiced because I'd thought I was different from the club girls. They did what they did because they wanted to, but also because it was expected. Apparently, I'd read that situation completely wrong because, if it had been wanted or expected by all the guys, Vincent wouldn't be embarrassed by me.

And yes. My thought processes were so skewed right now it wasn't funny. Nothing was making sense. The only thing I could fully process was that I'd fucked up when I thought I was being exactly what Vincent wanted in a woman. I'd followed his lead and enjoyed myself more than any other time in my life. Now, I was relegated to being a club girl? And no man in the club claimed a club girl as his. Likely because most of the brothers had already fucked them and the men didn't encroach on each other's territory.

"H-he said h-he w-wanted us t-to b-be t-together," I said through bouts of crying.

"What happened, child?" Mrs. McDonald tried her best to get it out of me, but I couldn't bring myself to form the words, "Vincent is embarrassed by my behavior." It was just too humiliating.

Dimly, I heard her speaking softly to someone. Mr. McDonald? The next thing I knew, I was being lifted from the floor where I sat in front of the stupid toilet. Tears blurred my vision, but gentle hands brushed my hair back and washed my face with a cool cloth. Then I was lifted again, cradled against an impossibly hard chest. Soft words were murmured in my ear, soothing me. Automatically, I slid my arms around the neck of the man carrying me, buried my face against his chest and just sobbed.

I have no idea how long I was like this. Grief and scalding shame combined with utter loss and the feeling of rejection ate their way through my heart until there was nothing left. The only thing I could cling to was that I still had Holly. I'd done what I had to in order to protect and care for her. If that meant sacrificing my happiness with a man, then so be it. If Vincent… if *Wrath*, was that repulsed by what I'd done, then maybe it was better this had happened now. Better now than after he was so deeply entrenched in our lives he broke Holly's heart like he'd done mine. She'd miss him now, but she was still making up her mind about him.

Finally, I exhausted myself. No more tears came. I just sat in a kind of shocked lethargy. That was when I realized I was in the lap of a man, being held close. His chin rested atop my head and his arms were tightly around me, holding me securely while he ran one hand up and down my arm in a soothing caress.

"There," he said. "Is my girl back with us now?"

That smooth, soothing accent…

"El Diablo?" I looked up and, sure enough, the enigmatic leader of Black Reign MC looked down at me with concern in his dark eyes.

"Sweet Celeste," he said, brushing away a tear that leaked from my eye. He reached beside him and brought a tissue box, letting me snag a couple before getting his own and setting them back on the couch beside us. "What has you so upset? You're breaking my heart."

The sincerity in his voice and eyes brought forth a fresh flood of tears. He just wrapped me up tighter, pulling a blanket from the back of the couch to secure around me. He rocked me slightly, letting me cry as much as I needed. Occasionally, he'd wipe at my tears, but otherwise he just let me continue to cry.

The next time I stopped, he looked down at me, a curious look on his face. "Is this about Vincent?"

"He's embarrassed by me," I said softly. I had no idea why, but I did. I never expected it, but El Diablo had a way of making me feel secure in telling him anything. "He tried to get me to quit camming, but I insisted on paying my part for Holly's treatment. I never did it without him, though. He was always with me, and the other men never came on to me or tried to get me to do anything without him or anything --"

"Hush, Sweet," he said, laying a gentle finger to my lips. "If he's embarrassed by you or what you did to help my little Holly sweetness, then he doesn't deserve you. Now. Tell me why you believe this. What has Vincent said to hurt you so?"

"He didn't really say anything, but I didn't even know he was the Assistant District Attorney. Then he went to that big charity dinner without me. Not that I'm really interested in that sort of thing, but if we're together, wouldn't he have wanted me to go with him?" I was rambling, but once the words started, they seemed to just trip over each other.

"Did he not tell you what was going on, sweet Celeste? There was a reason he didn't want you with him and not for the reasons you think, my dear."

"He just said it was club business." I didn't really intend to go on with my whining, but I couldn't seem to help it. "I don't want to know his stupid business, but, after tonight, I'm pretty sure he's going to put the club before me in his life. I know I'm not much of a trophy, but I deserve to have Holly and me be first in his life. We should be important to him too." I sniffed. "Whatever he feels like he has to do is fine. But I refuse to let my daughter grow up watching a man who should love her and her mother constantly put us second. I won't let her see me be with a man who constantly breaks my heart. If I do, she won't know she doesn't have to settle for being second best in someone's life." And there went the tears and snot and crying again.

El Diablo pulled me back against him, wrapping me up in strong arms like a father might a distraught daughter. It was weird, really. There was nothing sexual about his touch or the affection he showered me with. It was truly like that of a father or a favorite uncle comforting me.

I had been alone since I was fifteen. When I'd found out I was pregnant with Holly. My father was dead, my mother refused to let me stay once she discovered my secret. My boyfriend, a senior while I was a freshman, had plans after high school that didn't include being a father. So, I'd quit school at sixteen, just a few months before I'd given birth to Holly, gotten my GED, and gotten a job. Not long after her first birthday, I found out about the leukemia, and my whole world focused on Holly. Everything, including work, had taken a back seat. To say I had no social time to build relationships was an understatement. The only people I'd been able to grow close to had been Mr. and Mrs. McDonald. They'd practically dragged me in off the streets, given me a place to live, and only charged me rent because I insisted on paying my way. I must have been craving the attention because it felt like El Diablo really cared about me and my hurt feelings and pride. Maybe that was the problem with me and Wrath. Maybe I mistook his interest in me because I wanted him to love me. With the amount of pain I felt now, I was certain I loved him. If this wasn't love, I'd hate to feel what it was like to lose someone you truly loved. Because, if I was right and he was embarrassed by me, then not only had I lost him, I'd really never had him to begin with.

Finally, when I was once again quiet and still in El Diablo's arms, he spoke to me. "Black Reign is in the middle of a long investigation into the District Attorney's office in Palm Beach. Vincent is a plant. We got him noticed by the firm representing the DA the night he met you, then things took their own course. He was invited to a private meeting where he was met with the DA, Harold Collins, the night you had the falling out about his interaction with a certain club girl."

I gasped, pulling away from him. "You knew about that? Oh, my God. Could this day get any worse?"

He chuckled, "Sweet Celeste, there is very little that happens inside this club that I don't know about." Pulling me back to him, he continued. "That night, he managed to clone the phones of three out of four of the participants in that meeting. Tonight's charity event was just one more opportunity for him to get the information we need to shut down some very bad people, including the District Attorney. The man has just been elected, so if we can take him out, we will be in a position to move Vincent into the DA's office and not have to win an election for four years. Which will give us some time to complete our investigation."

"Why are you telling me this? Isn't it club business?" I asked the question with more than a little bitterness in my voice.

"Technically, yes. But you're Vincent's woman.

This is something you need to know. Lyric worked in the DA's office. Not now because it's not safe for her while another club has a foothold in the office, but once we gain control, she'll be back and be an asset to us. I have many long-term plans, but for now, I want control of this office. There are some really bad people there. We've already determined Mr. Collins has a liking for young boys. I'm hoping Vincent can gather more information tonight. He doesn't want to involve you because there is the potential for the other club, Kiss of Death, to get wind of our operation and try to… eliminate the threat. While Vincent can take care of himself, if he feels he has to watch out for you, his attention would be divided, and he could put you both in danger."

"I understand that. Why would he not just tell me?" What El Diablo said made sense, but it didn't explain his cold attitude toward me tonight.

"Because he's a man of his word. Club business has always been club business."

"But you told me."

"And I'm the president. I can tell whomever I want, Sweet Celeste."

"He was still a jerk," I sniffled, unwilling to let him off the hook. "I'm not sure I want to stay with him anymore."

"I don't blame you. But you leave all this to me. If he doesn't come around the way he needs to, I'll kill him for you." He smiled down at me, but I didn't think he was kidding. "I'm the president of Black Reign. I take care of those under my protection. That includes you and my little sweetness, Holly." He tilted his head, as if deciding whether or not to say something else. "Celeste, where are your parents?"

The question caught me off guard. "Well, my

father's dead. My mother didn't want her fifteen-year-old pregnant daughter to ruin her reputation in the neighborhood." I shrugged. "I left. After that, I didn't keep up with her."

"And your grandparents?"

I frowned. "My mother's parents are both dead. I never knew my father's parents."

"Well. You may not know them, but they know you. If Vincent can't make this right between the two of you, I'll take you to your grandparents. They're eager to have you with them anyway."

"What? My... grandparents? My father's parents?"

"My beautiful Celeste. You are loved. From afar, but you're much loved."

Chapter Ten
Wrath

This shit fucking sucked. I couldn't get the look on Celeste's face out of my mind when I'd walked out on her. The only way I could pull this off was to put her out of my head. Out of my heart. I knew I did it all the time. I guess it was a defense mechanism, but when my brothers brought club business to me, I just shut my emotions down. It was how I'd always done it. Celeste had noticed it. Had called it my "Wrath mode." She even tried to help me be conscious of it so I didn't hurt Holly's feelings unintentionally. Now, I'd hurt Celeste.

The event was a success for Black Reign. I'd gotten everything I'd been told to get and a few more just in case. But I couldn't celebrate. Not knowing that I'd left Celeste like I had.

Fuck! If there had ever been a time I regretted not being able to share club business, this was it. If I'd just told her what was happening, she'd have been fine. Hell, usually the "club business" line worked with her, but I could see her point here. It looked bad. I just had to get to her and soothe any hurt I caused.

The second I walked in the clubhouse to hand over my phone and the other little gizmos I'd used, I could tell there was something wrong. Shotgun accepted everything without a word. Everyone else seemed to be watching intently. There were no club girls anywhere to be found.

When I walked farther into the room, I saw El Diablo sitting on a couch in the center of the room. He had a scotch in one hand, a smoking cigar in the other. One ankle was placed on the opposite knee, and he looked as relaxed as anyone could. The hardness in his dark eyes told another story. As did the atmosphere in the room.

"Greetings, Vincent," he said mildly. The man rarely used my road name. "I trust all went well at the dinner?"

"I got everything I went after and more. If there is something to be used against those men or Kiss of Death, it's there."

"Good. Perhaps your success will be worth the price you paid for it." That didn't sound ominous or anything.

Then I stilled. "I suppose," I said, slowly, carefully. "It all depends on the price."

"How about if the price is a good woman and the child she holds dear? Was the success you garnered for the club worth losing them?"

Everything inside me rebelled at his words. They nearly made me physically ill. "What did you do?" If he'd hurt Celeste or Holly, I'd kill the motherfucker.

"Oh, I did plenty. In fact, I did your job with Celeste."

My job? "If you've touched one hair on their heads…"

"Be careful, Wrath. You're about to write a check your body can't cash."

"I think that's the first time you've ever called me by my road name."

"It's the first time I've ever thought of you as more of a club member and less of a trusted friend."

I was tired. So fucking tired. "You're going to have to explain what has happened with Celeste and Holly. I know I'm in the doghouse with Celeste. I couldn't explain why I hadn't invited her to come with me and I know it hurt her."

"So, you knew what you were doing? You hurt

her intentionally?" He said it matter-of-factly. Like he was just getting all the facts. I'd used the technique many times in court. Underneath, El Diablo was seething. Everyone in the room could see it in his eyes.

"What else was I supposed to do? You gave me the invitation. You told me to attend even though you knew I hadn't planned to. I admit now that it was a wealth of information for the taking, but I had no plans on going for this very reason." I was starting to get pissed. This was a fucking cluster fuck.

El Diablo surged to his feet and crossed the space between rapidly as he yelled at me. "You were supposed to fucking tell her what the fuck was going on!" El Diablo rarely swore, though he wasn't above it. It was yet another tool he used. Like me. Hell, I'd learned the technique from the man in front of me. "What the fuck were you thinking?"

"This was club business!" I tossed back. "I never tell club business!"

"Sure, it was club business, but it wasn't anything the entire club didn't know! Hell, I'd bet my next blow job every club girl in the fucking place knew about it! Everyone but the one person it mattered to."

"Are you saying I should keep her in the loop about what you have me do? Because, no matter how much I trust her, there are some things I don't want her to know."

"I'm saying that, if you were unsure if you should tell her what was going in, before you shut her out, you should have fucking come to me, Goddammit! Do you realize how badly you've hurt her?"

I blinked. Yeah. This was bad. "I know she was hurt. I could see it in her eyes when I left, but it's just one dinner. It can't be as bad as this."

"Oh, really?" El Diablo leaned into me, his nose

nearly touching mine. I'm a big guy, but El Diablo is every bit as tall and muscular. Maybe more so. "Sweet little Celeste thinks you're *ashamed* of her because of what she does here at the club to pay her part in Holly's medical treatment. She's beating herself up for not stopping the webcamming when you tried to get her to. Even though you've been with her every single session and have joined her more than once, that girl thinks you're *ashamed of her*!"

Swallowing, I shook my head. "I'm not. Not at all. I --"

El Diablo backhanded me so hard my ears rang. OK. Wasn't expecting that. I shook my head and faced him again. He backhanded me with the other hand, harder than the last time.

"Tell me right now," he said, taking another step, forcing me to go nose to nose with him -- where he was within stabbing range -- or retreat like a coward. I chose to back off, mainly because I recognized what he was doing. Looking like a coward was as bad to me as my being ashamed of Celeste would be to her. If punishing me meant getting Celeste to forgive me, I'd take anything he dished out and more. "Do you want her? Because, I have to tell you, I've grown rather fond of my sweet Celeste and her little Maddog. If you're not willing to care for them, I can tell you now, I intend to make them both mine."

You could have heard a pin drop in the clubhouse. The bombshell El Diablo just dropped was nuclear.

"You... want... Celeste? Like for your woman?"

"That so hard to believe? She's a beautiful, passionate woman. If she flourished under your tender care --" he made that a derisive sneer "-- she'll thrive with mine. I will make her feel like she's the only woman in the world. In my world, she will be. I'll raise little Maddog as if she were my own, and I'll find the bastard who fathered her and slit the fuck's throat."

"She is a beautiful, passionate woman, El Diablo. But she's mine. As is Holly."

"She wants to be called Maddog!" El Diablo roared. This time, the president of Black Reign laid into me. Punch after horrible punch. I tried to defend myself, but it was more a reflex than anything else. Try as I might, I could not just take his raining blows. Not from El Diablo. Not from anyone.

I kicked out, hitting the side of his shin. It should have numbed his leg and at least slowed him down, but he just kept coming. Roaring in furry, El Diablo hit me with a brutal strength. I got in a few good licks, but mostly, it was just El Diablo beating the fuck outta me. He started out with form and cunning. It rapidly devolved into an animalistic pummeling.

When I was finally on the floor on one knee, he slammed his fists onto my shoulders, making me double over, then my back. Like an enraged gorilla, he pummeled me. Every time I tried to fight back, he'd come at me from a different angle. The fight was so one-sided, I was beginning to realize I was truly being humiliated. I might lose standing in the club after this. I'd definitely be fighting a lot more. Would Celeste still want me after this? She and Holly needed a strong man to protect them. Would this drive her to El Diablo?

I lay on the floor, barely conscious. My ribs hurt like a mother, and I was certain more than one was broken. Blood pooled on the floor where it dripped steadily from my nose. There wasn't a place on my body that didn't hurt. It was then I realized the beating had stopped.

I looked up, my vision a little blurry, to find El

Diablo standing over me. Blood splattered his immaculate, white shirt. His knuckles were bruised, and his fists were still clenched. The man looked as scary as his namesake.

"You done?" I wheezed the question.

"Depends. What are you going to do about Celeste?" The fucking bastard wasn't even winded.

"Beg her to take me back. Explain to her how precious she is to me."

"Good. I expect a yard full of fucking Saint Bernard puppies as well." He knelt before me then, getting down to look me in the eyes. "Do you know who she is, Vincent?"

"Celeste?" I was confused.

"Yes. She's MC royalty, though she has no idea. She's an outcast. Her father was legendary in the clubs when I first came to America after leaving the Brotherhood. He was a notorious boss of his territory. When the Brotherhood tried to take over his city -- much like they're doing to Palm Beach now -- he stood up to them. Fought them. It cost him everything. Including his only child. When the Brotherhood finally got the better of him, it wasn't because they bested him. It was because he lost the will to fight them. One too many brushes with death turned his wife against him. She became bitter and, as their daughter grew into a very young woman, she did everything she could to rein in the rebellious teen who was too much like her father. Even now, Celeste believes her father dead. I'm not so sure. His body was never found, and the man was simply too cunning to have gone quietly to his death." As El Diablo spoke, I could feel the weight of responsibility he was handing me. "When Celeste got pregnant at fifteen, her mother disowned her, thinking Celeste would be afraid and bend to her will. But she has too much of her father in her for that. Celeste delivered her baby at sixteen, got her GED, and went to work providing for herself and her child. Luckily, her paternal grandparents tracked her down. They knew their granddaughter wouldn't accept their help. So they put trusted friends in her way."

"The McDonalds."

"Yes. Glinda McDonald is the sister-in-law to Ruth McDonald, the estate manager for Azriel Ivanovich of the Shadow Demons. Glinda's brother and Ruth's husband ran together back in the day after Vietnam. They were MC brothers. When I came along as a young kid, they took me under their wing. Taught me their way. They introduced me to two very special people. They're with Bones in Somerset, Kentucky. No one there knows their real name except Thorn from Salvation's Bane. Even he doesn't know everything about the pair. They were never married legally, but they've been inseparable for as long as I've known them. Mama and Pops are Celeste's grandparents. They know you've not claimed their granddaughter publicly, and they're not happy." He stood then, rising to his full height. Reaching out a hand for me, El Diablo helped me to my feet. "The only thing I can caution you about is that you will believe Pops is the threat. You'll have your entire focus on him, but Mama will stab you in the kidney before you even realize she's on you. Of the two, you better fear Mama."

"Wait. Are they coming to kill me? Because I'm not going to fight Celeste's family." I'd meant it as a joke. Mostly. But, when I thought about it, it was a real fear. I could fight back against El Diablo, assuming I could get my bearings long enough to actually punch the bastard, but I couldn't fight a man and woman in their seventies, no matter how hard and heavy they came after me.

"They're reserving judgment. I suggest you get to your woman, Vincent. You've got a lot of ground to make up and very little time to do it. Once Mama and Pops get here, it's out of my hands."

"Is she in our suite?"

"She's in Holly's. I suggest you tread carefully."

"Any advice?"

"Yeah. Don't fucking make her cry again. You do, I'll kill you myself.

* * *

Celeste

I had everything packed, but hadn't yet left. Then Mr. McDonald called someone and told them where we all were, but wouldn't say who he talked to. He just said to trust him and Glinda, and they'd take care of everything. They'd left me for a while, giving me some time alone before Holly woke. I wasn't sure how I was going to explain this to her. Though she still said she was undecided about if she liked Vincent or not, I knew it was far too late to leave without her getting hurt.

The door opened. Expecting Mrs. McDonald, I turned to find Vincent standing in the doorway. I glared at him before turning back to the window.

"What do you want?"

"To apologize," he said. He sounded funny. Like his nose was stopped up. I turned to look at him again and realized he'd had the shit beaten out of him.

"Oh, my God! Are you…" I stopped clearing my throat. "Looks like you had a rough evening. Must have been some dinner." What did I care if he was hurt? As far as I was concerned, he deserved it. He'd hurt me just as badly. I felt as battered on the inside as he looked on the outside.

"It's nothing," he said. "Got an attitude adjustment. We need to talk."

"Got nothing to say to you, Vincent. Everything that needed to be said was said."

"No, it wasn't. I was an ass and didn't tell you anything I should have."

"Perhaps, if you had, we wouldn't be where we are now. I'd like you to leave. I'm done."

"This isn't over, Celeste."

"Why?" I got to my feet, needing to pace. I was jittery inside and I had to get a grip on it. Otherwise, I'd give him that second chance he was asking for. "Because you say it's not over? I've got news for you, Wrath. This is over when I decide. You don't trust me enough to tell me why you can't take me with you, then there's nothing to discuss. Relationships are built on trust, and you obviously didn't care enough about me to build any kind of trust. El Diablo had to be the one to explain things to me."

"He make a move on you?"

I laughed. "No. But he showed me kindness and caring during one of the darkest moments of my life, and I'll forever be grateful."

"Celeste…"

"Wrath?" Holly chose that moment to wander out of her bedroom, her stuffed frog in one hand, the other rubbing her eye sleepily.

"Hey, Maddog."

Holly smiled through her sleepiness and ran to Vincent, jumping into his arms. "Missed you at bedtime."

"I know, honey. I'm sorry."

"Were you mean to Mommy? Because if you were you need to get her a puppy. That makes everything all better."

"Honey," Celeste said. "There are some things even puppies can't fix."

Holly glanced back at me, then leaned close to Vincent's ear. "Don't listen to her. If you were a lame-o, puppies will make it better, and Mommy will love you again."

My breath caught in my lungs. Holly. My little Holly. Leave it to the four-year-old to see the one thing you want no one finding out.

"You think that will make your mommy love me, huh? A puppy?"

"Not just any ole puppy," she confided. "A Saint Bernard puppy."

"If you think it's best."

"I do. Besides, you can get Mommy's when you get mine. You still owe me one for not letting Doc or Blade have Mommy."

Vincent looked at me, holding my daughter in his arms. Holly wrapped her arms around his neck and leaned in to kiss his cheek.

"Good. Because I have something to tell your mommy first."

"Is it good? Because, if it's bad, you might want to wait." The child looked solemnly at Vincent. "She was crying earlier, and I don't think it was because she was scared I was sick this time."

"You're too perceptive for your own good, Maddog," Vincent said, looking at me. "She wasn't scared for you. She was hurt and angry with me."

"You better say you're sorry." Holly sounded belligerent this time, wiggling out of his arms. When she got down, she gave him a fierce look. "Don't you hurt my mommy again, or I'll get Blade to do surgery on you. He said if it hurt when I woke up, it would hurt even worse if he hadn't put the needle with the medicine in my arm to make me sleep."

Of course, she'd equate her life experiences to a means to torture Vincent if he were bad. Angry and hurt as I was, I nearly smiled.

Vincent looked at me, meeting my gaze with a sincerity I'd rarely seen in anyone. "I'm sorry, Celeste. Truly sorry. You're a treasure. A fantastic mom, willing to do whatever it takes to make sure your daughter has the care she needs. I couldn't be prouder of you. Holly, though a little terror," he said with a wry grin, "is an intelligent, challenging kid. You've managed her well. Made it so her spirit was never broken. It could have easily happened, but you've given her a normal she can live with and others can relate to."

"Any mom would have done the same thing."

He vehemently shook his head. "No, Celeste. No mother I know would have sold herself so her kid could have medicine. They might have pestered the hospital or pharmacy or some bureaucratic agency who might have eventually approved something for her, but you refused to wait on something that might never happen. Like it or not, Blade told me everything you went through to get help with payment for Holly's treatments. He helped. But you did what you had to do to make it happen immediately. Working two or three jobs. Then, when you were out of options, taking that job the night we met. I knew there was something different about you from the second I saw you." He approached me slowly, like a predator stalking his prey. "I wanted you for my own. Still do. But I want more than just your body. I want you heart and soul. I want your daughter to be my daughter. I want it all, Celeste. And I'm not going to stop until I convince you to give me one more chance."

"Wow. You must've taken lessons from Uncle El. That was pretty good."

"Uncle El?"

I cleared my throat. "Uh, yeah. El Diablo spent a lot of time with us this evening. He told her to call him that."

He sighed. "He said if I didn't want you, he did. Do you want him, Celeste?"

Did I? El Diablo was charming, intelligent, sexy, and mysterious. He was rich beyond anything I could ever conceive and was willing to throw any amount of money into whatever Holly needed. There was only one problem. Wonderful as he was, I didn't love El Diablo. And he didn't love me.

"No. I don't."

"Then, can you give me another shot? Let me prove to you how much I love you?"

"Do you love me, Vincent? You've never said it, and every time I think I can tell that you do, you pull back."

"I struggled with it -- I won't lie. Not because of you, but because admitting how much I love you means I have a glaring vulnerability. Nothing can happen to you, Celeste. You or Holly. It's the main reason I didn't want you with me tonight. I couldn't control that room. If you were with me, if Kiss of Death had realized exactly what I'd brought with me, they'd have done everything in their considerable power to take you from me." Vincent shook his head. "I'd have killed everyone in the place to get to you, Celeste. That's no exaggeration. If that didn't work, I'd do whatever it took, including giving my life, to get you safely back to Holly."

Mrs. McDonald opened the door. Seeing Vincent, she frowned. "Is everything all right?"

Holly piped up before Vincent or I could say anything. "Wrath was just groveling for Mommy. Trying to get us back." She shrugged. "He's willing to get both of us a puppy, so I'm willing to give it another shot." Holly looked over her shoulder at Vincent. "But if he hurts my mommy again, I'm telling Uncle El. He said he'd take care of everything if Wrath decided to be a lame-o again."

"Well," Mrs. McDonald said crisply. "I think that would be warning enough for him not to be a lame-o again." She held out her hand for Holly. "Come, dear. There are some people I want you to meet. They didn't bring puppies, but they did bring pixie sticks. Next best thing."

When we were alone, Vincent held out a hand to me. The man was battered and bloody and was favoring his left side. His knuckles weren't scraped, but everywhere else seemed to be either bloodied or bruised. I took the hand he offered but didn't let him pull me into his embrace. Not yet. I had to hold out just a bit longer. For my own sanity.

"What happened. Who beat you up?"

He snorted, then winced. "El Diablo. The man is both a both a technical fighter and a fucking brawler. And he can just plain beat the shit out of anyone he wants to. I thought I was pretty good, but that man kicked my ass hard."

"You deserve it, asshole."

"Yeah. I did." This time I let him pull me in for a hug. It felt wonderful to be in his arms again. His heart beat under my ear, that slow, steady rhythm that had lulled me to sleep more than a few nights. I wanted to cry again but held myself in check. Just.

"Don't do this again, Vincent. My heart couldn't stand it, and El Diablo gave me a not-so-subtle hint that he'd kill you for me if I wanted him to."

"I believe it, baby. But don't worry. I'll never let anything like this happen ever again." He kissed the top of my head gently. His lip was swollen so I'm sure the tender gesture hurt. "Come on. There are some people you need to meet."

"What's going on? Mrs. McDonald had said that to Holly."

"You'll see. Let's go."

Vincent led me down to the common room where there was a considerable crowd gathered. It looked like every member of Black Reign was there as well as another club I didn't recognize. According to their colors, they were from Bones MC in Somerset, Kentucky. There was also a club from Palm Springs. Salvation's Bane. The name Bones seemed vaguely familiar to me, but I had no idea where I knew it from. Something a long time ago. Maybe before my father died. I stepped closer to Vincent, needing his arm solidly around me as I fisted his shirt in my hand.

"Sweet Celeste," El Diablo said in welcome. He held his hand out to me and Vincent urged me to take it. "I have someone I want you to meet."

"Mommy!" Holly bounded to my side. She was practically vibrating with excitement. "This is Grandmama and Pop-pops!" The child grabbed my other hand and practically dragged me to an older couple. Both were grey, though Pops had a scarf tied around his head. His hair was longish, but stopped well short of his collar. His full, grey beard was neatly trimmed but hung down his chest. He was tall and wiry, but very fit. Mama's hair was woven into a thick braid that hung over her shoulder down to her waist. She wore a tank under her plain leather vest. No club colors on the back. Her arms were thin but, again, fit.

Both of them had leathery skin that spoke of many days in the sun on their bikes. Both of them had hard eyes that could look through a person, but when they gazed on me or Holly, warmth spread over their feathers like a warm breeze.

"Celeste." Mama breathed my name. "It's so good to finally meet you."

"Who are you?" My voice was small. The woman didn't look familiar, but the man looked exactly like my father. Just older. "Are you my father's parents?"

"We are," the man said. "Everyone calls us Mama and Pops."

I just stared at them. I had no idea what to feel or what to say.

"We've watched over you," Mama said, looking back at Pops as if unsure of what to say or do. I got the feeling she wasn't an indecisive woman. That she was trying very hard not to say or do the wrong thing.

"I never knew about you," I said, lamely.

"I expect you wouldn't," Pops said. "Your father never brought club business home, though, I'd have hoped Jacinda would have told you about us."

"She never talked about my father after he died."

"We figured as much," Mama said, softly. Everyone in the place seemed transfixed by the reunion. Mama just seemed nervous. Once, she clasped her hands in front of her and I could have sworn she'd started to wring them. Then she stopped herself and clasped them behind her back. Pops just laid a hand on her shoulder.

"El Diablo says little Holly here is entering her final treatments for leukemia and that, other than chemo sickness, she is doing well." Pops was obviously grasping for something to say. "Mama was a surgeon in the army. She might not be able to treat your daughter's illness, but she can help her manage the symptoms of the chemo. All you have to do is tell her what you need, and she can get it." Mama stood a little taller when Pops spoke.

"I appreciate any help." I looked at El Diablo, then at Vicious. "I can pay you --"

"Hush now," Mama said. "I'm a doctor. The very least I can do is help my great granddaughter with something as simple as nausea medication and fluids." Then, to my surprise, the older woman dissolved into tears. She reached for me as if I were her lifeline. And maybe I was. "I'm so sorry I missed you growing up, child," she cried into my shoulder. "I wanted to help you so many times, but every time I reached out to your mother, she refused to speak to me. Then you ran off and I lost you for a time. Until Data joined Bones. He found you and we kept tabs on you. Trying to throw helpful people in your way."

"Like Mr. and Mrs. McDonald?"

Mama pulled back, wiping at her eyes, but not letting go of me. "Yes. They kept us informed about you and little Holly as much as they could. We knew Holly was sick, and I tried my best to make sure the right people were treating her."

"Dr. Muse," I said. "He wasn't originally her oncologist. We saw a different doctor the first time. Then Dr. Muse said he was taking over her care." I looked around until I spotted Blade, then asked the couple. "Did you send him to us?"

Pops nodded his head. "We did. He's MC, and his father is a trusted friend of ours."

"And Dr. Muse had Dr. Collins met us at the ER when Holly was so sick." Blade met my gaze and gave me a little salute.

Tears filled my eyes. So many of these people

had helped me and I had no idea. I turned to El Diablo. "Why have you been so nice to me?"

"Sweet Celeste. I protect those in my club. I told you that."

"But I'm not a member."

"No, but you belong to us. More importantly," he indicated Vincent, "you belong to that man. He's stubborn and can be a complete ass at times, but he has a good heart. He will cherish you as long as he lives and will raise Holly as his own."

I glanced at Vincent, who reached out to El Diablo. The president handed him a small box that Vincent opened. Inside was the most beautiful diamond ring. It was surrounded by deep blue sapphires in a gold setting. Vincent got down on one knee and reached for my hand. I was so shocked, I surrendered it willingly.

"I ain't good at this shit so..." He fumbled with the ring a little but managed to slide it onto my finger. "Marry me."

I gave an exasperated huff. "You're supposed to ask, you lame-o." Snickers all around.

Holly sighed, looking up at Mama. "We got a lotta work to do on that on, Grandmama."

Mama just looked at Vincent, her eyes narrowing. "Yes, child. Seems we do." She turned to Holly, who took the older woman's hand in a firm grip, smiling up at her. "Where to start?"

"Well, I'd say with the puppies. 'Cause I still ain't seen any yet."

That got more than one guffaw out of the bikers in the room.

"If you've promised this child puppies and not delivered, Vincent Black..."

Vincent looked equal parts exasperated and

amused. "I'm trying to propose here."

"Really?" Pops said, crossing his arms over his chest. "'Cause it seemed to me you were ordering her to do your bidding. Ain't heard no question yet." More snickers.

Vincent looked up at me. His face was grim, but his eyes seemed to be begging me to put him out of his misery.

I sighed. "Fine. I'll marry you, Vincent."

That got some cheers and more than one hard slap on the back for Vincent. A couple of the brothers tried to take a kiss from the bride to be, saying it was some kind of tradition, but Vincent shut that shit down with a growl and a possessive arm around me. I hugged him back for long moments before going to Mama and hugging her. Pops followed and, yes, tears flowed.

I had a family. They'd had my back all along. Mama and Pops, as well as El Diablo, promised to tell me about my father. Or rather, tell me about the side of him I'd never seen or known. I had the feeling I had a lot to learn and that I'd be surprised where it led me.

Right now, though, I just wanted to be with Vincent. I was tired and emotionally drained. Much as I wanted to stay up half the night with the three clubs, I wanted to have some quiet time with Vincent more.

"Let's go," he said, reading me so well.

"I don't want to snub anyone."

"You won't. Mama and Pops are going to be here for a while. Mrs. McDonald is staying with them and Holly tonight. Go say your good-nights and let's go to bed."

I grinned up at him. "Sounds like a plan to me."

He looked at me very seriously then. "I love you, Celeste. I hope you really feel that. You're the most beautiful, most courageous woman I've ever met."

"I do," I said softly, cupping his cheek and standing on my tiptoes to kiss his mouth. "I love you, too."

Epilogue

Celeste
Two Weeks Later

"Holly, get off the dog! He's not a pony!"

"But she likes it, Mommy. See?" Sure enough, the big Saint Bernard Holly had named Tiny was prancing around the yard with my daughter on her back. Behind them, four Saint Bernard puppies frolicked and chased their mother.

"Not sure I'd agree with that. Besides, Mama and Pops are here to take you to the movie."

"Oh, boy!"

That got her attention. Since we'd met my grandparents, Holly had been as foolish over them as they were her. Mr. and Mrs. McDonald hadn't left us either. Even though they now went home during the day, most days they were at the Black Reign compound to visit with my new family. Vincent included. In fact, they were meeting the trio tonight. El Diablo had made sure everyone had a place to stay away from the debauchery that could often occur in the club. As for me and Vincent, I found that, occasionally, I liked participating in said debauchery.

Like tonight. There was a party planned with Salvation's Bane, and Vincent and I were attending. I'd found that, most times, those parties devolved into orgies. At least, orgies among the men and women not attached to anyone else. Even if they were mated, they still participated, fucking each other while watching everyone else.

"I got all my stuff packed," Holly said. "Me and Grandmama and Grandpops are staying at our old house."

"That's what they tell me," I said, grinning.

"Come on. They'll be here any minute. You don't want to keep them waiting." She hugged Tiny and each of the puppies before hurrying to me.

By the time I got Holly on her way, I was nearly as excited as she was. Vincent smirked as he watched me preparing myself. I'd shaved everywhere and showered. Vincent had watched avidly but refused to join me.

"If I get in that shower with you, Celeste, we won't be going anywhere." So I'd bathed alone, taking great care to wash my bare pussy, even coming close to orgasming before Vincent stopped me. "Little witch."

I'd dressed in shorts, a tank, and sandals. No underwear. Vincent palmed my ass several times under my shorts before we even got out the door.

"I'm not sure we're gonna make it to the party," he growled at me. "This pretty little ass is just begging to be fucked."

"I thought you wanted to do this?" I laughed, but I honestly didn't care. I'd grown to love showing off for the guys in the control room when we were camming. Vincent knew I was a little bit of an exhibitionist.

"Are you kidding? I'm looking forward to it. Fuckin' you in front of my brothers. Showin' them who you belong to. Besides, I know you get off on being watched."

"Yeah," I admitted. "I kind of do."

We made it to the common room to a party in full swing. There wasn't a single woman in the place who wasn't partially or totally naked. I saw several of the Black Reign men, including El Diablo and El Segador, with women all around them. The scent of sex and alcohol seemed to permeate the air. Moans and laughter were everywhere.

"Wrath! You really did bring your woman." Razor approached us, grinning as he did. "As insatiable as she is on camera, I'm not sure you can handle her in this kind of an environment."

"Fucker," Wrath snarled. "I can handle my woman anywhere, anytime."

"Well, you decide you need help…"

"Get your own woman, you prick."

"Oh, I've got plenty of women." Indeed, as if he'd summoned them, two naked club girls sidled up to Razor, one of them palming the front of his jeans, the other kissing him deeply.

"Guess I'll get to see you fuck tonight, Razor." When he winked at me, I giggled.

"Come on," Vincent led me to the bar where he ordered two shots of whisky. He raised an eyebrow at me. "You wouldn't drink before. You willing to now?"

I grinned. "Sure. I admit I'm a little nervous knowing what's going to happen. I mean, I want it, but it's still a little scarry."

"You afraid? Because I can fuck you just as hard in our room as I can down here."

"No! It's not that. It's just… I don't know. Good girls don't fuck in public."

"Is that all? 'Cause I don't see any bad girls here. Just women having a fuckin' good time with men." He grinned. "And each other."

"Ahhh," I said. "I see how it is. You imagining me with one of the club girls?"

He shrugged. "Ain't saying I am and ain't saying I'm not. But a man who says he hasn't jerked off to the mental image of two chicks goin' at it is lying."

"Well, I'm not doing that."

"Didn't say I wanted you to, honey."

He shot his glass, then pulled me in for a kiss,

sharing the liquid with me. I took it much more eagerly than I would have from the glass. The alcohol still had a burn, but was much less bitter to me mixed with Vincent's taste. He did it several more times until I was able to shoot my own glass. I hardly winced. Much.

Vincent's grin turned positively wicked. "Tell me when it starts to hit." He shot his own glass, never taking his eyes off me. For some reason, I found the situation erotic as fuck. In between shots, Vincent kissed me. Slowly at first, just his lips. Occasionally, he'd slip his tongue into my mouth.

I did another shot -- that made four. I was definitely starting to feel it now. "I'm all warm inside." I giggled. "And the room's starting to spin a bit." I leaned into him to whisper at his ear. "And I think I might be a little wet."

Immediately, his hand went to my pussy. When he groaned, I knew I'd been right. He brought his fingers up between us, letting me taste myself as he did the same. Then he did it again. When I moaned, he took my mouth again. This time, he wasn't so gentle. And I didn't want him to be.

Wrath -- he'd definitely become that persona now -- pulled me hard against him, shoving his thigh between mine so my sex rubbed up and down his muscular leg.

"I'm gonna get your jeans wet," I whimpered between kisses.

"Get 'em wet. Don't care." He sat back on a barstool and pulled me onto his lap, straddling his hips. "Plan on gettin' wet with your juice any-fucking-way."

I let my legs dangle as I got as close to him as I could. My pussy found the ridge of his cock and I simply slid up and down, grinding myself on Wrath.

His big hand palmed my ass, rubbing and squeezing roughly.

"That's it, baby. Feel good?"

"I need to come," I panted. And I really did. The whisky and the friction on my clit were an explosive combination. I reached between us to his pants. "I want to put your cock in my pussy, Wrath."

He fisted my hair, pulling me back to look at him. "You need to come?"

"Yes! Oh, God!"

"No." That simple word nearly made me weep in despair.

"Wrath!"

"You don't come until I tell you. You got it?" As he spoke, he snapped his fingers at the bartender. He got another full shot glass and held it to my lips. I drank eagerly, never taking my gaze from his. When it was gone, Wrath pulled me back for a kiss, his fist tightening in my hair. Everything around me had tunneled. I could hear others around us, but I was only truly aware of Wrath and his kisses and his hard cock pressed so tightly against me through his jeans.

He stood with me. "Wrap those sexy legs around my waist, baby." I obeyed, and he carried me across the room. The next thing I knew, he sat me down on a pool table. He kissed me once before whipping my tank off and pulling me back to him.

I sat on the edge, my legs still locked around his waist. His hand plucked at my nipples, turning me on even more. There was a woman laid out on the table already, a man's head between her thighs. When the man lifted his head, I realized it was Razor. Beside Razor, Iron had a woman bent over the table, fucking her with sharp, fast thrusts. Her tits were mashed against the green felt, and she gasped and cried out with every jarring motion of her body. When I turned my head, I saw more couples and threesomes all over the room in various stages of fucking.

Looking up at Wrath, I whimpered. "You're going to fuck me, aren't you?"

"Oh, yeah, baby. You good?"

"I'm horny," I said. There was a feeling of euphoria hitting me as the whiskey did its job. My clit also throbbed like a son of a bitch. "I need to fuck."

He shoved me back with a hand on my chest. I lay back on the table next the woman Razor was fucking. She screamed over and over as Razor fucked her, her body quivering as she orgasmed.

"Like watching her come?" Wrath swatted my ass as he stripped off my shorts, leaving me naked on the pool table.

"Yes," I gasped. My hands seemed to go to my tits on their own, my fingers finding and tugging my nipples.

"Fuck, that's hot. Fucking play with those luscious nipples." Even as he spoke, he bent over me, taking one tit into his mouth and sucking the peak until I arched my back and cried out. Then his mouth was between my legs, tonguing my pussy and clit until I thought I'd die. But he never let me fall over the edge.

Two fingers entered me, stretching my cunt. Then three. Wrath was back at my breasts while he finger-fucked me. My head spun, a combination of the alcohol and my hyperventilating. Each time Wrath would ease me away from the edge of orgasm, I'd swear at him, screaming obscenities until he once again started me on that steep climb.

"You better let her come, Wrath," Razor commented from across the table. "She's liable to throw you to the floor and have her way with you."

"She's not coming until I say," Wrath bit out. "And that's gonna be with my dick deep inside her."

"Fuck." Iron was still pounding into the woman he had. "I thought she was hot in the cam rooms." He smacked the ass of his woman, fucking her even harder.

"Yeah," Razor bit out. "You've got to do a full show fuckin' her, Wrath. We could make a fortune off you two. She's gaining a huge following. Already made three times as much as any other woman in the club on her shows. You get her looking like she does now, we'll bring in three times that."

"Ain't promisin' nothin'," he said. Then he wrapped one big hand around my neck. "You ready for me to fuck you now?"

"Yes," I gasped. "Do it!"

He did. I was so fucking wet he slid home easily. Once inside me, he wasted no time setting a hard, driving pace. My tits shook with the force. He wrapped his free arm around my thigh, holding me to him when his hard pounding into my body tried to slide me across the table. He let go of my throat to grab my other thigh, using his hold as leverage to pull me to him with every thrust of his hips.

Mercilessly, he pounded into me. My brain shut down somewhere in there, and I just lay there and felt. *Screamed.* Sweat soaked my body, my hair sticking to my face when I thrashed about trying desperately to come.

Wrath pulled me up, spinning me around. He shoved my upper body down to the table, lifting one of my legs so my knee rested on the edge. Then he fucked me again, pulling me back to him by my hips with every surge forward of his body.

The sound of skin slapping skin was loud in the

room, as were the moans, cries, and screams of women all around us. Men's more aggressive shouts and growls were just as loud, providing the perfect soundtrack to the haze of lust blanketing me.

"I love it when you fuck me," I said to Wrath. I didn't look at him. I'd long ago closed my eyes and just let him do with my body whatever he wanted. "My little pussy is greedy for your cum, Wrath. Please. I need it!"

"My slutty little woman," he said at my ear. "So fucking greedy for my cum."

"I am, Wrath. I'm your woman, right?"

"You definitely are, Celeste. My fucking woman."

"Then come in me. Make me come and fill me with your fucking cum!"

"Fuck yeah! Fuck yeah!"

Wrath picked up the pace, slamming into me with brutal force. I could feel his cock swelling inside me. "Gonna fill you so full of the stuff you'll never get it all out!"

"Yes! Wrath!"

He slid his hand around to find my clit. The second he found it, my orgasm detonated. I screamed and screamed. It seemed like the louder I got, the more the noise around me increased as well. Men and women both getting louder and louder. I have no idea if it was real or only my perception of the whole thing. I was more than a little drunk. Thank God, too, because I'd have never been able to let go like this otherwise. Sure, I liked having sex while other people watched, but this was more than I was used to. Way the fuck more. I knew this. I knew that I'd be so embarrassed in the morning, but right now, there was only me and Wrath, and that fucking amazing orgasm he'd just given me.

Wrath gave one bellowing roar before he finally slammed deeply into me and held himself while his cock pumped jet after jet of hot cum inside me. I did my best to hold it inside me, to hold him inside me. His cock pulsed and spasmed, making my pussy ripple with pleasure until, finally, we were both still.

Around us, the sounds of sex still echoed. Wrath pulled me up, still deeply imbedded in my pussy. He wrapped his arms around me from behind, my back to his front.

"Are you OK?" His voice was hoarse. No wonder, with that fucking war bellow he'd just given.

"I'm wonderful," I sighed. Was my voice hoarse, too? Probably.

Next thing I knew, I was being lifted into Wrath's arms, cradled against his chest. "You're fucking beautiful, Celeste," he whispered as we left the party. The noise started to fade as he walked down the hall. Our suite was on the other side of the compound, but Wrath took me to another room and locked the door.

He sat me down on the bathroom counter before washing me gently. I was still buzzing pretty hard, so I just let him. Once we were both cleaned, he took me to the bed and crawled in beside me. I snuggled against him, nuzzling his bare chest with my face. By pure accident, my mouth found his nipple and I lapped at it. It pebbled under my touch and he groaned.

"No more of that, little witch. Not until I rest."

"Pussy," I said, yawning. "I think you're losing stamina in your old age."

Wrath barked out a laugh before rolling us over. He wedged his hips between my thighs and rubbed his rapidly hardening dick over my mound. My clit throbbed in response to the friction.

"Old?"

"Yeah. 'Cause you're way older than me."

"I'll show you old." He found my mouth with his and started kissing me over and over. I giggled, then sighed as he continued his sweet assault.

"I love you so much, Celeste. I'm going to marry you and adopt Holly. Then we'll have more kids to spoil."

I sighed happily when he slid his cock inside me gently, moving in slow, languid strokes. "I love you too, Vincent. With all my heart."

"Show me," he whispered wickedly at my ear. "Come for me and take me with you."

I did. Over and over and over…

Marteeka Karland

Erotic romance author by night, emergency room tech/clerk by day, Marteeka Karland works really hard to drive everyone in her life completely and totally nuts. She has been creating stories from her warped imagination since she was in the third grade. Her love of writing blossomed throughout her teenage years until it developed into the totally unorthodox and irreverent style her English teachers tried so hard to rid her of.

Marteeka at Changeling: changelingpress.com/marteeka-karland-a-39

Changeling Press E-Books

More Sci-Fi, Fantasy, Paranormal, and BDSM adventures available in e-book format for immediate download at ChangelingPress.com -- Werewolves, Vampires, Dragons, Shapeshifters and more -- Erotic Tales from the edge of your imagination.

What are E-Books?

E-books, or electronic books, are books designed to be read in digital format -- on your desktop or laptop computer, notebook, tablet, Smart Phone, or any electronic e-book reader.

Where can I get Changeling Press E-Books?

Changeling Press e-books are available at ChangelingPress.com, Amazon, Apple Books, Barnes & Noble, and Kobo/Walmart.

ChangelingPress.com

Printed in Great Britain
by Amazon